Washed *Away*

J A S O N   G R A Y ,   J R .

PAGE PUBLISHING, INC.
New York, NY

First originally published by Page Publishing, Inc. 2019

ISBN 978-1-68456-987-8 (Paperback)
ISBN 978-1-68456-988-5 (Digital)

Printed in the United States of America

If you can watch the things you gave your life to,
broken, and stoop and build them up with worn-
out tools...then yours is the earth and everything
that's in it...

—Rudyard Kipling

Dedicated to Kathleen who rebuilt her life and the lives of her children through courage, perseverance, and the all-enduring devotion of a mother, with love and admiration from her dad.

ALTHOUGH THE STORY UNFOLDS IN a historical setting, *Washed Away* is a work of entertainment and should be read as nothing more. The disaster in Austin, Pennsylvania, on September 30, 1911, was an actual event. The author has used names of persons residing in Austin at that time and referenced streets and locations of that era. The story, however, is strictly the product of the author's imagination. There were no criminal convictions as a result of the event. Rusty, Katie, and Brady existed only in the author's mind.

Acknowledgments

THE HISTORICAL FRAMEWORK FOR *WASHED AWAY* was based upon of the works of historians Gale Largey, Paul E. Heilmel, Marie Kathern Nuschke, and John and Denise Owens. I am indebted to each of them for their diligent research into the history of Austin, events preceding and subsequent to the disaster, eyewitness accounts, and reproduction of newspaper reports. Professor Largey's comprehensive collection of journalistic coverage *The Austin Disaster 1911* is filled with real-time reports, some sensationalized, some fact-based from local, national, and international newspapers. His printed work is complemented by a video featuring stories from survivors, *The Austin Disaster of 1911: A Chronical of Human Character*. Mr. Heimel's *1911: The Austin Flood* and Ms. Nuschke's *The Dam That Could Not Break* are comprehensive records of history and personal reflections. The Owens's have presented a complete listing and genealogy of the victims. Once again, I am immensely indebted to my lovely and supportive wife, Libby, for her proofreading and constructive comments. Thanks again to multipublished author Kristine Gasbarre whose suggestions strengthened the final manuscript and to Marianne Fyda whose artistic abilities transformed my rough drawings into a finely finished detailed map of Austin. I extend much-deserved appreciation to publication coordinator Gretchen Wills and the Page Publishing team of copy editors, layout designers, and cover artists for their contributions. It is a pleasure to work through the publication process with such talented professionals. And finally, I extend heartfelt thanks to friends and family for their encouragement and expressions of support.

Contents

Before I could tell what was happening, the water was tearing down Freeman Run, a wall fifty feet high, and sweeping everything before it. I never imagined there could be such a force. And over and above it all were the shrieks of people who could not escape.

—Harry Davis

The wall of water seemed fifty feet high. Above it rose a great cloud of spray. Houses were tossed, bumping together, spinning and turning as they fell to pieces or were swept out of my sight. The noise was appalling.

—Lena Brinckley

I watched the flood sweep down the valley. It was terrifying. Because of the debris it was pushing ahead, its speed was slow, but its force was terrific. The strongest building did not seem to possess the resistance of an eggshell.

—George Sutton

I went back and told Mama that a man said the dam had broken. She told me to run and that she would come. She had her coat on and was standing in the doorway when I left her. It was the last time I ever saw her.

—Faith Glaspy

I saw dozens who made frantic efforts to free themselves from the timbers and wreckage. Dead bodies floated on the surface and went downstream fast. Most of the people who lost their lives were caught like rats in a trap.

—C. F. Collins

And the sad part is no one in those families in Austin who lost people got anything for it. They didn't get a dime. Babies – they found babies in that wreckage!

—Bink Fowler

Prologue

AT 2:30 ON AN UNSEASONABLY cool, partly cloudy afternoon in late September 1911, the three–hundred–fifty–foot-wide cement dam located a mile above the mill town of Austin, Pennsylvania, started to breach along two eighth-inch surface cracks, then gave way unleashing a wall of water cascading down the narrow valley toward the town and sweeping away everything in its path with the explosive power of a nuclear bomb.

Lulled by the assurance of engineering experts that the two-year-old dam would forever withstand the pressure of the pent-up waters above the town, three thousand unsuspecting residents of Austin went about their slow-paced Saturday routines.

Some floundered and drowned in the raging waters that consumed the town, some were battered to death by logs and debris swept up by the torrent along its route to the town, and some, the lucky ones, raced to the safety of higher ground. Stories of heroism, sacrifice, cowardice, and selfishness emerged from the aftermath. The residents of Austin represented, after all, simply a crosscut sample of humanity exposing the best and the worst in times of crisis.

Reporters from newspapers, large and small, from nearby towns and faraway cities flocked to the scene with cameras and notepads to record the death and destruction. Most reports focused on the struggles for survival and the agonies of loss. A few speculated on the causes for the catastrophic failure of the dam. But none pursued the issues of accountability of the owners of the Bayless Pulp & Paper Mill who had constructed the dam to create a reliable source of water for their operation.

What follows is a story of what might have happened had two enterprising reporters reached beyond the sensational journalism of the time to investigate, not only the underlying causes of the catastrophe but also the motivating forces of deceit and greed of those responsible. In seeking accountability, justice, and restitution, they placed themselves and a reluctantly recruited curmudgeonly lawyer in grave danger. Block by block, not unlike the very way the dam was constructed, they built a case with the knowledge that any structural flaw could cause a collapse that would wash away so much: the evidence, their reputations, and even their lives.

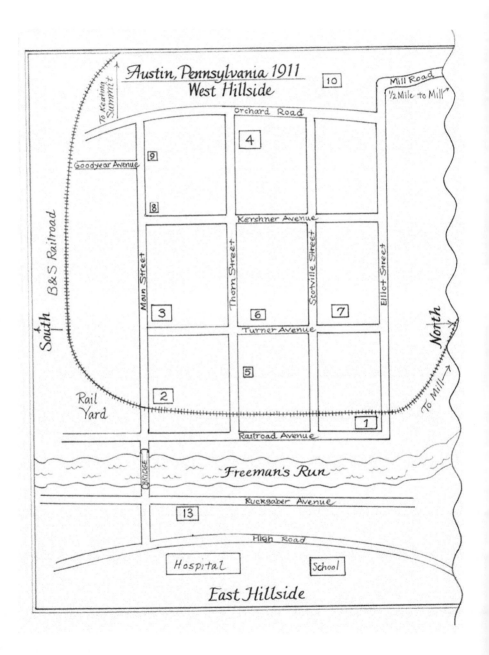

Austin, Pennsylvania 1911
West Hillside

10

Mill Road
½ Mile to Mill →

To Keating Summit

Orchard Road

4

9

Goodyear Avenue

8

Kershner Avenue

Main Street

Thorn Street

Scotville Street

Elliot Street

B & S Railroad

South

North

3

6

7

Turner Avenue

5

Rail Yard

2

To Mill →

1

Railroad Avenue

BRIDGE

~ Freeman's Run ~

Ruckgaber Avenue

13

High Road

Hospital

School

East Hillside

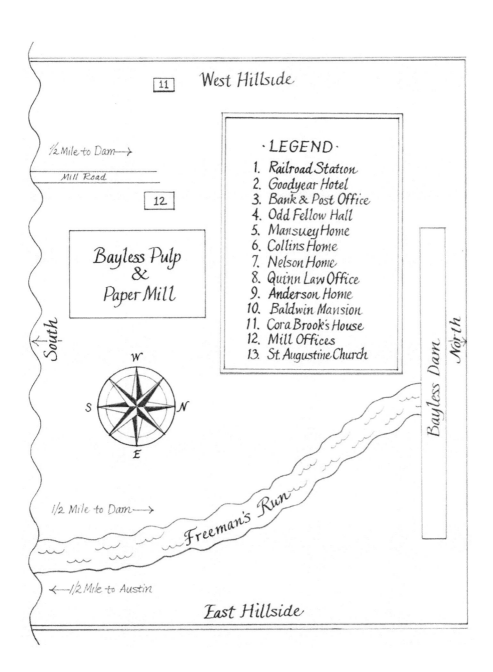

West Hillside

11

· LEGEND ·
1. Railroad Station
2. Goodyear Hotel
3. Bank & Post Office
4. Odd Fellow Hall
5. Mansuey Home
6. Collins Home
7. Nelson Home
8. Quinn Law Office
9. Anderson Home
10. Baldwin Mansion
11. Cora Brook's House
12. Mill Offices
13. St. Augustine Church

½ Mile to Dam →

Mill Road

12

Bayless Pulp & Paper Mill

South

Bayless Dam

North

W
S
N
E

½ Mile to Dam →

Freeman's Run

← ½ Mile to Austin

East Hillside

Thursday
September 28, 1911

BOB PEARSON, HEAD OF MAINTENANCE, for the Bayless Pulp & Paper Mill in Austin, Pennsylvania, leaned over the railing of the spillway platform atop the midpoint of the breast of the Bayless dam as far as he dared desperately trying to peer through the veil of water cascading down the fifty-foot concrete wall. Despite the water's deafening roar, he could still hear rain pelting like a machine gun on his broad-brimmed rain hat. Unrelenting now for four days, the driving rain streamed onto his broad, furrowed forehead, and spilled into his eyes. It further blurred his vision as he searched for any signs of weakness in the integrity of the dam's surface.

Two days ago, concerned about the mounting pressure of the rising waters of the man-made lake behind the dam while standing at this very spot, he had conducted a similar inspection before the pent-up waters began spilling over the breast. What he observed sent a chilling sensation across his shoulders and down his spine: two pencil-wide cracks approximately eight feet to the right and left of the platform extending as far as he could observe toward the base.

At that time, with the water level at forty-six feet, still four feet below the breast, he had reported his observations and concerns to Fred Hamlin, his supervisor, who gruffly waved him off.

"Don't bother me with that bullshit, Pearson. You take care of your precious machines in the factory, and I'll take care of the dam. Now get back to work and don't ask me again to open the spillway. Ever! Ain't gonna happen!"

Now having risked crawling on the four-foot-wide breastworks to the spillway platform with overflowing water splashing around his hands and knees, he squinted to see if the cracks had widened or additional cracks had been created by the increasing pressure. He couldn't be sure if what he saw were cracks, stains, or illusions. Perhaps it had been his imagination. He grasped the wheel that controlled the relief valve, delayed momentarily, then stifled the impulse to turn it a few revolutions to relieve some pressure. He decided against incurring Hamlin's wrath again by disobeying orders.

He released his grip, shrugged in frustration, wiped his eyes, and dropped to his knees to retreat, inch by slogging inch, across the breastworks to the relative safety of the sloping embankment on the mill side of the breastworks. He slid on the bottom of his pants to the streambed beneath the dam and muttered obscenities as he watched the once-placid stream, known as Freeman's Run, pound down the narrow gorge toward town.

* * *

T. CHALKLEY HATTON, SENIOR PARTNER of the engineering firm of Hatton, Bixby, & Rollins, LLC of Wilmington, Delaware, known to his business associates as Chalkley and to his close friends as Whitey, glared at the phone ringing on his cluttered office desk. He was sure of the identity of the caller. The caller had already phoned three times today. Five times yesterday. Hatton had an intense personal dislike of Fred Hamlin under any circumstance and was further irritated today by his arrogant persistence. Of course, he had to admit, these were not ordinary circumstances.

Hamlin, the superintendent of the Bayless Pulp & Paper Mill, was demanding that Hatton travel to Austin, an arduous full day's train ride to the backwoods desolation of North Central Pennsylvania to assess the condition of the dam that Hatton had designed and then acted as consultant during construction some two years ago. Hatton removed his spectacles, massaged the bridge of his nose, and reluctantly reached for the receiver knowing full well that his stalling tactics over the past two days wouldn't work this time.

"Yes, Marie."

"Mister Hatton, Mister Hamlin is on the line. He's in a nasty mood, sir."

"I know, Marie." Hatton sighed. "Put him through." Hatton held the receiver at arm's length anticipating the abusive verbal barrage to come.

Hatton let him rant for a full two minutes, then as the eruption began to subside, he slowly brought the receiver closer to his ear and waited for an opening. "Look, Fred, you don't need me there. My advice would be the same at the site as it is now. Gradually open the relief valve at the base of the spillway and lower the water level."

"You realize, Hatton, what a public relations nightmare that would be? You remember the flooding it caused in town when we allowed a partial release last spring? Freeman's Run is already a river. It's flowing over its banks and up to the bottom of the bridge on Main Street. If I release more water than is already overflowing the spillway, I put Main Street and the entire business district underwater. George Bayless, my boss, says no, so I say no. You're the one who designed the goddamn thing. Come up here and tell me that it's going to hold at full capacity. Christ, this rain won't stop. A solid week of this shit. Now get your ass up here."

"Any sign of structural distress, Fred?" came the soft reply. It took more than one of Hamlin's tirades to ruffle Hatton's trademark demeanor of calm.

"My seldom sober maintenance man says he saw surface cracks. Who knows? That's why we need you here pronto."

Hatton listened with mounting alarm. *Damn Hamlin and Bayless. I pleaded for a deeper trench into the bedrock. I warned them not to fill the lake until the concrete was fully cured. No shortcuts to save time and money! Pocketbook-based decisions without regard to safety!*

Hatton wanted to be done with Hamlin. Done with Bayless. Done with the dam he had designed. Reasoning overrode emotion, however, as he stifled the impulse to slam down the receiver. Instead he heard himself saying, "All right, Fred, I'll check on train schedules and leave as soon as I can. I can't promise I can get there tomorrow. It may be Saturday, depending on connections. I'll do my best."

"You do that, Hatton, and call me along the way. Goodbye."

The line went dead. A temporary blessing. He walked to the outer office. "Marie, see what train connections you can make for me for departure tomorrow morning from Wilmington to Philadelphia, connecting with the Pennsy to Harrisburg, and with the Buffalo branch to Keating Summit in Potter County. God willing, I can make it in one day. I'll let Hamlin know along the way when to pick me up."

He wandered aimlessly back into his office and fell into his cushioned desk chair. *I'm too old for this, but I really need to make the trip. I need to see if there are signs of structural weakness. I need to see if water is percolating from the ground below the dam. I need to persuade Hamlin face-to-face to open the relief valve. And I need to go on record that my recommendations have been ignored.*

An inner voice, "conscience" some call it, abruptly chastised him. *Shame on you, Whitey Hatton, for placing your own self-interest ahead of your concern for the safety of those poor souls in Austin.*

* * *

CORA BROOKS, PROPRIETRESS OF THE most famous, and only, brothel in Austin, studied her ladies while they stood lined up in the parlor of her house on the hill. Cora always inspected them before business hours that would commence shortly after the five o'clock afternoon blast from the whistle at the mill signaled shift change.

Cora was a smart businesswoman, learning the trade as a "fallen dove" as these ladies were referenced with disdain by some and with affection by others, in mining, lumber, and mill towns throughout Western Pennsylvania. Now in her early forties, Cora had advanced from the bedroom to the management side of the business, applying her lifetime of experience to the successful operation she ran today.

No need for the thirsty mill workers to seek out a tavern in town to whet their appetites for the pleasures Cora had to offer. Cora provided both the whiskey and ladies afterwork hours. Local tavern owners protested continuously to Chief Dan Baker, the persona of the law in Austin, but Cora was happy to pay the monthly fine for providing the booze illegally. That, and some cash across the palm to the liquor suppliers from Olean across the border in New York state, took care of the problem without digging too deeply into Cora's profits. Besides, Dan himself was an occasional customer who didn't wish to shut down the business.

The other rather brilliant piece of her marketing strategy was location. Situated on a hillside above the mill, Cora's place was a convenient detour for a mill worker on his half-mile walk into town. Such stopovers had been known to result in enduring marital pain and suffering for some husbands whose wives had literally stationed themselves behind trees to spy on those who stopped at Cora's.

Needless to say, Cora's popularity in town was confined to a small but very loyal segment of men who refrained nonetheless from public acknowledgment of their fondness for her. The much larger segment, comprised of all the women and many of the churchgoing citizens, on the other hand, were quite vocal in their disdain for both Cora and her business.

None of this bothered Cora in the least and certainly didn't enter her mind now as she surveyed her ladies, four today—one for each upstairs bedroom and prepped them with warnings and advice prior to the arrival of the first customers.

"Florence, for goodness sake," she purred to a slightly over-weight big-bosomed teenage girl standing at attention before her. (Cora never swore or raised her voice.) "Pull down that bodice and display those assets."

"Alice," she continued, marching down the line, "take off some of that makeup. You look like a whore." The remark was not intended as humor, nor was it received as such. Cora referred her ladies as "ladies" and expected them to appear and conduct themselves accordingly in her presence. What they did in the bedroom to keep their gentlemen satisfied and returning was not of particular concern to Cora and long as they presented a clean and neat appearance and bathed regularly. Cora treated her ladies with respect and paid them fairly. She had no trouble recruiting.

"And, ladies, remember that the gentlemen stepping across our threshold tonight will be sweaty from a day's work and muddy from slogging in here from that rutted bog out front passing as a road. Before you let them in the door, they must remove their boots. Before you offer them a drink, I must collect the fee. And before you take them upstairs, you must have them wash in the downstairs bathroom."

Turning her back on the ladies, signaling that the inspection was complete, Cora adjourned to her office and shut the door, deadening the sound of girlish twittering from the parlor. She looked out her window with an unobstructed view of the mill and the towering dam in the distance. "When will this rain ever stop?" she murmured to herself, then turned her attention the full-length mirror on the wall. She straightened her floor-length lace-ruffled dress, reapplied lipstick, and mentally prepared herself for a busy Thursday evening. The mill whistle blew. The rain continued.

* * *

FATHER PATRICK O'BRIEN LACKED THE typical enthusiasm of a newly ordained priest. He prayed for the oppressive weight of lethargy to be lifted from him. *Surely, God,* he prayed each morning, *you must have sent me to this last outpost on the edge of civilization for some reason. Show me why. Please give me a sign that I may know my purpose here as a minister of the Lord.*

God had been slow to answer Father O'Brien's prayer. Ordained by Bishop John Edmund Fitzmaurice of the Diocese of Erie, Pennsylvania, on the first of April in 2010, a mere seventeen months ago, and assigned as pastor of St. Augustine Parish in Austin on the anniversary of his ordination, he was still desperately seeking that sign. At thirty-two, a young man by most standards, he felt old beyond his years. Encouraged by the strong Irish Catholic tradition of his immigrant parents, he had turned at a time of personal crisis to the refuge of the seminary and finally to ordination in what his younger priestly brethren characterized as "a retarded vocation."

Upon graduating summa cum laude from Wilson College with a teaching degree in secondary education, Patrick returned to his hometown of Erie to accept a position in the public-school system, living at home with his parents. Patrick loved teaching mathematics, but he struggled with relationships both with his older peers in the teaching profession and with his students, mostly high school seniors, not many years his junior.

Shy by nature, he found himself quite alone among the more elder, entrenched, clique-driven faculty members who made no effort to reach out in welcome to the newcomer. Conversely, he was well-liked by his students. He was consciously guarded, however, oftentimes awkwardly so, in maintaining professional distance with students and parents further solidifying his social isolation after school hours. The isolation ceased with the arrival of Katie Keenan.

Katie burst into his math class with bubbling enthusiasm on the first day of school in September of 1902, his second year at Erie High School, and brightened his life in an instant. A raven-haired beauty at seventeen with cream-like complexion and emerald green eyes that could be alternately soft or piercing depending on her mood, she captivated his heart.

Of course, this captivation was nothing he could express or even inwardly acknowledge. He simply delighted in her presence, in the classroom, in the cafeteria, or in the lively hallway discussions, sometimes related to classwork, sometimes not. He encouraged her progress as his star math student and kiddingly tried to dissuade her from pursuing her passion for journalism.

He lost that battle as she enrolled the following year at Allegheny College, sixty miles from Erie, with a major in journalism the following year. He would run into her occasionally during her return to Erie in the summer months and watched as she grew in confidence and flowered into adulthood. It was at such a chance meeting during the summer between her sophomore and junior years, when he was twenty-five and she nineteen, that he first thought about asking her for a date.

It was she that made the approach later that summer by inviting him to a family picnic. Her father was enraged by her ill-considered indiscretion. Imagine, inviting such an older man as a date, and to make matters worse, her former teacher! It would be scandalous! And so the invitation was withdrawn, but Patrick was thrilled nonetheless to know of her interest.

Their relationship did blossom, quietly and without her father's consent, however, through constant correspondence and Patrick's frequent secretive trips to her college campus throughout her junior year. The crisis occurred in the spring of that year when Katie told her parents that she was in love with Patrick and wanted to marry him.

The result was predictably explosive. Patrick was confronted by her irate father, a prominent attorney in town, in the high school principal's office, ordered to stop all communications with his daughter under threat of prosecution, and summarily dismissed from his teaching position by an intimidated and highly embarrassed principal.

Patrick departed from the school, and from Katie's life, broken and brokenhearted, and immediately enrolled in the seminary.

Now six years later, the Reverend Father Patrick O'Brien stood in the nave of the small, wooden church in Austin, staring at the barren altar. Discouraged and disillusioned, his youthful idealism and passion gone, feeling the crushing, almost unbearable weight of failure, first as a teacher and now as a priest, he stood as a study in self-pity.

"Excuse me, Father. Will you be hearing confessions now?" The voice from a frail, shawl-draped widowed parishioner kneeling in the pew next to him, startled him back to the present. He smiled weakly at her and brought into focus a line of kneeling bodies stretching toward the front of the church, all waiting for him to enter the confessional. All asking for forgiveness. All anxiously awaiting absolution from their sins, real or imaged.

"Of course," he sighed, opening the door to the confessional a few steps away as the rain continued to beat on the stained-glass windows of the church. The unabated dismal downpour matched his mood. The elderly lady rose and followed him, not knowing that this would be her last confession.

* * *

FRANK E. BALDWIN, ESQUIRE, DISTINGUISHED member of the Pennsylvania Senate from the forty-third district, legal counsel for the Bayless Pulp & Paper Mill, and self-acknowledged leading citizen of the borough of Austin, paced the office floor of the mill's owner. Senator Baldwin was not used to waiting on anyone for any reason.

"Where is he?" Baldwin shouted through the open door to the outer office.

The thoroughly intimidated, mousy secretary, frozen in a huddled position over her typewriter, managed to squeak back, "He should be here any minute, Mister Baldwin, sir."

Baldwin continued to pace, ten quick steps by his count from door to desk to door, moving quite lithely for a man of such massive size. At six feet three and close to three hundred pounds, Baldwin's frame alone brought attention to his presence but was no match for the intimidation of his bombastic manner. As he made the turn toward the door for perhaps the twentieth time, there was a bustling noise in the outer office, and the mouse named Edith squeaked again, "Good morning, Mister Bayless."

George C. Bayless, a portly physical presence himself but of shorter stature than Baldwin, burst across the threshold. "Good morning, Baldwin."

"Where the hell have you been, George?" Baldwin fumed. "I've been waiting half an hour."

Actually, it's only been ten minutes, thought Edith as she closed the office door but remained standing close behind it, positioned to eavesdrop on the ensuing conversation. Seconds later, she soon withdrew to the sanctuary of her desk as the booming voices from men, impeccably dressed in three-piece suits and starched collars, could be heard clearly enough even at that distance.

"Dressing down my superintendent for passing on some gibberish from, a willy-nilly, worrywart maintenance man if you must know." Bayless was one of the few men who could parry any thrust from Baldwin without flinching and had no concern about keeping him waiting. In Bayless's mind, Baldwin was merely another employee. He motioned to a chair as he moved behind his desk. "Sit down, Frank, and stifle the attitude."

"Don't lecture me, George," came the quick response as Baldwin slid into the chair. "I'm here because we have an issue…a major issue. How convinced are you about the integrity of that damn dam because if it breaches. you are going to drown in a sea of litigation."

Bayless rubbed his thumb against the cigar-stained index figure of his right hand, the only sign of nerves visible in his stoic demeanor. His hand moved to the corner of his manicured mustache as his paused to formulate a response that finally came is his clipped, staccato style.

"Fred Hamlin's been talking to Hatton. Got a report from him just an hour ago. Hatton says not to worry. The dam is solid. Designed to withstand the pressure to overflowing and beyond."

"Well, you didn't seem that certain last spring during the heavy rains, George, and neither did he. You remember, he advised opening the relief valve to reduce the pressure."

"And you saw what happened then, Baldwin. Flooding in the town. Over the bridge on Main Street. Lots of pissed off people with water damage. Cost me a bundle in restitution. And it sent a message that we lacked confidence in the dam. We're not doing that again. No way."

"What did Hatton advise we do this time?"

Bayless paused again, evading the question. "I'm going to insist he get his ass up here to look at the dam. We need to consult in person. In the meantime, Baldwin, keep your mouth shut about his coming here. That'll make the people nervous. We don't need that. We need to promote calm in the town. Business as usual, you know."

"Well, I won't keep my mouth shut when it comes to giving you advice, George. That's my job. It's my job to protect your ass, remember. And I am concerned about the situation, very, very concerned."

"I'll call you when Hatton arrives," Bayless responded dismissively, rising from his chair to signal the end of the conversation. "I want you to meet with Hatton, Hamlin, and me at that time but not until then." The two titans stood facing each other wordlessly. A standoff.

Baldwin turned and marched out the door, grabbing his umbrella propped against Edith's desk. She flinched as he blew by and then looked out the window. *When can we put the umbrellas away?* she wondered. The rain was relentless. When mill's whistle blew late that afternoon signaling the end of a shift for the mill workers and the end of the day for Edith, she said good night to an empty office (Mini Porky had long since departed to the Odd Fellows Hall for some brandies and cigars), slipped on her galoshes and rain gear, and stepped out onto the water-logged boards serving as a sidewalk. The rain had not diminished. It continued unabated through night and into the next day.

Friday
September 29

IF GEORGE BAYLESS WAS CONSIDERED the king of this little fiefdom of Austin, and Senator Frank Baldwin a knight in shining armor, then most folks considered William "Willie" Nelson—some called him "Crazy Willie"—the court jester. He made the people of Austin laugh.

It wasn't because of his wit or ability to tell a good tale but because of his odd obsession with the Bayless Dam. Nelson simply didn't trust it. His apprehension was heightened in the spring of this year when the mill superintendent had ordered an unprecedented release of water. That's when Willie started his daily morning ritual of unauthorized and unappreciated inspection of the dam.

His mile-long slog on Mill Road began this morning, as it had for the past two weeks, in a wind-driven downpour. He pulled up the hood of his slicker and leaned into the wind as pelts of water stung his face in an unrelenting but unsuccessful, effort to drive him back to the comfort of his home. As always, with a postman's dedication and the will of a St. Bernard on a mission of rescue, he was not deterred. In the early morning half-light, dimmed further by a veil of rain, he could not see the dam but felt its presence looming ahead of him.

A giant, he thought, *but not simply a giant. More like an ogre. A giant, menacing ogre ready to pounce on me and my town behind me.*

The analogy struck him as strangely funny, and he laughed out loud despite his discomfort and foreboding. *Maybe I am Jack climbing the bean stock, but god save me, this is a giant I cannot slay.*

He trudged past the mill, the machinery behind its walls processing pulpwood into paper that would be fed into the hungry printing presses of newspapers throughout Pennsylvania and New York. The tracks of the muddy road disappeared into a maze—row after row—of thousands of cords of four-foot lengths of pulpwood stacked above him. He wound his way through the stacks suddenly overcome with exhaustion and a sense of futility.

He had never seen the pulpwood inventory at Bayless Mill this expansive. *They must have had another rail delivery yesterday. How far does it stretch? An acre? Two acres? God help us if the pent-up waters behind the dam were to sweep up these missiles and hurl them toward the town.* The thought further numbed his senses. Disorientation morphed into confusion, and then momentary panic until he finally stumbled out of the maze into open ground.

He plodded on until it came into sight. The giant, the ogre, the monster looming before him. He fell to his knees on the muddy embankment slopping upward to its base as if in supplication to a deity, awestruck by the sheer enormity of thirty-two million tons of concrete, quarry stones, and steel rods cobbled together through engineering genius, or so it was said.

As a self-appointed inspector, Nelson would normally approach the dam close to its base and walk nearly half its length to the spillway at its center, carefully surveying its fifty-foot-high surface for any cracks or signs of weakness. Now one hundred feet from the base, impeded by the gushing waters of the widening outflow stream on his right and gripped by a paralyzing fear within, he had no desire to proceed.

At that distance, and with such limited visibility, any kind of meaningful inspection was impossible. He scanned instead for something he had seen yesterday—something that bothered him immensely. There had been a man on top of the breastworks leaning out over the railing of the spillway platform obviously looking for signs of trouble. It confirmed what he suspected. There were others—others from within the mill's workforce—who shared his concern. Maybe he wasn't "Crazy Willy" after all.

No one appeared on top of the breastworks this morning, but there was something he did observe that was equally troubling. The water pooling at the base of the spillway before it sped off toward town was agitated, not only by the overflow spilling into the pool but also a bubbling turbulence from below.

Nelson's heart seemed to clinch and skip a beat as a chilling thought coursed through him. He was no engineer, but his instincts told him that such percolating meant that water had found a breach through the bedrock beneath the dam, weakening the structure—perhaps fatally—in a way that was not obvious. He rose, turned, and began his journey back to town, shivering from cold and fear.

Later that morning, after opening his grocery store on Main Street, he tried to explain this phenomenon to a legion of disinterested customers. Some listened politely. Some walked away shaking their heads. Willy was such a regular guy most of the time, congenial as a good grocer should be. Sane as hell until he started talking about the dam. Crazy Willie. Paranoid Willie.

* * *

IT WAS A SMALL SPACE on the third-floor rear corner of Austin's most substantial and prestigious edifice at the corner of Main Street and Turner Avenue, two blocks from the Main Street bridge, housing two federally regulated institutions, the First National Bank of Austin and the United States Post Office. Bank officials had rather magnanimously—in their opinion, at least—allocated the space as a public service for the town's telephone exchange.

Pauline Lyons, full of youthful enthusiasm and unfettered curiosity, sat behind a desk facing a board of cords and receptacles, a telephone operator's workstation, filing her long, bright red fingernails—quite unsuited to her job in the catty opinion of her colleagues.

Pauline, in her confident, sometimes flamboyant style, was mostly immune to such criticism. And while her enthusiasm was a public relations asset, endearing her to many of the town's customers on the exchange, her curiosity, a penchant to monitor many of the conversations she connected, was not appreciated nearly as much. As a consequence, most folks were both charmed and guarded when they heard Pauline's cheery "number please."

The one-windowed space on the Turner Street side of the building overlooked a two-block vista of one and two-story commercial buildings clustered along Main Street up to the bridge over Freeman's Run. The bridge spanned the creek, now swollen to river size by the outflow from the dam upstream. The bridge connected the commercial center of Austin on the west bank to the east side where houses dotted an increasingly steep slope leading to the hospital and school

The window was on the right side of Pauline's corner workstation, providing her a welcome cool albeit damp breeze and a view of the town. She welcomed both on this rainy autumn day. It would take more than raindrops to dampen her spirit. Two more workstations were positioned on her left, the first chair empty, and the one against the far wall occupied by the prim middle-aged Lena Binckley who was currently observing Pauline's nail buffing with undisguised disgust.

Pauline remained oblivious to Lena's frown and body posture, content with the breeze and the slightly less crowded atmosphere without a third operator on duty.

Lena broke the silence. "I wish you wouldn't do that, Pauline. It's annoying."

Pauline turned to Lena with an apologetic smile and dropped the nail file onto her lap. Determined not to let Lena get under her skin, she adjusted her headset and turned her focus to the board in front of her, noting the appearance of several flashing lights. "I'll get these, Lena," and then with the slightest hint of sarcasm, continued, "just relax."

She connected the calls, stifling the urge to linger on the line on a call from Burgess Michael Murrin to Cora Brook's house. What she could tell many unsuspecting wives or confirm to many suspecting wives in town! But that was not Pauline's style. She accumulated information on these little eavesdrops that was useful or interesting to her and discarded the rest to her mental trash bin.

Calls to or from Cora's house of pleasure were of passing interest to her, but the juiciest tidbits usually came from the long-distance calls. The next caller had her full attention.

"Austin operator, please connect me to the offices of the Bayless Mill."

"Yes, ma'am, right away." Pauline hung on the line as she connected the call hoping that Lena would not notice.

"Fred Hamlin speaking," answered a gruff voice. Pauline barely recognized the clipped, stress-filled voice of the plant supervisor.

"Mr. Hamlin, this is Mr. Hatton's secretary calling from Wilmington."

"Yes, where the hell is he?"

"Ah, that's why I'm calling, sir. Mr. Hatton asked me to call you regarding his travel plans to Austin."

"Thank God. He's on his way then?"

"Yes, sir. He drove to Philadelphia last night and called me from the Broad Street Station early this morning before boarding the Pennsy express to Harrisburg. He will transfer to the Buffalo Division there and arrive in Keating Summit this evening at seven ten. He asked if you could pick him up."

Pauline knew that Keating Summit was a scheduled stop on the Buffalo Line, eight miles from Austin with a one-room train station, a water tank to quench the thirst of the steam-driven locomotives, and a nearby telegraph office. Passengers bound for Austin could hope for a reasonably good connection on the Buffalo Susquehanna line, but Pauline knew that no trains ran after six o'clock

"Okay," Hamlin grumbled, then paused.

"Mr. Hamlin?"

"Yeah."

"You will pick him up then?

"Yes, I'll pick him up."

"And he also requested that you reserve a room for him at the Goodyear Hotel."

"Boarding house not good enough for him?"

"Sir?"

"Never mind. I'll pick him up and book him a room. Anything else?"

"No, sir."

"One more thing. Is he traveling coach or parlor car?"

"Parlor car, sir."

"Pretentious son of a bitch." Hamlin shocked the secretary with his response and hung up knowing that Hatton's travel expenses would be passed on to Bayless at the end of the day.

Pauline unplugged simultaneously. She was not surprised at the reaction of the notoriously cheap mill superintendent. She was surprised, however, at the content of the conversation. She knew of the reputation of T. Chalky Hatton of the esteemed Wilmington engineering firm and of his close connection with the Bayless organization as primary architect of the Bayless Dam.

Even so, her suspicion meter might not have spiked into the red zone, had she not connected some dots provided by her friend Edith at the mill office. Edith, it seems, had overheard a rather heated discussion between Edith's boss, George Bayless, and Bayless attorney Frank Baldwin yesterday afternoon.

Pauline began to make the connections signs of turmoil in the upper ranks of the Bayless organization. An urgent summons to the design engineer of the dam. Something was wrong. Something was scary wrong.

She thought she should share her concerns with someone but realized she had no idea who to call or what to say.

* * *

"IS THAT GRACE COLLINS CALLING again, Ed?"

Doctor Edward Mansuey, holding the phone receiver to his ear and phone set in his other hand, turned to his wife, Mary, mouthed "*yes*," then turned away. He couldn't deal with two impatient ladies at the same time. He turned his attention back to the one on the line.

"Yes, Grace. I see. I'm sure it's another symptom of cognitive decline in your mother, Grace. Yes, Grace. Yes, Grace, it's not unusual for a woman of seventy-four. No, no, of course, no offense intended. Well, perhaps I could look in on her tonight. Yes, I'll be there shortly."

Grace was off the line before he could say goodbye.

"You let her bully you, Ed," Mary huffed as she set a casserole of pot roast and potatoes on the kitchen table. "Please sit down while dinner is hot."

"Just keep it warm for me, Mary. I need to pay a visit to calm her down. God knows she has a enough hardship taking care of her aging parents. I'll be back as soon as I can." He picked up his black medical bag, grabbed his rain gear, and turned toward the front door without waiting for a response. Mary's attention was already diverted, however, as she ran to the bedroom to attend to the cries of their infant son. He felt a touch of guilty relief knowing that the ensuing argument would be postponed until his return.

Doctor Mansuey, the younger of Austin's two resident physicians, quickly paced the two blocks through the puddles and light ran to the residence of Grace Collins and her parents, John and Josephine Baldwin. The Baldwins, the parents of the Honorable Frank Baldwin, had maintained a degree of prominence in the social circles of Austin until their deteriorating health kept them homebound in recent years.

Frank, to his credit, took good financial care of his widowed sister Grace and their aging parents but was precluded by his busy schedule (and some would say his conceited nature) from any measure of caregiving. That was Grace's job to which she was not well suited either.

Nervous, impatient, and tending toward hypochondria, Grace called the good doctor frequently and at all hours for issues more often perceived than real. Doctor Mansuey, the junior doctor in town with a newly established practice, always responded, much to the growing annoyance of his wife.

Grace was waiting for him on the top step of her front porch. "Oh, Doctor, thank you for coming. Let me take your raincoat. You can leave your galoshes on the porch." Grace always voiced appreciation for his visits that made it somewhat easier for Doctor Mansuey to overlook her demanding nature. Not so for Mrs. Mansuey.

Grace led the doctor into the sitting room of her substantial home, the closest thing to a mansion by Austin standards with the exception of her brother's recently constructed stately manor on the east side of town. Her father, John, crippled by rheumatoid arthritis, sat in his wheelchair near the entrance. The walking cane he had used in years past gathered dust now, propped against the stairwell bannister. Grace had moved him into a downstairs bedroom. He gave Mansuey a vacant smile.

Grace took little notice of her father as she quick paced across the sitting room to a couch where her mother Josephine was squirming restlessly.

"Hello, Doctor," Josephine piped up in greeting as she waved her hands in front of her. Doctor Mansuey at first mistook the gesture as a handshake offer but withdrew his hand quickly as he recognized she had something else in mind. "He's somewhere in the house," she continued, pointing first to the stairs and then at the kitchen."

"Who, Mrs. Baldwin?" the young doctor asked politely.

"Why my son, James, of course."

Mansuey knew that James, the third and youngest Baldwin sibling, had succumbed years ago to scarlet fever. Grace and Frank were careful not to mention their deceased brother in the presence of their parents who harbored a grief undiminished by the passing years. Mansuey looked to Grace for help.

"Now, Mother, you know that James lives in Buffalo."

Mansuey winced. He would have preferred that Grace try to keep her mother in the world of reality. He didn't believe in unnecessary confrontation with patients suffering from dementia, but neither did he believe in creating a fantasy world for them.

The game was played by Grace's rules, however, and so a bizarre conversation bouncing between fact and fantasy continued for the next hour. Finally, Mansuey, after checking temperature and heart-rate of both elderly patients and knowing that his pot roast was cold and his wife distressed, attempted to bring the meeting to a close.

"Your mother can take two of these pills before bedtime, Grace. You can do that every night from now on. It should calm her and make her rest easier." With that, Mansuey rose and headed for the door."

"Doctor," Grace pleaded as he reached for the door knob. "You will come again when I need you, won't you?"

"Of course," he replied with full knowledge that his visits were more about Grace's loneliness than her parents' medical condition.

He marched hurriedly off the porch, galoshes in hand and rain-coat collar open before she could summon him back. He noted that the rain had picked up again.

* * *

AT THE GOODYEAR HOTEL ON the corner of Main Street and Railroad Avenue, Barney Anderson, bartender and sometimes front desk attendant at the Goodyear Hotel, bored, yet restless, trudged at an arthritic pace along the thirty-foot distance of the dark, distressed wood bar sweeping its surface in circular patterns with an overused rag. He figured he must have wet-ragged the bar twenty times in the last four hours since coming on duty slightly past two o'clock on this dreary Friday afternoon. As he moved to the center of the bar, he raised the rag to his nose, suppressed a reflexive gag, and threw it in the corner.

A few stragglers from the four o'clock end-of-shift mill-worker crowd remained at the far end of the bar. Barney turned his attention to a newly arrived customer seating himself in front of the bartender. "The usual, Brady?

"The usual, Barney," came the weary response from Brady Quinn, punctual, disheveled, and anxious as always for his afterwork beverage. Quinn's arrival at ten minutes past five on weekday after-noons and ten minutes past noon on Saturdays—liquor wasn't served on Sunday—was determined by the closing time of his law office on upper Main Street and a ten-minute walk down the hill to the Goodyear.

Why Quinn, the senior and only partner of the Quinn Law firm, maintained such a rigid office schedule was a mystery to towns-people who rarely saw a client coming or going beneath the battered shingle over his door. In appearance and style, Quinn was the polar opposite of Austin's only other barrister—the honorable Frank E. Baldwin, Esquire.

Barney squinted at the bottles stacked in neat rows behind the bars searching for Quinn's favorite whiskey in the dimming light of early evening. He switched on the two chandelier ceiling lights as he reached for the bottle. The artificial illumination, meager as it was, seemed to startle two businessmen seated some distance from the bar at a corner table.

This mix of clientele was not unusual for the Goodyear. Located near the bridge at the corner of Main Street and Railroad Avenue, it attracted both higher-end customers for its accommodations and dining as well as local mill workers (some of whom were detained at Cora's place on their way) for an end-of-shift beverage or two. On the few occasions when a lady entered the dining room, Barney cautioned the bar crowd to tone down and clean up the language. It was one of the few dining establishments, and certainly the only tavern, that was deemed socially acceptable for a lady with, but only with, a gentleman escort.

There were no ladies tonight and, in fact, not much of a crowd at all. By eight o'clock, the two businessmen had departed followed in short order by the cook and the night clerk. At ten o'clock, Barney announced to one very inebriated attorney and one remaining mill worker in a similar state that the bar was about to close. The mill worker wobbled off his barstool and headed for the door. Quinn did not move, partly paralyzed by alcohol but mostly fixed on his stool in stubborn Irish defiance. After a few moments of impatient pacing, Barney unceremoniously heisted Quinn up by the back of his crumpled collar and marched him to the front door, ignoring the profanity-laced objections.

For the next half hour, Barney washed glasses, wiped the bar for the last time, and swept the floor. He was about to collapse in one of the overstuffed lobby chairs to give his swollen knees a rest when Fred Hamlin burst through the outside entrance. Hamlin, angst-ridden on his calmest days, now drenched in a mixture of sweat and rain, carried a suitcase in either hand. He was followed by a distinguished-looking gentleman in a tailored three-piece suit and stylish homburg hat. The gentlemen shook off his umbrella, folded it, and smiled at Barney.

"I have a guest here with a reservation," Hamlin sputtered, dropping the bags at the front desk. "You on duty tonight, Barney?" Hamlin knew full well that it was part of Barney's duties to register late arriving guests.

"Yes, sir, Mister Hamlin," replied Barney limping behind the desk. He turned to the approaching gentleman. "Name please?"

"Hatton. T. Chalkley Hatton from Wilmington, Delaware, sir," the gentleman announced in a quiet, confident voice.

Barney put on his "let's see" expression as he shuffled through some papers, knowing full well that he had only one reservation for the evening. "Ah, here it is, Mister Hatton, the executive suite." Out of the corner of his eye, he noted a flinch of disgust from Hamlin. "Would you sign here, please? And how long will you be staying? The reservation didn't specify."

"Not long, I hope. Let's say two nights"

"It may take you longer than that, Chalkley," Hamlin snorted.

"Yes, make it two nights. I'll let you know if I'm detained," Hatton addressed Barney, turning his back on Hamlin

"Very good, sir. Here is your key. Would you like…"

"Not so fast, Barney," Hamlin interrupted. "Open up the bar and give us a drink, then take the bags to Mister Hatton's *suite*." He spat out the last word for sarcastic emphasis.

Barney never liked Hamlin, and his bossy attitude now might have triggered a challenging response but for the sake of the polite and polished gentleman with him. Barney glared at Hamlin but bit his lip as he limped across the lobby to reopen the bar. He seated the two at a table and delivered two tumblers of top-shelf whiskey before he lugged the two bags up to the stairs.

Returning to the bar, he maintained a discreet distance but close enough to gather snippets of the conversation. The hushed tones denoted a serious and confidential matter under discussion, but occasionally Hamlin's voice would rise in extreme agitation.

"Need to get your ass to…office…early…thorough inspection…assurance…damn well…no more bullshit."

Barney's usually reliable radar began beeping. It signaled trouble. And by the time the conversation broke off, and Hatton headed to his room, Barney was pretty sure he was onto a juicy piece of gossip for tomorrow's bar crowd. He wondered about the man from Wilmington and what his presence had to do with the Bayless Mill. He decided to call Willie Nelson in the morning to see if he could connect the two.

Saturday morning
September 30

"WHITEY" HATTON ROSE EARLY TO the dull gray light of predawn. He hurriedly washed, shaved, reached into the small hotel closet, pushed aside the two hangers of herringbone tweed suits, and selected denim bib overalls instead. Wool socks and a frayed, heavy turtleneck sweater completed his dress for the day—an ensemble never seen in the offices of Hatton, Bixby, & Rollins.

Slipping into knee-high rubber boots, he grabbed a hooded rain slicker draped across the room's sole sitting chair, stepped briskly into the hallway, and tromped down one flight of stairs to the lobby. There he was greeted by a sleepy-eyed night clerk seemingly oblivious to the unusual attire worn by the businessman registered in suite 200.

"Morning, sir," came a yawn-stifled greeting from behind the registration desk. "Cook hasn't arrived yet for breakfast, but I have a hot pot of coffee fresh brewed on the stove in the kitchen. Pour you a cup?"

Hatton nodded assent. "Thank you. May I use the desk phone, my good man?"

"Certainly, sir. I'll be right back with your coffee. You like it black?"

Another nod, and the clerk disappeared into the kitchen. Hatton reached for the phone, lifted the ear piece and double clicked the receiver.

At the Telephone Exchange, Hazel Knapp watched the blinking light on the board in front of her. It was the first sign of a town awakening and the first call to the Exchange in nearly six hours. Hazel liked the solitude of the night shift, sometimes called the dead shift, and although the shift was assigned on a rotating basis among Austin's six full-time operators, she voluntarily traded for the bulk of these shifts. She couldn't remember the last time Pauline or Lena worked the dead shift where the gossip they relished, except for the few calls from Cora's house, was nearly nonexistent.

"Number pa-*leaze*," Hazel drawled sweetly into her headset.

"Please connect me to the home of Fred Hamlin. I don't know his number."

"Yes, sir. One moment, sir, while I look up that number." Hazel paused to give the impression of diligent research for her customer though she had no need to look up the number, nor for that matter numbers for the majority of the nearly three thousand residents of Austin. "Yes, sir. The number is 1738-J if you would like to make note of it, and fortunately, no one is on this party line at this moment."

Hatton shifted his weight impatiently from one leg to the other as he waited for the call to be connected. Finally, he heard Hamlin's gruff voice on the other end of the line. "Yeah, this is Hamlin."

"Where are you, Fred? You were to pick me up at six o'clock."

"Obviously, I'm at home, Hatton. Put a rein on those horses. What's the rush, anyway? The dam isn't going anywhere."

Hatton abandoned his usually genteel demeanor. "Listen, Fred," his voice raised half an octave, "I told you I wanted to start the inspection at first light. I traveled nearly three hundred miles at your request yesterday, and I have a job to do. From what I've heard, I don't think we can afford to waste a minute."

Hamlin, quite unused to taking orders but taken back by the urgency in Hatton's voice, stifled an instinctive vulgar retort. "I'll be there in a minute," he snorted and hung up.

Sliding one arm into his rain slicker, Hatton accepted the mug of hot coffee offered by the clerk, nodded appreciation, and headed for the front door to wait on the hotel porch.

"No need for the rain gear, sir. The rain has stopped, and the sun is coming up."

Hatton stepped outside. Indeed, it was a beautiful crisp morning in early autumn.

* * *

COLOR DRAINED FROM WHITEY HATTON'S normally ruddy complexion giving him a pallid appearance not unlike his nickname. Clearly shaken by the twenty-minute crawl across the overflow washed breastworks of the Bayless Dam to its center platform, Hatton grasped the railing for support as he rose weak-kneed to his feet. Bob Pearson, a relative veteran of that journey, stood composed and alert by his side.

"Catch your breath, Mister Hatton," Pearson offered, peering down at the cascade of water rushing over the spillway a few feet below where they stood.

"We've got to relieve the pressure, Bob. When did the water breach the top of the dam?"

"On Thursday, sir. First time ever. Scared the shit out of me, excuse my French, which is what I told the Super. He kinda shrugged me off."

"Well, that was a mistake, Bob, and we're going to do something about that right now." Hatton turned and took a stride toward the horizontal wheel centered on the platform designed by Hatten himself to open the valve to release water through a thirty-six inch clean out pipe through the center of the dam at the base of the spillway. He clamped his shaking hands on the waist-high wheel. "Take hold on the far side. We're going to crank open the relief valve."

"The Super won't like that, sir."

"To hell with Hamlin. It's got to be done, and it's got to be done now."

Together they strained to move the wheel counter clockwise, both men's feet slipping on the wet deck. The wheel wouldn't budge.

"When's the last time the valve was opened, Bob?" Hatton was gulping air and feeling the scream of seldom-used core muscles.

"Little over a year ago," came the reply. "Caused some flooding in the town, and Super took a lot of flak for that from the old man."

"Damn the both of them! I told Hamlin this wheel had to be greased, and the valve opened at least once a month to keep it serviceable. Now put some ballsy effort into it this time, man." Resenting Hatton's rebuff, Pearson tightened his grip, lowered his shoulder for more leverage, and pushed forward with all the force he could muster.

Hatton wasn't sure if the groaning sound came from the wheel or the muscular maintenance man opposite him, but it was encouragement enough for him to redouble his own aching effort. The wheel budged. He was sure of it.

They paused to recover. Then slowly at first but with increasing momentum, they marched in a circle, pushing the wheel one full revolution. After the second revolution, the wheel locked.

"That should be full open, Mr. Hatton."

Together they peered over the platform's railing down the outward sloping face of the dam expecting to see a rush of water from the outlet pipe churning in the pool at the foot of the spillway. They saw nothing more than the constant soft turbulence, the same percolation seen yesterday by grocery store owner Willie Nelson. Unlike Nelson, who only suspected that seepage through an insufficient bedrock base was the cause of the percolation, Hatten was sure of it. He was now certain of something else as well.

"Son of a bitch! The valve's open, but the cleanout pipe is clogged." He sunk to his knees in exhaustion and frustration.

"Those vertical cracks below us, Bob. Are they wider than what you saw two days ago?"

"Yes, sir, I think they are. No, I mean I'm sure they are. Last week they were just hairline cracks on either side of the spillway. The further down they extend now, the wider they get."

"Bob, you've got to go back and get help. I'm staying here. I've crawled across the breast once and the next time for sure will be my last. Bring Hamlin back with you along with men to carry the material I'll need. Tell him I said to get his ass up here if he wants to avert a disaster. And Bob, listen closely, what I need are ten pounds of dynamite, a sack of sand, one hundred feet of strong rope, an equal length of electric wire, blasting caps, and a plunger detonator box."

Pearson's eyes widened.

"Don't ask questions, Bob. Just do it!"

* * *

"DO THIS IN MEMORY OF ME." The good Father O'Brien's soft voice floated from the altar of nearly vacant church as he raised the chalice at the most solemn moment of the eight o'clock Mass at St. Augustine on Ruckgaber Avenue. Kneeling parishioners, the same faithful few who routinely attended daily Mass, touched their hearts with closed fists in signs of reverence.

Looking past the chalice in his hands, Father O'Brien scanned the faces of the sparse gathering before him, marveling at the peace evident in this space during such time of stress. Momentarily distracted from the liturgy, he was absorbed with a longing, so strong it approached the threshold of the cardinal sin of envy for such simple, unquestioning faith.

He was sure that the faith-filled prayers on their lips and in their hearts this morning, a mixture of petitions of thanksgiving and pleas for deliverance from harm, would be heard. He was less certain that the prayers he offered, corrupted by cynicism and uncertainty, would be so received. As he paused to reflect upon the comparative weakness of his own faith, Father O'Brien bowed his head and asked for forgiveness. Would the Almighty protect him and his flock from the ravages of nature and the sins of man? He had his doubts.

* * *

AN HOUR AFTER FATHER O'BRIEN concluded the Mass with a final blessing, Bob Pearson returned to the platform, leading a party of four across the breast of the dam. Behind Pearson marched a surly, stoutly built Fred Hamlin followed by three burly workmen carrying the material Hatton had requested.

During Pearson's absence, the water level behind the dam, no longer fed by relentless rain, had subsided below the rim allowing the early morning sun to semidry the walkway surface. With much improved footing, the men approached the platform at a relatively brisk pace. What Pearson now observed removed any doubt about the courage of the architect/engineer from Wilmington as abruptly and completely as the rain had ceased hours ago. Fred Hamlin's reaction was not as generous.

"Sweet Jesus! What are you doing out there?" Hamlin bellowed as they stepped onto the platform. Unable to hear over the roar of water still cascading down the spillway, Hatton, lay prone on the catwalk extension of the platform over the face of the dam. As they watched, he inched further out, now bending over the edge to get a better view of the dam's outer surface.

Pearson, still in the lead as their feet hit the platform, ran onto the catwalk, fell to his knees, and grabbed hold of Hatton's ankles. "Jesus, Mister Hatton," he screamed, echoing Hamlin, as he pulled him back to the platform. "What are you doing?"

"I'm trying to get a closer look at those cracks on either side of the spillway," Hatton announced as he righted himself squarely in the contorted face of the Supervisor of Bayless Mill.

"Are you nuts, Hatton?" Hamlin spat, spraying spittle in his rage. "What's the meaning of dragging us all up here?"

"In language you might understand, Fred, I'm trying to save this dam and your fucking sorry ass in the process." Hamlin stepped back. The never-before-heard profanity from the dignified engineer stunned all of them into temporary silence. "The structure is seriously close to failure, Fred, and in large measure because you refused to open the outlet valve routinely. Now when we desperately need to reduce the pressure, the cleanout pipe is clogged."

Hatton abruptly clapped his hand on Hamlin's shoulder, and the others cowered backward sure that a brawl was about to erupt. Hatton used such force to direct Hamlin to the side of the platform that it appeared he was dragging him. In shock, Hamlin neither responded nor resisted.

"There, Fred! There! Do you see that crack beyond the spillway? There's another one on the other side, Fred. Pearson tells me they were hairlines last week. Does that look like a hairline to you now, Fred? I was trying to see how far they extend toward the base, and the answer is as far as I can see. This dam is in danger of breaching, Fred!"

The color seemed to drain from Fred Hamlin's face. "What do you propose we do?"

"I don't propose you do anything, Fred, but stay out of the way. I am going to try to lay an explosive charge near the mouth of that pipe to clear it." He paused. "Actually, there is something you can do. Pray it works."

* * *

AT THAT VERY MOMENT, TWO miles from the drama unfolding at the dam, Clare Benger, following her usual Saturday morning schedule, arrived at Austin's one-room schoolhouse on High Road, located on the hill east of the Main Street bridge. Clare was extremely meticulous as a teacher and in her personal habits. Saturday morning was her quiet time when she readied the classroom and prepared lesson plans for the coming week.

Clare bustled about in a carefree manner, generally reflecting the mood of most of the townspeople buoyed by the sunshine. Four days of continuous rain had been depressing. She dusted the desks for her thirty elementary students. Now only four weeks into the school year, she was just getting to know the first graders and missing last year's eighth graders who had moved on to the high school in Costello five miles away. She felt badly for those students who had to endure the long walk to and from school, especially in the frigid winter months to come.

The room was cramped and excessively noisy on school days, certainly not the teaching environment she would have preferred. She wished she had more desks, at least one per student, but the space would not permit it. What she really wanted was a new school house, but her pleas to the school board and the town's board of burgesses fell on deaf ears. "Why don't you ask George Bayless to build us one? The tightwad can afford it, but we can't." was the response. Disappointed, but not defeated, Clare remained hopeful.

Dusting completed, Clare turned her attention to lesson plans. Because she was so exacting, it would take her hours, but she didn't mind. She was a middle-aged single lady who had plenty of time. She loved the work, and she loved her students.

Sitting at her desk in front of the blackboard, she looked out the window toward the Bayless Mill and the dam beyond. Her friend Pauline Lyons had told her of the strange call she overheard yesterday from the mill supervisor to an engineering firm in Wilmington, Delaware. Clare's interest had peaked. She loved a good piece of gossip as much as Pauline. She wondered what was happening at the dam.

* * *

T. CHALKLEY "WHITEY" HATTON, the senior partner of the distinguished firm of Hatton, Bixby, & Rollins, shed his rain slicker in deference to the clear skies and rising midmorning temperature. He crawled once again to the edge of the catwalk. This time, Pearson insisted upon tying a length of rope around Hatton's waist and securing the other end to a platform post. On his knees, holding the end of a longer rope coiled on the platform, Hatton shouted over his shoulder, "Hand me the sandbag."

A line of men formed a bucket brigade with Pearson and one man on their knees behind Hatton on the catwalk, and Hamlin and another standing on the platform. The sandbag was lifted, deposited on the catwalk, then dragged hand to hand out to Hatton. He tied the sandbag securely to the end of the rope. The brigade followed the next set of commands by passing to Hatton, in this order, ten sticks of dynamite bound together, a box of blasting caps, and a roll of thin copper wire. The plunger detonator box remained on the platform

Hatton, his hands beginning to shake as the adrenaline rush of his anger wore off, attached the wire to a blasting cap and carefully inserted it into the end of one of the dynamite sticks. Next, he tied the dynamite package to the rope approximately ten feet behind the sandbag. He asked for gloves and then passed the coils of wire and rope back down the line.

Hatton cautiously nudged the sandbag over the edge. As gravity took hold of the sandbag, and the rope slipped a few feet through his gloved hands, he tightened his grip to arrest its descent, nearly losing his balance. Pearson grabbed Hatton's belt to steady him. Taking a deep breath, Hatton turned to address the two men standing on the platform. "Now slowly uncoil the rope and the wire as I lower, or rather," he paused with a deferential nod to Pearson, "*we* lower the dynamite."

The rope and wire uncoiled simultaneously. The sandbag, followed by the dynamite, descended slowly down the face of the spillway. Twenty-five feet from the top, halfway to the base, the sandbag touched the face of the outward sloping spillway, and the cascading water nearly ripped the bag from the line. The force yanked at the men on the other end.

"Pull her up," Hatton shouted frantically. They raised the bag a few feet out the clutches of spillway water.

Pearson had a death grip on Hatton's belt. "What do we do now, sir?" he shouted back.

"We can't drop it directly from here into the pool where the pipe outlets," Hatton responded in a more controlled tone. "I need to get it out beyond the angle of the spillway so the waterfall won't shred the sandbag and the dynamite. Hold that rope in position and have the two men on the platform lower me on the rope tied around me."

"What?" came the astonished reply.

"How long is the rope I'm tethered to?"

"I cut off about thirty feet, I think. I saved the rest for the dynamite."

"Good. Now tell Hamlin to lower me and hang the fuck on. Tell the other guy too. I don't trust Hamlin."

"Mr. Hatton, I…"

"Just tell them, damn it. I need to swing that bag out over the pool."

Pearson complied, and seconds later, Hatton was dangling spread eagle and out of control fifty feet above the base, fighting for breath as the rope cut into his gut, and praying that Pearson's knot would hold.

* * *

CORA BROOKS, SLEEPING SOUNDLY IN the comfort of her quilted covers, bolted to a sitting position, knuckled crust from her bloodshot eyes, and squinted at the bright midmorning light streaming through her bedroom window. Cora hadn't seen sunlight in so long that the vision seemed almost surreal. Her brain wasn't prepared to greet the day either.

Early morning to Cora's nocturnally conditioned biorhythms meant something after the noon whistle at the factory. Midmorning was usually that lazy period those of higher breeding associated with afternoon tea. If she were to get up at this hour, she would need some steaming, sailor-strong coffee, but none of her ladies, all fast asleep after a hard night's work, would hear her call. Resigned, Cora rose to close the window curtains, opting for more sleep instead.

What she saw as she reached for the curtains shocked her awake more abruptly than any jolt of nitro-level java. Her dam-facing window clearly framed a sunlit body dangling from a length of rope attached to the spillway platform. *Somebody hanged himself*, was her first thought.

Further scrutiny, however, convinced her that a man was being lowered down the face of the dam. Her second thought turned from alarm to annoyance. *Damn fool*. Thoroughly agitated at such ignorance, she decided to dress. There would be no more sleep for Cora this day.

* * *

HATTON HAD NO TIME FOR feelings of self-conscious folly or fear. He stayed laser focused solely on his efforts to steady himself and the package of sandbag and dynamite ten feet beneath him. *Get control of yourself first*, he thought but found it impossible to quiet the inertia-fed spin and the wind-fed sway of his body. It occurred to him how much easier it would have been had he been in a harness. As it was, his only protection from free fall was the rope around his waist, and his only connection to the package were the rope and wire inching through his gloved hands.

He reflexively tightened his grip, thus arresting the descent of the package. He was relieved to feel the tension of the line and the added weight of the package begin to stabilize his movement. He took two deep breaths to assess his situation. As the spin and sway diminished, he freed one hand to signal the men above to lower him further.

When he was approximately fifteen feet below the platform with the bag of sand again nearly touching the outward-slanting spillway overflow, he signaled to stop the descent. Carefully, he began to swing the sand and dynamite like a pendulum in an ever-wider arc parallel to the face of the spillway.

He fought to keep both his nerves and the rhythmic motion of the package under control. He knew the next move would be crucial. Did he have the strength? Could he maintain his balance? He clenched his teeth in mental preparation.

When he felt he had the package swinging at the maximum arc he could manage, he muscled an abrupt change in the angle of the forward motion. He directed the package out away from the face of the dam and released his grip. The sandbag and dynamite, rope and wire attached, sailed upward and outward from the spillway before gravity guided it down toward the ponding water at the base of the spillway.

It wasn't exactly a perfect hit, not quite in the center of the pond but close enough to satisfy Hatton. Crucially, he had avoided contact with the waterfall and its ripping effect on the package. He waited for the sticks of dynamite to disappear below the surface and delayed another moment to allow the sandbag to hit bottom, positioning the dynamite, he hoped, close enough to the mouth of the cleanout pipe to be effective.

He jerked one thumb upward as a signal to pull him back to the platform. It would be a matter of debate later as to whether the signal was misinterpreted or whether Hamlin purposely ordered the man at the detonator box to push the plunger.

The result was the same, and at that particular moment in time, the cause made little difference to Hatton. The tremendous concussion of an underwater explosion blasted through the air tossing him helplessly out of control.

* * *

DOCTOR EDWARD MANSUEY, STARTLED BY the loud clap echoing down the valley, flinched a bit with stitching needle in hand as he pierced the skin of thirteen-year-old Madge Nelson. He was performing this minor surgery in his home, sewing up a forearm wound sustained this morning. Madge, renowned for high drama and low pain threshold, wailed as her mother, bending over her, whispered comforting words and her father, seated with her on the Mansuey's living room couch, struggled to restrain her.

Willie Nelson, grocery store owner and self-appointed protector of the town, was also distracted from his daughter's theatrics by the sound. An ominous feeling, emanating from the pit of his stomach, gripped him.

"Sorry," Mansuey mumbled to no one in particular and proceeded patiently, without missing a beat, to close the gash while trying to ignore as much as possible the whining, cooing, and struggling around him. Applying antiseptic and a protective bandage, he breathed, "*There*," signaling a successful completion of the surgery. Nelson loosened his restraining hold on Madge. Immediately, she sprang sobbing into her mother's arms. "Poor, poor dear," Mary Nelson repeated over and over as she smothered Madge in her bosom.

"Poor kid. Practically her first time outdoors after days of rain and look what happened," offered Nelson to break the awkward moment. "Fell off the backyard swing."

"Playground accidents happen, Willie," responded Mansuey. "Can't blame the girl with all this rain. We'll keep it clean and take out the stitches next week."

Hearing the doctor's words and imagining more pain, Madge's wails erupted again.

Nelson motioned for the doctor to follow him from the living room to the front porch. Once safely beyond his wife's hearing, Nelson confided, "Let's let things settle down in there, doc. The missus is much better at that stuff than us men folk."

Nelson turned away from Mansuey and peered north toward the dam that was now clearly visible in the distance, no longer cloaked in the perpetual mist of rainfall. "What the hell was the noise we heard a minute ago? It came from the direction of the dam, didn't it?"

Mansuey nodded.

"It sounds like trouble to me, doc. I need to hustle up there to see what's happening."

Mansuey nodded again, fully aware that Nelson was a perpetual worrywart. Still, he thought, it might be a cause for genuine alarm. "You go ahead, Willie. I can take it from here. Old Bessie and your buckboard are tied over there. I'll load your wife and child on board when we're finished. Bessie knows the way home well enough."

Nelson hurried across the porch, down the steps, and broke into a sprint toward the livery stable on Main Street without a thought of explanation to his wife and daughter.

Mansuey, watching Nelson turn the corner, felt a certain unease. Nelson, running at full speed, felt a heightened anxiety. Their feelings would be magnified a thousand times this day.

Saturday morning
Buffalo, New York

IN THE PAST TWO YEARS since Roy Durnstine, editor in chief of the *Buffalo Evening Times*, had hired the spirited young reporter, Katherine "Katie" Keenan from the *Erie Daily Times*, he considered her addition to his newsroom one of his very best staffing moves. There were times, however, that Katie's shoot-from-the-hip investigative style caused his stomach ulcers to stir and his balding head to flame red with anger.

Durnstine's blood pressure was just recovering from the most recent of such incidents when Katie's front page "scoop" involving alleged embezzlement of funds by a prominent banker's daughter caused such community blowback that he endured a rather scathing rebuke in the publisher's office. Durnstine's defense of his reporter's investigative initiative curried little favor with the boss and even less with a group of irate Daughters of the American Revolution (of which the accused was an officer in good standing) picketing outside the *Evening Times* building. The whole episode nearly cost Durnstine a demotion and Katie her job.

The publisher was ultimately appeased by the newspaper's uptick in circulation, a welcome event in the ongoing competition with the morning *Express*, and Durnstine's promise to keep his "ditsy, headstrong" reporter in check. Durnstine, in deference to his rarely expressed admiration both for Kate's dogged perseverance of a story and her writing skills, relayed a toned-down version of the publisher's message. He would simply be more judicious on what he assigned and what he approved for print.

On balance, Durnstine happily endured his occasional frustrations in exchange for the talent and aplomb that Katie brought to the newsroom. The publisher, he knew, mistook her enthusiasm for the mark of a lightweight and her style of dress as sign of a lesbian-leaning lifestyle. Wrong on both counts.

Her enthusiasm for the job was contagious, and it challenged all her peers to be better journalists. And her choice of tailored suit pants and jacket, accented by a no-frills, starched white blouse with tastefully embroidered collar, for her working attire was simply her statement of confidence in herself, equality in a male-dominated profession and defiance of the norm.

She's simply a one-of-a-kind, be-damned-with-conventional-standards self-assured young lady who can be both businesslike and feminine at the same time, Durnstine thought as he glanced in her direction from his central position at the editor's desk. He likened her to a fresh flower in a garden of testosterone-laden, smelly weeds.

A prurient thought entered his mind. He envisioned her in a steamy shower with her lustrous raven hair untied, flowing water drenched below her shoulders, casting droplets down her delicate, fair skin, beading on the nipples of her ample breasts, curving down the shape of her flat stomach and rounded hips, and finally passing through the softness between her shapely legs on its way to the drain.

A hand on his shoulder brought him out of the shower and back to the newsroom. The smoke-induced gravelly voice of his city editor came from behind him. "Chief, I'm headed out to make the rounds of the precinct blotters. We're pretty close to deadline. I could use some help."

Durnstine acknowledged the request with a nod, mildly annoyed to be startled back to reality. "Yea, an hour away to be exact. Go to first and second and call it in, Rappaport. I'll send Keenan to third."

Durnstine squinted through the smoky haze of the newsroom at the wall clock above Katie's desk, and then at Katie. His eyes registered ten o'clock and Katie fully dressed. She and other reporters were picking up the pace to put a final polish on their reports or complete a routine task. In Katie's case, the task, which she despised, was assembling the day's obituary notices.

Katie loved the syncopated background beat of the newsroom: the pounding rhythm of Underwood typewriters, the constant chatter of UPI and AP teletype machines, a cacophony of ringing telephones, and the occasional cry of "copy" above the din. The flurry of activity was no less energizing: the copyboy scurrying from desk to desk picking up copy paper from waving hands, editors ripping off chunks of wire copy from the state and national news feeds, and the dynamic of bodies in continual motion. The sounds and sights, mixed with the smell of cigarettes, sweat, and stress, combined to stimulate, not distract her from her work.

Finished, she snatched the paper from her typewriter, sprang to her feet, and hurriedly bypassed an approaching copyboy on the way to Durnstine's desk.

"Here's the last of the obits, chief," Katie chirped, slamming the paper down on the spike protruding on a stand beside him. "What's next?"

In a rush of guilt from his still-vivid mental fantasies, he avoided eye contact with her. "You're going to spike yourself doing that someday, Keenan. Slow down. I want you to help Rappaport with the police blotters. He's covering first and second precincts. You take the third and call in anything beyond the level of a scratched bumper or a domestic quarrel."

Slow down did not register with Katie. She flew out the door and down the street.

* * *

IN ANOTHER NEWSROOM LESS THAN two blocks away and in sharp contrast to the hectic pace at the *Evening Times*, Russ "Rusty" Shephard, city editor of the *Buffalo Express*, rocked back on his beat-up swivel chair, propped his feet on his desktop, and began chewing on a pencil, mentally decompressing following the close of the morning news cycle. Rusty, aptly nicknamed by his newspaper colleagues for his short-cropped auburn hair and his deliberate, meticulous style of reporting, savored this after-publication quiet of the newsroom. The *Evening Times*, publishing early afternoon, was peaking in its news cycle. At the *Express*, presses were silent, papers were on the street, and the newsroom wouldn't spring to life again until early evening.

Rusty's fingers followed a gold chain on his chest to a vest pocket and retrieved a gold-plated watch, a legacy from his father—also a newspaper man. "Guess the family has ink, not blood in its veins," Rusty was prone to say on occasion although neither his brother nor his sister had followed their father into the business of the fourth estate. Rusty was more like his father in other ways as well: intelligent, sometimes introspective, always quick-witted, meticulous, adverse to knee-jerk judgment, mild-mannered, and a lightening three-fingered typist. He was the golden boy journalist at the *Express* and on the fast track at age thirty, many colleagues thought, to be youngest editor in chief in its storied history.

Part of that history included an intense rivalry with the *Evening Times*. In Rusty's somewhat jaded opinion, the editorial credo of the *Evening Times* reporters was "get it first and at all costs." Rusty's personal mantra was "get it right at all costs." Most of the time, he got it both ways—first and right—much to the chagrin of Roy Durnstine. Rusty's widespread reputation as a quality journalist irked Durnstine. Anxious for any competitive advantage and determined to knock Rusty off that perceived pedestal, he closely scrutinized Rusty's prodigious output of copy, alert to any vulnerability. To date, he had found no misstep in accuracy or ethics to exploit.

Rusty's watch showed five minutes past ten. He slowly swung his feet to the floor, rolled down his sleeves, straightened his tie, picked up his suit coat, and headed for the exit. He was looking forward to a hardy breakfast at Al's Café, a brisk walk to his bachelor's pad on the second floor on the Main Street Pool Hall, a much-needed shower, and a savored few hours of sleep. The sharp first break of pool balls from below served as his alarm clock to start his daily cycle again.

On Saturdays, he retrieved his prized Model LD Maxwell Runabout car from a rented garage space for an escape to his widowed mother's house in Rochester for a good night's sleep and a home-cooked meal. If the publishers of the *Express* ever decided to print a Sunday edition that relaxing part of his weekly routine would be history.

In no hurry and not particularly hungry on this Saturday morning, Rusty strolled leisurely toward Al's place. His route took him directly past Police Precinct Three entrance on Main Street, and on a whim, he diverted up the steps with the intent on trading barbs with the officer on the morning desk, his old pal Sergeant Sweeney. Two steps from the entrance door, he was overtaken and rudely brushed aside by an attractive woman in a business suit with a stack of thick dark hair tied up in a bun.

He swore. She swore back at him as she rushed through the door.

* * *

EUGENE "SARGE" SWEENEY WAS IN a surly, end-of-shift mood when he head snapped his attention from the paperwork scattered on the desk before him to the commotion at the front door. He wasn't pleased to see the female pest from the *Evening Times* bolting toward him.

"Slow down, Keenan, and show some respect for an officer of the law," he growled as she approached.

"Sorry, Sergeant, but I'm on deadline and need to check the blotter."

"Yeah, well how about a 'Please, Sergeant, sir'."

"Come on, Sarge. It's a public record."

Sweeney was about to respond with sarcasm when he noticed that another visitor had entered the lobby behind her, lost in the dust of her explosive entrance. The slightest of smiles began to form on the corners of his compressed lips. Standing several paces behind Katie, still fuming from his encounter with her on the steps, Rusty Shephard managed a nod toward Sweeney.

Katie, oblivious to Shephard's presence, tapped her foot impatiently waiting for a response from the sergeant. When it finally came, it wasn't what she expected.

"Turn around, Keenan, and meet your opposition from the *Express*. He has an appointment. You'll have to wait your turn." Sweeney's expression now blossomed into a full-blown impish grin, accentuating the lines of his deeply furrowed features.

Katie whirled around to face Shephard. "And who are you, mister?"

Shephard bit his tongue and decided his best comeback was to play Sweeney's little game. He waved his credentials in front of her. "Rusty Shephard from the *Express*, miss, and I do have an urgent matter to discuss with Sergeant Sweeney."

Katie stood speechless as Sweeney took the lead. "She's no *miss*, Rusty. She's a pain-in-the-ass reporter from the *Times* who thinks she owns this place."

"Never heard of her," Shephard lied in response, fully aware of Katie's reputation for sensational journalism.

Katie, uncharacteristically flustered, cautiously eyed the tall, auburn-haired man now moving forward to stand beside her. She finally found her voice. "Look, you two, I don't have time for this bull crap. All I want to do is look at the blotter and report back to my chief."

"Sorry, Keenan, Shephard here had an appointment. He's first."

Katie looked pleadingly at Shephard. "Look, I know I made a bad first impression, but I need to see that list of police reports. I'm on deadline."

"I do know what a 'blotter' is, Miss Keenan. And I understand you push people around like you're always on deadline," came the response. "I agree with the sergeant. It's time you showed your superiors a little more respect."

"Superiors? Superiors?" Katie stammered. And then again, as if they hadn't heard her. "Superiors?"

"Yep, that means you are outranked here. Better get used to it, rookie. Now how about an apology to the good sergeant and a polite request to me."

Sweeney, trying to look serious again, was savoring the exchange from behind his desk.

Katie could feel the blood rushing to her face, her complexion now approximating the hair color of the man beside her. She knew of his reputation as well—highly regarded in the male-dominated ranks of the profession—but her feisty Irish pride would allow only a partial retreat. She turned to Sweeney.

"Okay, Sergeant. I came on a little strong. I'm sorry. Now may I see the blotter?"

"You'll have to ask the gent behind you if he's willing to wait."

Silence reigned for what seemed like half a minute. Then without turning, a flimsy gesture of holding her ground, she whispered, "May I please see the sergeant first?"

"I can't hear you, Miss."

Slightly louder. "May I please see the sergeant first?"

"I can't hear you. You'll have to turn around."

Slowly she turned to face Rusty. Her body language spoke of resentment and defiance, but she forced out the words. "I said, may I please see the sergeant first, Mr. Shephard, sir."

"Stifle the sarcasm, and I'll consider it."

Katie's defensive hard shell began to crack. "I need to see the blotter, Shephard. Please." Tears registering resignation and humiliation welled up in her emerald green eyes.

Rusty relented. "Sure. Go ahead. I don't mind, Sergeant."

Sweeney waived toward the register beside him and swiveled it around to face Katie. Her vision too blurred to read, she faked scanning the latest entries. "Nothing there," she croaked as she spun around, brushed past Rusty on her way to the door, and exited with the same speed as she had entered but now with far less attitude.

"Maybe we were a little harsh on her," offered Sweeney.

"Maybe. A little." Rusty wished they had met on better terms. He did admire her spunk, not to mention her good looks. Perhaps he should invite her to coffee and apologize sometime next week. He could not know that their paths were destined to cross again far sooner than that.

Saturday afternoon
Austin

WILLIE NELSON RARELY RODE HORSEBACK, not for plea-sure, not for transportation. As far as he was concerned, horses were meant to pull plows or carriages or wagons or buckboards, not to be ridden. Nelson's disdain for horseback riding was second only to that for Henry Ford's recent invention. He would have nothing to do with the expensive, unreliable, and unsafe automobile.

This morning was different. In his rush to get to the dam, he would gladly have cranked up a model T, if one had been available. Discarding another alternative, he dashed past his horse and buck-board, hitched outside Doctor Mansuey's home, in favor of borrow-ing a horse at Wolcott's Livery. Desperate times called for desperate measures. Silas Wolcott obliged.

It was slightly past noon when his horse galloped past the Bayless Pulp and Paper Mill on his way to the dam. He pulled up short of the dam, breathless and sore from the one-mile jarring journey aboard a little-exercised, spirited stallion. As he reined in the horse, he was stunned by what he saw ahead: a line of men descending the sloped embankment of the dam. Two men in the middle appeared to be carrying a body on a makeshift stretcher.

Nelson nudged the horse forward to get a closer look and soon approached the bizarre parade. He recognized Fred Hamlin, the mill's superintendent, leading the group on the road toward the mill. Hamlin glared at him as he passed by. Nelson returned the stare in kind. The mutual disdain was apparent.

Nelson sighted Bob Person in the midst of the group. He knew Pearson as a quiet, likable sort who visited his grocery store occasionally.

High astride the stallion, Nelson caught Pearson's attention. "Bob, who's on the stretcher and what happened?"

Pearson paused, allowing the stretcher to pass. "That's Chalkley Hatton, Willie."

"The design engineer from Wilmington?"

"Yep. He was inspecting the dam."

"Did he fall?"

"Not exactly. We lowered him on a rope from the spillway platform, and he ignited a couple sticks of dynamite trying to dislodge the cap on the clean out pipe." He paused again. "Actually, he didn't ignite it. One of the boys touched the wires too soon, and it pretty much shot Hatton up in the air like out of a cannon. He's breathing but out cold."

"Jesus, Hatton came all the way from Wilmington to inspect the dam?"

Pearson nodded.

"Does he think there's a problem, Bob?"

Pearson nodded.

"Do you think there's a problem, Bob?"

Pearson nodded for the third time and headed up the road without another word.

Nelson shivered, reined his horse around, and headed back to town at the same breakneck pace. *Not good, not good*, he thought. *I knew this day would come.*

He needed to close the store and warn anyone who would listen. He needed to warn Mary and Madge who should now be home from their trip to see the doctor.

* * *

T. CHALKLEY HATTON, STILL DAZED from the concussive blast that spun him out of control at the end of a rope above the base of the dam, lay on his back on a cot in the office of George

Bayless. He heard a muted voice somewhere in the distance, but with his vision blurred, he remained disoriented. The bright ceiling light above sent daggers into his already-throbbing head. He desperately tried to focus, and finally some detail began to emerge. He recognized that the bulky silhouetted figure at his side was Bayless, but he still could not make out the words.

"Damn foolish thing to do," finally came through the humming in his ears.

"Can you sit up?" came the request from the other side. Hatten turned his head to see a balding, gray-bearded man seated on a stool next to the cot. Hatten saw a black bag at the man's feet and concluded he was being addressed by a physician.

In response, Hatton jerked to a sitting position and immediately passed out. Doctor Horn, Austin's other resident doctor and close friend of Doctor Mansuey, tipped forward on his stool and cradled the slumping man, preventing him from toppling to the floor. Doctor Horn eased Hatton back to a prone position on the cot.

"This man is obviously suffering from severe physical trauma, and I suspect brain concussion," mused the doctor. "We must keep him absolutely still when he awakes again. I suggest he be bound to the cot to prevent him from doing more damage to himself." Not waiting for affirmation from those assembled in the room—George Bayless, Fred Hamlin, Frank Baldwin, and Bob Pearson—he reached for a folded linen sheet on the floor next to him and began tearing it into strips.

Pearson, obviously ill at ease in the presence of men of such influence, shuffled his weight from foot to foot in the corner of the room. "Do you really think that is necessary?" he murmured meekly. At once, he was sorry he called attention to himself.

"Yes, I think it's necessary, or I wouldn't have suggested it!" Horn bellowed. "Who is this fellow anyway?"

"One of my maintenance men," Hamlin retorted, glaring Pearson into silence.

The doctor resumed his task. "Would someone help me with this?"

"Pearson, for god's sake, take the strips and tie the smart-ass engineer to the cot," growled Hamlin.

Without protest, Pearson crossed in front of the three men huddled in the center of the room, knelt across from Doctor Horn, reached for the pile of linen strips, and begin fastening Hatton's wrists and ankles to the legs of the cot.

"Make 'em good and tight, Pearson."

"Now, Fred, show a little compassion for an injured man." Baldwin offered in a conciliatory style befitting a state senator.

"Compassion, my ass, Frank! This asshole tried to blow up George's dam. He's been a downright pain from the outset."

"Well, you were the one who invited him here, Fred," Bayless boomed.

On your orders, boss, Hamlin thought. Instead he remained silent.

"Now let's all calm down and assess the situation," Bayless continued, waiving them to follow as he moved across the room. He lowered his bulky frame into a leather-padded desk chair behind an enormous ornately carved mahogany desk.

Baldwin squeezed himself between the arms of a straight-backed wooden chair in front of the desk. Hamlin settled into a matching chair beside him. Pearson remained across the room with the doctor and patient, knowing that he was not included in the invitation.

Bayless directed his remarks to Hamlin. "What the hell was he doing on the spillway platform? And come to think of it, why the hell were you there?"

"Damn fool tried to blow a chunk out of our dam, George. Unfortunately, he failed to blow himself up at the same time. He did give it a damn good try though." Hamlin allowed himself a smirk before continuing. "Look this guy is dangerous. We can't allow him near the dam again."

"You didn't answer the second part of the question. Why were you there, and why didn't you stop him?"

Hamlin, realizing that blame had suddenly shifted from Hatton to him, squirmed in discomfort on the wooden seat. "I dunno. He was out there. I wanted to see what the hell he was up to. I didn't understand what he was doing." Hamlin knew it was a lame response. His pressure-cooker anger and resentment of Hatton was building within him.

"Okay, Fred, let's just say you screwed up and leave it at that." Bayless turned his attention to Baldwin. "I'm paying you a hefty amount for your counsel, Senator Baldwin." The sarcasm was not lost on Baldwin. "How can we keep this bastard from tinkering with our dam?"

Hamlin showed relief that some heat had transferred from him to Baldwin. Unlike Hamlin, however, Frank Baldwin was a thoughtful person, slow to express himself, and reasoned in his responses. He collected himself and purposely paused for dramatic effect.

"I agree that Chalkley acted recklessly and precipitously, George, but we have to consider that his concerns may have merit."

"What concerns?"

"Concerns that the integrity of the structure is at risk. He's an engineer. He designed the dam, and he should know what stresses it will tolerate. We should hear him out when he revives. And one more thing, George. We should be concerned about protecting ourselves from liability," he paused again, "should the dam give way."

"Give way? Give way? What kind of bullshit is that? I paid for the best engineering plans and construction methods that money could buy. That dam is solid as Gibraltar," Bayless sputtered.

"Actually, George, you cut a lot of corners. You ignored Chalkley's recommendation to sink the pilings a minimum of twelve feet into the bedrock. You opted for six."

"That was sufficient."

"Again, to save costs, you used one-half-inch steel reinforcing rods rather than the one-inch rods recommended and spaced them four instead of two feet apart."

Bayless sat expressionless, enduring the rebuke like a guilty school child.

"In your haste to fill the dam, you poured the concrete in cold weather, then ignored the recommendation to allow it to cure for at least six months. And finally, and perhaps most critically, you opted for a valve cap rather than the more effective, albeit expensive, gate mechanism."

"You done, Frank?"

"No, I'm not done, George. If liability occurs, the engineer is going to pass the blame on to the owner who ignored his advice and altered the specs. His testimony in court would be damning, and we have no substantive defense."

"Well, the dam will hold, and we're not going to court," Bayless snorted.

"Perhaps we should have released some water," Hamlin interjected with new-found boldness.

"Remember what happened last time we did that, Fred. Flooded Main Street with all hell to pay. Cost me a thousand dollars in damages. Besides, we needed to store as much water as possible to operate the mill to during the dry months ahead."

Hamlin continued to probe for a foothold in the discussion. "Well, at least we need to contain Hatton. He's a loose cannonball who could cause a lot of problems with the employees and with the town folk."

"I do agree with that, Fred," was Baldwin's measured response. "Think we could detain him for medical reasons, doc?"

Doctor Horn, across the room, diverted his attention from the patient to Baldwin. "Yes, he certainly needs rest. I could admit him to the hospital with instructions for complete bed rest."

Hamlin couldn't wait to add. "Until we can load him on the first train back to Wilmington."

"Agreed," said Bayless rising from his chair to signal the meeting was over. "Doctor Horn, Fred, please make those arrangements. Now let's go to lunch. It's nearly one o'clock. Pearson, you stay here and make sure Hatton doesn't leave the room."

"In fact, keep the bastard tied down," Hamlin bellowed as an added thought.

Baldwin shaking his head in disgust at Hamlin's impertinence and vulgarity, rose from his chair. "That might solve a short-term problem, gentlemen. In the longer term, however, if the dam ever breaks, now or in the future, our soft under belly is exposed."

As if on cue, Edith opened the door and handed the men their hats and coats as they exited past her desk in the outer office.

Hamlin lingered for a second and shot a glance back at Bayless. "Maybe we should take care of the long-term problem now."

Pearson, even at a distance, noted the almost imperceptible nod in response.

* * *

BAYLESS USHERED THE GROUP OUT the door of the outer office and into two separate cars. Doctor Horn was bound for the hospital in his car; Bayless, Hamlin, and Baldwin to the Goodyear Hotel for lunch.

When the door closed, it took but a moment for Edith to pick up her phone. She clicked the receiver repeatedly in an effort to rouse her friend Pauline at Central. Finally, she heard a connection and the familiar greeting, "Number, please."

"Pauline, Pauline, this is Edith. You can't image what just happened!"

"Sorry, Edith, this is Lena. Pauline's busy on another call, but you can tell me. What just happened?"

It was true that Edith was an inveterate gossiper, but she had a certain code of conduct, more like a pecking order actually, and this was just too juicy to share with anyone but Pauline. Besides, she wasn't fond of Lena because Pauline wasn't fond of Lena.

Edith took a deep breath to compose herself. "Sorry, Lena. I got carried away. It was nothing really, but I would like to talk to Pauline when she's available. Ask her to call me."

"Well, all right, Edith, if you ask nicely."

Pauline's right. She is a bitch. Edith repeated the question with exaggerated politeness and then waited for the return call. It finally came ten minutes later. Lena had been too busy to give Pauline the message immediately.

"Pauline, is this you?" Edith wasn't about to make that mistake again.

"Yes, Edith, it's me. What's up? Little Porky been harassing you again?"

"Not funny, Pauline. This is serious. That man from Wilmington, the engineer gentleman, he's strapped to a cot in the old man's office. I saw it myself."

"What?"

"I said he's tied up, lying on a cot in Bayless' office. Doc Horn just left. The man got hurt up on the top of the dam, and they brought him in here unconscious. Did you hear the explosion?"

"I did hear something a while ago that sounded like thunder."

"That was it. Something exploded at the dam, and this man named Hatton was hurt. But there's more, Pauline. When they brought him back, they brought in a cot and tied him to it.

Pauline's silence on the other end signaled skepticism

"It's true. I saw it myself," protested Edith. "They tied him to the cot with strips of bed linen and left him there alone. Well, not quite alone. Bob Pearson is still in there."

"Edith, you should go in and help them!"

"Ah, yes, you're right. I should go in." Feelings of guilt were washing over Edith. She had been more interested in the gossip than in the well-being of the poor man. "I'll go in there now. Talk to you later, Pauline. And Pauline, please don't tell anyone about this."

Pauline unplugged the connection with one hand and reach for a handful of cords with the other. Soon phones were ringing all over Austin.

* * *

BARNEY ANDERSON WAS SURPRISED TO see Bayless, Baldwin, and Hamlin enter the dining room at the Goodyear Hotel, not because they were infrequent clients at the hotel—they had lunch here often—and not because they arrived shortly after one o'clock—they usually arrived at the stroke of noon—but because they were not accompanied by Mister Hatton. Barney wondered if the gentleman from Wilmington had already departed after such a short visit. It was strange.

Barney went back to washing glasses at the bar across the room from the entrance. He watched while they were seated at a table and noticed their unusually somber mood.

The conversation between Bayless and Hamlin picked up through the course of the lunch, facilitated by a liberal amount of liquor. Only Baldwin remained sober and somber. Barney was very attentive to the beverage needs and the conversation at the table but rarely heard a word from the senator.

A half hour (and two bourbons apiece for Bayless and Hamlin) later, Doctor Horn rushed in. Barney joined the rush to the table, elbow to elbow with Horn, to find out what was happening. Barney finally backed off but remained within earshot.

"All right, gentlemen," Horn interrupted somewhat breathless, "I have made arrangements at the hospital. I'll leave it up to you to transport the patient. They have my instructions."

Barney wondered if the patient could be Mr. Hatton. That might explain his absence. But if it was, what happened to him?

Horn departed as abruptly as he had entered, and Barney, back at the bar, stewed over his concerns for the next ten minutes. He leaned across the bar to address his regular Saturday afternoon customer, Brady Quinn. "What do you make of that, Brady? Pretty strange."

Quinn, reasonably sober at midday, had also observed the encounter. He nodded.

Baldwin exited shortly after Horn at the same time lunch was being served to Bayless and Hamlin. Minutes later, Barney heard the phone ring in the lobby and rushed to answer. Reentering the dining room, he approached Bayless who was hovering over a juicy steak and showed obvious irritation at the intrusion.

"The phone is for you, Mister Bayless," Barney intoned timidly. Bayless swore before following Barney to the lobby to pick up the phone.

"What do you mean he's gone?" Bayless growled into the phone. "He can't be gone. Where's Pearson? Son of a bitch!" He slammed down the receiver into its cradle.

"Hamlin," he shouted into the dining room, "we need to leave. Now!" "Son of a bitch!" he repeated.

Barney was too intimidated to remind him he had yet to pay the bill.

* * *

EDITH POPPED INTO BAYLESS'S OFFICE just as Bob Pearson was removing the restraints on Hatton's wrists and ankles.

"My god," she exclaimed and then covered her mouth as if appalled by her own expression.

"It's okay, Edith," Pearson reassured her. "I think he's going to be all right. Hand me that glass of water on the table please, and see if he'll take a sip when I raise him up."

Hatton sputtered and coughed as the water passed his lips. Pearson held Hatton's shoulders as the spasmodic coughing continued.

Hatton finally found his voice. "Jesus, Bob, are you trying to drown me?" Then looking at Edith. "Sorry, ma'am." Then back to Pearson. "Where are the others?"

"Take some more water, Mister Hatton, and lay down for a while."

"There's no time for that, Bob. Let go of me. The dam is in danger of breaching."

Hatton swung his legs over the edge of the cot and tried to stand. His legs wobbled and gave way. Pearson caught him and gently seated him on the edge of the cot.

"Edith, please give us some privacy. I need to talk to Mister Pearson alone."

Edith, overwhelmed by what she had seen and heard, meekly marched out of the office and closed the door. She sat down at her desk to compose herself, too shaken to even think of calling Pauline.

"Mister Hatton, there's nothing more we can do," Pearson continued once they were alone. "None of the men are willing to go back out there." Pearson pointed in the direction of the dam. "And we certainly can't get more dynamite without Hamlin's okay. Besides, my orders are to keep you in this room until they returned to take you to the hospital."

"I'm not going to the hospital, Bob, and I'm not staying in this room. Is there anyone else in town who might help?"

"Willie Nelson certainly would, but I'm not sure how we can reach him. He was hightailing it to town the last I saw him, and he's probably nowhere near a phone. Nearly everybody else in town either works for Bayless or takes orders from him."

"Does that connect me with central exchange, Bob?" Hatton asked gesturing to the phone on Bayless's desk.

"I believe so, sir, but who do you know in town that would help?"

"Nobody, Bob. It's people out of town that I know. And by the way, Bob, I don't want you to have any part in what I'm about to do. That would cost you your job, and I'll have none of that."

"What are you planning to do, sir?"

Hatton stood, steadier now, hands at chest level, and faced Pearson. "I'm sorry, Bob."

"About what?"

He barely got the words out when Hatton's right fist shot out, cobra like, landing on Pearson's forehead. The first strike dazed him, and the next strike from Hatton's left fist to his jaw put his lights out. He collapsed.

"Sorry, Bob, that was for your own good. I'll apologize when I see you next." No one in Austin, very few in this state, and certainly not poor Bob Pearson, were aware that the dapper T. Chalkley Hatton, senior partner at Hatton, Bixby, & Rollins and an officer of the Society of Engineers, was also a retired amateur middle weight boxer of some accomplishment.

Hatton proceeded to hogtie and gag Pearson with the same linen strips that had bound him minutes ago. Then he reached for the phone.

Ten minutes later, Hatton doffed his homburg, straightened his tie, stepped briskly over the still-unconscious Bob Pearson, and exited the office. He politely doffed his hat as he passed Edith on his way out. Further bewildered by another in a series of bazaar events in a totally bazaar day, she rose from her desk to ask Bob Pearson what was happening. She opened the office door and petitioned God for the second time today.

* * *

AT ABOUT THE SAME TIME that Hatton was exiting the Bayless Mills offices, Frank Baldwin was marching out of the Goodyear Hotel in the same brisk fashion. Oblivious of the casual greetings of passerby, he stared unfocused into the distance on his way to his Main Street office two blocks away. He was angry. He was frustrated. He was seriously concerned. Angry at the shortsighted stubbornness of George Bayless, frustrated with the irritating insolence of Fred Hamlin, and concerned that both of them had recklessly dismissed Chalkley Hatton's warnings. He respected Hatton, his expertise, and his reserved and understated manner. If Hatton said there was a serious problem, it could be translated to mean impending disaster

Disaster in Baldwin's mind didn't include any imminent danger to him, his elderly parents and sister, or the residents of Austin. *Disaster* meant property destruction, huge liability, shutdown of the mill, and ultimately job security for him as chief counsel for Bayless Pulp & Paper.

Massive shoulders slumped, consumed in a swirling caldron of emotion, he continued his march, directly underneath the shingle of Baldwin & Baldwin, Esq. (in deference to his retired father), through the front door, past the desk of his startled secretary, and into the seclusion of his back office.

There Baldwin collapsed into the desk chair, folded his hands in front of him, and bowed his head. Frank Baldwin, the confident and proud leading citizen of Austin, the distinguished barrister of untarnished reputation, the articulate orator in the state Senate, and the self-aware spineless puppet of George Bayless trembled in rage and indignation.

Behind him, the seal of the Commonwealth of Pennsylvania emblazoned on the wall plaque seemed to vibrate in rhythm with the tremors of the bulky body below. Baldwin turned to look at the emblem. He was overcome by a feeling of dread. An omen perhaps? Might Hatton's *impending disaster* mean something far more devastating than he had imaged. It had been a bad day for the senator. Could it become a bad day in the history of the state as well?

* * *

EDITH WAS HAVING A BAD day as well. She looked out her window and saw Bayless's car approaching. She closed her eyes, grasped the sides of her desk to steady her shaking hands, and braced for the firestorm entrance of her boss. He might be furious with her for what she had done or not done in the past fifteen minutes. After removing the cloth from Bob Pearson's mouth, she had acted upon Pearson's requests: leave him tied and call Bayless.

Pearson was no fool. He realized that Hatton had given him not only a sore jaw but also a defense against the wrath of Bayless. He wasn't about to ask for the bindings to be removed until Bayless arrived to see for himself.

To Edith's relief, Bayless blew by her on his way for a confrontation with Pearson.

"What the fuck, Pearson! What are you doing on the floor? Where is Hatton?"

Lying on his stomach, hands, and feet tied together behind his back, Pearson tried to explain what he thought should be obvious, "He overpowered me, sir, and left. I don't know where he went."

Hamlin, close on the heels of Bayless, paused to give Edith the icy glare he thought she deserved for being complicit by her mere presence, then joined in the verbal pummeling of Pearson. "You let that pathetic invalid overpower you, Fred?"

"He's no invalid, believe me, Mr. Hamlin. He untied himself when I wasn't looking and then about knocked my head off. That's the last thing I remember until I woke up tied like this. Would someone please untie me?"

"You deserved it, you moron," Hamlin fired back without any move to free him. "If you had tied him up good and tight like I told you, he couldn't have loosened those knots."

Pearson, writhing in discomfort, decided to risk taking some of the blame. "He asked me for water, so I untied his hands so he could sit up to drink. Then he untied his feet when I was distracted."

"Distracted! Distracted!" It was Bayless this time. "I ordered you to do one thing and one thing only. Not to give him water. Not to turn your back. But to keep him here with a close eye on him until we returned. That's all you had to do! Did you do that, Pearson?"

"I tried, sir. Please untie me."

"Untie the bastard, Fred."

Hamlin reached under his coat and pulled a hunting knife from a sheath on his belt. He slashed the bindings and then kicked Pearson in the midsection as he rolled on his side.

"Always have this handy for the rattlers around here," Hamlin boomed over Pearson's moans. "Good for gutting pigs too."

"Enough, Fred!" said Bayless. Then in a softer tone, "Pearson, get on your feet and back to the mill."

"Jesus, George. You're not going to let me fire him?"

"No, I'm not, Fred. He's paid a price. Now help him up. We need to turn our attention to finding that meddling engineer and getting him out of town."

Without further protest, Hamlin jerked Pearson to his feet and escorted him out of the building. He glared at Edith a second time as he passed her desk on the way back to Bayless's office. He slammed the door behind him. Edith cowered behind her desk.

"You should have let me fire him, George. Or beat him to a pulp. Or both."

"That won't solve our problem, Fred. Our immediate problem is Hatton."

"Let me take care of that, George. I think I know where to find him."

"When you do find him, forget about taking him to the hospital. Just get him on the first train out of town. And keep him quiet. He's scaring the bejabbers out of everybody with his "cry wolf" nonsense. The rain has stopped. The dam is holding. We don't need him anymore."

"No, we don't, George. Indeed, we don't," Hamlin repeated for emphasis as he left.

* * *

BOB PEARSON THREW UP ON his way back to the mill, the result of Hatton's gut punch. He stumbled through the entrance and reached for the wall-mounted rack of time cards to steady himself. With shaking fingers, he searched for his employee card, intending to punch it into the adjacent time clock. *Not punched in, won't be paid*, was the mantra at the mill. *Ironic*, he thought. *The tightwad bastard won't even pay me for what he ordered me to do for the past two hours.* He inserted his card. *Bang*. The stamp read 2:20.

"You look like hell, Pearson," growled the voice of a worker behind him. "You should be clocking out and going to sick bay, not clocking in."

Before Pearson could respond, a figure flashed by beyond the open entrance door splashing through mud puddles and screaming obscenities.

"What's that maniac doing?" was all Pearson could manage.

"I think that maniac is the Super, and we never know what that crazy ass is up to."

Pearson retreated to the entrance in time to see Hamlin, rifle in hand, running toward the dam. *This sure can't be good,* he thought, and then covered his mouth as another wave of nausea swept over him.

"I think you're right on both counts, Smitty," he gagged. "Hamlin is a crazy ass, and I better go home." He clocked out.

As he exited the plant, Pearson could still see the receding figure of Hamlin on the uphill path toward the dam. His eyes drifted to the dam itself where he spotted something else that alarmed him. Pearson wasn't certain, but he thought he saw a glint of movement on the spillway platform at the midway point of the dam's three-hundred-fifty-foot length.

At a range of over eight hundred yards, even with sunshine breaking through intermittent cloud cover, he was unsure. Was it an illusion? Was it possible that someone was back up on the platform? He shook his head as if dismissing the absurdity of the idea and turned away from the dam to begin his long journey toward home on Orchard Road.

It was twenty minutes later that he heard a sharp cracking sound echoing through the valley. If he couldn't trust his vision, he most certainly could trust his hearing. Pearson recognized without any doubt the retort of a rifle.

He turned once again toward the dam when all hell broke loose. He scrambled up the hillside to save his life.

Saturday, 2:00 p.m.
Buffalo

RUSTY SHEPHARD CUPPED HIS HANDS around the steaming mug of coffee, toe-curling strong as only Al, the proprietor of Al's Café, could make it.

"What's the matter, Rusty? Cat got your tongue." It was Al leaning over the counter in Shephard's face.

"Just thinking, Al, that's all."

"Not like you, my man, 'specially on a Saturday afternoon with a weekend and mom's home-cookin' ahead of you. Not that Mrs. Shephard's cookin' is any better 'n mine, mind you."

"Let the record show that it is considerable better than yours, Al."

"Spoken like the rooky newspaper man you are, Shephard. And now that we've traded insults, tell Uncle Al what's buggin' you."

"You ever insult a lady, Al, then feel bad about it after?"

"Never."

"No. I guess you wouldn't, but someone with even a small measure of integrity might."

"You're sayin' you're somebody like that?"

"Right now I am. Ever hear of a reporter at the *Times* named Keenan?"

"Yeppers. Heard about her. Seen her. Read her stories. She ain't afraid to stir the pot, is she? Damned good lookin' too."

"Nailed it, Al. I didn't think you read newspapers."

"Decent newspapers I do. Not the *Express.*"

"Thanks."

"What's buggin' you about the dame? You don't like her style?"

"Nothing like that, Al. In fact, don't ever tell anyone, but I do admire her reporting style and spirit. A little out of control sometimes, but I admire it. I'm just feeling a little guilty for being so hard on her."

"You criticized her for her stories?"

"Nothing like that. I just put on my cocky hat and embarrassed her in front of Sarge Sweeney."

"Shame on you, Rusty…not for being a smart ass, but for feeling guilty. She needs to be chopped down a peg or two."

"You don't think I should apologize then?"

"Hell no!"

"Good enough for me. I've never taken your advice, and I'm not about to start. Hand me that phone."

* * *

KATIE KEENAN STUDIED THE HANDSOME features of Rusty Shephard trying to decide if he was being honest or mocking her. He sat across from her, a desk between them, in the now nearly vacant newsroom of the *Buffalo Evening Times*. Only she and Roy Durnstine, encircled in a wreath of cigarette smoke at the editor's desk some thirty feet away, remained in the aftermath of the bedlam of another news cycle.

While Katie was perplexed as well as a bit flattered by Shephard's invasion of this space, Durnstine was simmering in thinly disguised disgust. Shephard had sullied the hallowed ground of his newsroom by his presence. *The boy had some balls in coming here.*

Rusty didn't like it much either. His idea was to meet in a coffee shop, preferably Al's, but she had set the terms for a meeting. On her turf. Her advantage. He had delivered his apology and now waited for a response. He could see that she was assessing his sincerity.

"Well, Mister Shephard, you're right about one thing. You were indeed out of line. I'll go a step further in characterizing your behavior. Both you and Sweeney were chauvinistic jerks."

"Guilty, but since we're friends now, please call me Rusty."

"We're not friends now, Mister Shephard," she replied coolly. "You have a long way to go to achieve that status."

"Fair enough, but I have to start somewhere, so I'll try once more. I am truly sorry for my behavior."

Silence.

"Now you say, 'I accept your apology, Mr. Shephard.' Then I say, 'Call me Rusty'."

Silence.

"Okay, I was a jerk, not only for disrespecting you as a woman but for interfering with your work as a journalist. A journalist, I might add, whose work is remarkably good."

"For a woman?"

"No. No. Let's get past that. For a journalist."

"For a rooky journalist?"

"Damn it, Katie. You are simply a good journalist, a good writer, a good reporter, a thorough researcher, and a ballsy investigator who is not afraid to step on toes to get the truth."

"You mean it."

"I do."

"Then I accept your apology, Shephard, because you are right. I am good at what I do, but I'm far from perfect. I want you to be straight with me. I don't want false flattery. I want your honest opinion when I ask for it. And I'd like to learn from your experience."

Their conversation proceeded for the next hour, sometimes animated, sometimes relaxed with an obvious warming tone much to the chagrin of Durnstine who fired repeated dart-filled glances of disgust in their direction. The editor in chief wasn't about to leave Katie alone with this charlatan. He'd had enough. He rose to kick him out.

* * *

BEFORE DURNSTINE COULD REACH KATIE'S desk, a cacophony of bells rang out from the far end of the newsroom. The harsh ringing sounds reverberated throughout the near-empty room causing confusion as to the source. Durnstine was the first to react, running to a far corner where a bank of news-service teletype machines lined the wall. The teletypes from UPI and AP wire services were labeled for the specific type of news they carried: national, New York, Pennsylvania, weather, Op-Ed. The Pennsylvania state wire was filed from Philadelphia, the New York state and weather wires from Albany, the national and Op-Ed wires from Washington. The Pennsylvania wires of both services were ringing furiously signaling a major news alert.

Durnstine reached the AP machine first, fixing his eyes intently on the letter by letter copy being pounded out on the roll-fed paper. Katie and Rusty rushed to the UPI machine.

"Oh my god, oh my god," Durnstine kept repeating as the story unfolded letter by letter, line by line.

Katie and Rusty stood transfixed in front of the other machine, absorbing a similar story from the competing service.

"Where in God's name is Austin?" Durnstine asked, rubbing his forehead nervously.

"Potter County. God's country," Rusty responded and then posed a question of his own. "What's the source of the AP story?"

"Eyewitness phone-in from Costello picked up by the *Erie Times*?"

"Same source attributed by UPI," said Rusty, then added to save Durnstine from further geographically challenged embarrassment, "Costello is a small lumbering town just south of Austin. Austin's by far the larger town. Big paper mill there if I recall correctly."

"I know it," Katie added in a hushed, somber voice. "In fact, I have a friend there."

The bells on both machines ceased almost simultaneously signaling the termination of the news alert. Durnstine ripped the copy from one machine. Rusty did the same from the other.

"Let's bring them over to my desk and compare them side by side."

"I can't waste much time, Roy," Rusty said as the three moved across the newsroom I need to get to Austin for eyewitness reports. Reporters from every newspaper in the northeast are probably on the move already."

"Chief, may I cover this?" Katie pleaded.

"How are you going to get there, Keenan?" Durnstine growled.

"I'm going to hitch a ride with Shephard."

"You are?" came the response in unison from both men.

"I am."

"I guess she is if it's okay with the boss man," Rusty mused.

Durnstine nodded, knowing that it would take valuable time to find another available reporter and transportation.

Rusty looked at Katie as they approach Durnstine's desk. "We're likely to be there for a while. You have a change of clothes and a toothbrush and makeup or whatever you women need for traveling?"

"I don't need the makeup, Shephard. The other stuff I have here in my locker."

Rusty already had his weekend bag packed and in the trunk of his roadster.

"Let's compare the wire services reports," said Durnstine, laying them side by side on his desk.

Rusty had already fully absorbed the UPI report. He focused on the AP report.

Bulletin…bulletin…bulletin…bulletin…bulletin…bulletin:

Austin, PA—Paper Mill Dam breaks flooding town of Austin, population approximately five thousand in Potter County, North Western Pennsylvania, near New York border. Witnesses say significant casualties and loss of life. Fires are widespread from broken gas lines. Emergency crews stream in from Coudersport and surrounding towns. Updates to follow. Will feed Sunday morning news cycle papers ASAP.

Rusty was headed out the door. Katie detoured to her locker and chased after him.

Saturday, 2:30 p.m.
Austin

CORA BROOKS HEARD THE SAME sound echoing across the valley that Bob Pearson had identified as gunfire. She recognized it as well. Not unusual in these parts. It bothered her though that someone was shooting this close to her home. From the front porch of her famous house on the hill overlooking the mill and the dam, she turned toward the direction of the sound. An object appeared on the face of the dam falling toward its base.

Before she could comprehend the meaning, a more massive, surreal event began to unfold. On either side of the falling object, great cracks were opening, and in an instant, the center section of the dam blew outward and twisted at an oblique angle. The falling object was swallowed up in the release of a raging torrent of pent-up waters.

Additional sections of the dam instantly exploded outward with such concussive force and deafening sound that Cora clapped hands over her ears and fell to her knees. *God help us,* she thought. *The dam has burst.*

Stunned for an instant, she regained her senses and sprinted into the house. Her ladies lounging in the parlor were shocked from their midafternoon malaise by her screams. "The dam. The dam. It busted open. We have to alert the town."

One of her ladies, Florence, sat mouth agape, paralyzed, phone in hand in the process of scheduling an appointment with a client.

"Give me that damn phone. I need to call central," Cora shrieked at Florence and then into the receiver. "Get the fuck off the phone. This is an emergency."

Cora heard a click and then the voice of Pauline Lyons at central telephone exchange, already on the line monitoring the last call. "Cora, this is Pauline. What's happening?"

"The dam has burst, Pauline. God save us. The dam has burst." Cora's voice choked off in sobs.

* * *

PAULINE DISCONNECTED THE HYSTERICAL CORA and swung into action as if preprogrammed. Days later, she would reflect upon her response as being almost practiced, as if she had subconsciously prepared for the inevitable release of death and destruction from this monster slab of concrete hovering over the town.

First, she called the fire house and ordered them to sound the siren. Then for the next five minutes, her hands flew over the phone boards patching in as many homes as possible and repeating the message, "Head for high ground. The dam has broke. The flood is coming." She later estimated that she had alerted as many as one hundred homes before she looked out her third-story window to see a thirty-foot wall of pulpwood, structural debris, and sickly brown angry turbulence crashing down Turner Avenue toward her brick and mortar building. She knew that no building, however substantial, could survive that blow intact.

Hiking up her skirt, she ran down two flights of stairs screaming, "Get out of the building! Get out of the building!" into open office doors and then through the lobby of First National Bank on street level. Those who hesitated would not survive. It was near-certain death to be trapped inside a building or home in the path of the onslaught.

Out of the building, Pauline turned right, up Main Street, in an effort to reach higher ground. She passed people in panic running down the street toward the bridge, toward the center of the deadly deluge. She waved at them to turn around as they flew past her. She continued her uphill dash another block and a half before the buildings on her right began to crumble. She took two more steps and was knocked off her feet and swept away.

* * *

CLARE BENGER, STILL AT THE schoolhouse on High Road east of the Main Street bridge, didn't receive any warning. Pauline hadn't given a thought to calling the school. It was, after all, Saturday afternoon, and the children would be at home or out playing now that the rain had stopped. It wasn't a phone call, but the wail of a siren and a distant rumbling sound that drew her to the window facing upstream. In the distance, the tranquil flow of Freeman's Run had transformed into a thundering wall of water cascading down the valley toward the town.

Meek and passive by nature, Clare had always looked to her husband to make decisions for her. Since his death in a lumbering accident last year, she looked to others for direction. Now on her own in an isolated one-room schoolhouse, she was faced with a life-or-death decision. *Should I go, or should I stay?*

She opted to run. It was the right decision. Out the door and up the slope to higher ground she fled. She ran until her cramping legs would hold her no longer. She collapsed, chest heaving, on the muddy hillside. Her head throbbed with each pounding heartbeat as a deafening roar, no longer distant, overwhelmed her senses. On her knees, she looked over her shoulder to view the town on the other side of the bridge.

The tidal wave was crushing buildings on Main Street and houses on Kershner, Turner, and Ruckgaber Avenues. She could barely see the top of the submerged steeple of the First Baptist Church before it, and the church below were torn apart. The torrent slammed into the sturdy structure of the Goodyear Hotel, tearing away chunks of the exterior and blowing furniture and bodies out its windows. Across the narrow valley, she saw bodies scrambling up the opposite hill; some caught in barbed wire pasture fencing. Those lucky souls were still alive at least, not so for the bodies she saw washing downstream among the debris.

Some fifty yards below her, the old schoolhouse, surrounded by a swirling dirty-brown current, stood in steady defiance, high enough on this bank to survive the main thrust of the onslaught. Clare could not know then that the next time she entered that building would be to identify bodies of flood victims. Tomorrow the schoolhouse would become a morgue.

* * *

FRANK BALDWIN WAS SAFE ENOUGH, on high ground west of town across the valley from Clare Benger, at his estate off Orchard Road. It was the perfect location, he always thought, to build the aristocratic, pillared home a man of his stature deserved.

Following his luncheon with Bayless and Hamlin at the Goodyear Hotel, Baldwin had succumbed to a wave of nausea and came home to rest. He explained to his wife Gladys that he was not feeling well. She suspected he had been drinking, not an unusual circumstance for Baldwin on a Saturday afternoon.

He had washed his hands long and hard in the kitchen sink, a practice he knew infuriated Gladys. Thankfully, she had walked away, saving him from another confrontation this day. He felt sick and unclean. He wanted to wash away the stench of association with George Bayless and Fred Hamlin. He wanted to wash away the guilt of being bullied into ignoring the warnings of Chalkley Hatton. He had retired to the bedroom to lie down.

Wakened by Gladys' shrieks, he now stood on his front porch witnessing the same scene as Clare Benger. He peered frantically into the churning mass of debris that had been downtown Austin for any sign of his homestead on Ruckgaber Avenue. The home where he was raised. The home to his widowed sister and aged, infirm parents. Was it gone? Were they gone?

He threw up his hands in a gesture of frustration and helplessness. Gladys joined him on the porch, shocked, mute, dumbstruck by the scene unfolding in the valley below. The thunderous roar of the crushing wave of destruction had moved downstream beyond the town, replaced now by the ghostlike sounds of human suffering from below. Floating up from the valley came terror-filled, struggle-for-life screams, desperate pleas for help and anguished cries of despair.

* * *

BARNEY ANDERSON HEARD THE SIRENS, and unlike many others who disregarded or failed to react to the alarm, he sprang into action without the need to look out the windows. He sensed that disaster was on its way and knew instinctively the form it was taking.

"Out of the bar! Out of the building! Get to high ground," he screamed to the few remaining luncheon patrons at tables and Brady Quinn at the bar. He raced across the lobby and quick-hobbled painfully up the stairs to the second-floor rooms shouting the warning and banging on hallway doors. Breathless and retreating to the stairwell, he stumbled on the bottom step, recovered, and continued upward to the top floor. Several bewildered guests stepped from their rooms only to be forcefully shoved toward the stairway by Barney as he flailed and shouted his way down the hall.

He paused for a split second as he reached the corner window facing upstream toward the mill and the dam. For that instant, time stopped for Barney. What he sensed was coming, he saw for the first time. The monster wave, some thirty feet high, churning with debris from the pulpwood stock yard, crushing everything in its path, seemed to Barney to pause in its deadly descent halfway from the mill to the town. A still frame from a horror film frozen in his mind. Then slowly, frame by frame, he pictured its advance, subconsciously calculated its speed, and reckoned he had less than five minutes to save himself and his family.

Scrambling down the stairs and into the street, Barney encountered the same confused looks he had seen inside the hotel. Like Paul Revere without a horse, he continued screaming his warnings as he ran up Main Street toward his house and higher ground. He passed Nelson's Grocery Store, now vacated by the ever-vigilant Willie Nelson. He bounced through a crowd pouring out of the First

85

National Bank building on the corner of Turner Avenue. He staggered past the darkened window of the Quinn Law Firm. Finally, knees ready to buckle with throbbing pain, he emerged from the commercial district into a row of houses flanking upper Main Street.

The raging wall of water, closing in on his right side, threatened to engulf him and all in its path within seconds. Gasping from fear, pain, and exhaustion, he tried to locate his house. Images began taking shape in his blurred vision: his house, front door open wide, and beyond the house his wife and five-year old twin boys fleeing up the hill

Barney closed the distance step by painful step and reached for them as they neared a barbed-wire fence, marking the boundary of pasture land. In an instant, the surge, waist-high on this higher ground, knocked all of them off their feet. He grabbed for the boys as they floundered in the current. In desperation, he hooked onto the shirt collar of one of the boys and held fast. Stumbling to his feet, struggling to maintain his grip and balance, he toppled over again as the watery surge slammed the other boy into him. He braced his feet against a fence post, managed to right himself, and dragged both boys to their feet, one in each hand. He searched for his wife, Nancy. She was nowhere to be seen.

Barney whipped his head left and right in a frantic search for any sign of her. The two frightened, coughing boys dangling in his grip danced like puppets in unison with his movements. They were screaming and pointing at something further down the fence line. Barney saw nothing but calico material fluttering on the fence.

As he stared, the material seemed to take on shape and substance, forming into a skirt and then a woman inside the skirt. Nancy! The barbed wire had caught her dress saving her from being swept away.

Barney, boys in tow, wadded to her. She embraced the three of them and refused to release her vice-lock hold around Barney's waist even as he lifted the boys over the fence onto the muddy ground beyond. The water, no longer a brutal, rushing force, was subsiding. The boys stood wobbly but safe in the ankle-deep, mucky residue on the far side of the fence.

Barney lifted his wife over the fence, then hoisted himself over using the fence post for support. The Anderson family in a shaking huddle fell in unison to on their knees onto the muddy ground. Arm in arm, they cried and shook and prayed together in thanksgiving.

* * *

IT WAS A MIRACLE. THERE WAS no doubt in Father Patrick O'Brien's mind. The six-foot-tall marble statue of the Risen Christ stood upright, embedded in mud in the center of fallen timbers that once formed the steeple of St. Augustine Catholic Church. The sturdy side and back walls of his church, although damaged, had withstood the onslaught, protecting, miraculously Father O'Brien would say, the statue, once situated sedately behind altar. The altar, the pulpit, the communion rail, the pews, the kneelers, and the entrance doors were smashed or gone. The statue remained.

Father O'Brien knelt in the mud before the statue. Streaks of sunlight streamed between the few remaining ceiling timbers, silhouetting the lonely outline of his soiled black frock. Tears stained his usually ruddy, now pallid, cheeks. His hands, folded in front of him, trembled in shock.

His prayer was wordless. Words would not form in a mind overwhelmed by sensory overload and emotion. He could barely comprehend that he had survived. And now, with survivor's guilt, adding another crushing layer upon his fragile emotional state, he wondered why. Why had he been spared as he napped in his second-floor bedroom in the parish house behind the church? It appeared that the walls surrounding him now, sturdy as the faith of the pioneers who anchored them years ago, had protected both the statue of Christ in the church sanctuary and him in the house next door.

He gathered sufficient courage to raise his head and gaze into the eyes of the statue, a piece of art commissioned by the Erie Diocese that made its way across the ocean a quarter century ago from a sculpture's studio in Padua to this backwoods church in Potter County, Pennsylvania.

The sky darkened as a parade of gray puffy clouds marched across the face of the sun. As Father O'Brien contemplated the miracle of the statue, the cloud cover broke for a moment allowing a ray of sunshine to descend between the rafters like a spotlight on the face of Christ. It was then that the answer became clear. He was saved for a purpose.

He rose from his knees and went beyond the walls to tend to the needs of the suffering as he knew Christ would do.

* * *

AFTER DOCTOR EDWARD MANSUEY PACKED Madge Nelson, still whimpering and pouting, and her mother, still cooing and cajoling, into the Nelson family buckboard, fed a carrot to Bessie, and slapped her equine flank to start their journey home, he marched wearily back into his house.

Mary Mansuey greeted him at the front door with ten-month-old Eloise squirming in her arms. "God, what an awful child that Madge. Her screaming woke the baby from his nap. I wish you could afford an office, Ed, like a proper doctor, so we wouldn't have to deal with these things at home."

It was a bad beginning to a very bad day for the doctor as he set out on foot with his black medical bag to address the needs of his patients at their homes scattered around town. No office. No car. Those were luxuries that his young practice could not yet afford. He set a brisk pace departing his house on Thorn Street to start his rounds with his first visit to the Donofrio family down the street.

Four of Ralph and Angelina Donafrio's five children were down with the mumps. Only baby Antonio had escaped the virus and was being kept in strict isolation in the parents' bedroom as ordered by Mansuey. The others, Emma, age seven, Virginia, age six, Mona, age five, and Joseph, age three, were crammed in the other bedroom of their modest, one-level home now serving as an infirmary. Ralph, recently returned from a night shift at the mill, greeted Mansuey at the door and explained that Angelina was nursing her infant and trying to get some rest after an exhausting week with the children.

The doctor examined each child, then reassured Ralph that they were recovering nicely and were no longer contagious.

Emma and Virginia should be able to return to school on Monday... Continue plenty of liquids... Say hello to Angelina for me... Ralph, it looks like you could use some rest as well.

On went Mansuey to the Broadt residence, also on Thorn Street, to look in on Adam and Jennie, an elderly couple in failing health. He then proceeded further up Thorn Street and turned right onto Turner Avenue where he stopped at the Rennicks' residence to call on Mayme Rennicks and her two children, Arnold, age seven, and Evelyn, age three. Arnold and Evelyn had escaped the dreaded mumps but were suffering from severe cold symptoms. Mansuey advised Mayme to keep the vaporizer going throughout the night and to rub the children's chest with Vicks before bedtime.

Is Charlie working at the mill today? ... Say hello to him for me.

Mansuey dreaded the next call, two houses down from the Rennicks. He slowed his pace almost to a stall as he approached the grand white-pillared home of John and Josephine Baldwin. If their daughter Grace was out, it would be a short visit. If not...he shuddered. Grace answered the door. It was indeed turning out to be a bad day.

After his tiresome visit with Grace, Mansuey walked back home for lunch. Sometime around one thirty, he crossed over the Main Street Bridge to visit families on High Road, first near the school and then southward as the road wound uphill toward Costello. It was at the Miller home, as he was talking to the ailing widow Edith Miller, that he was vaguely aware of a distant rumbling. *Strange*, he thought, *to have a thunder storm on a sunny day*. The rumbling intensified.

He excused himself from Edith's bedside and stepped onto the porch overlooking Austin and the Bayless Dam in the distance. He could clearly see breaches in the breastworks and a wall of water descending the valley toward the town. He knew at that moment that the worst of his day was yet to come.

Hours later, when he completed his anguished hike back to town, he would discover that each of the souls he had visited that morning, including his wife and baby girl, had perished.

Saturday evening

WITHIN THE FIRST SEVERAL HOURS of their trip to Austin, Katie Keenan concluded that there was no room in Rusty Shephard's life for romance other than his fire-engine red two-seater Maxwell Runabout automobile. She soon tired of hearing about its gold-chrome grill and headlights, its pneumatic tires, its fourteen horse-power four-cylinder engine, its patented black canvass top, not to mention its superiority over the more popular Ford Model T, and its price tag of an astounding eight hundred and twenty-five dollars.

At first, Katie listened politely about his years of sacrifice and saving for this dream car and the generous bequest from his father's estate two years ago that enabled him to complete the purchase. She lost interest somewhere during Rusty's detailed account of his trip by rail to Tarrytown, New York, to view the assembly of his new car, his adventurous three-hundred mile, top-down return trip, and his consuming loving care for the vehicle.

It's only a piece of machinery for crying out loud, Katie thought as she turned her attention to the first hint of color in the trees covering the rolling foothills of the Allegheny mountain range on this sunny autumn day. The open sides of the Maxwell enabled her to turn on her leather-padded seat for full panoramic views.

Katie was far more interested in Rusty the man and Rusty the talented journalist than in Rusty's new machine. She tried to turn the conversation in that directions several times without success. They stopped late afternoon in Olean, New York, at a general store with a sidewalk gas pump, lunch counter, and bathroom. Katie hadn't thought about food, but Rusty insisted they eat and stock up on

90

water and provisions. He rightly presumed that it might be a long while before their next meal.

It wasn't until they crossed the state line south of Olean, viewed the headwaters of the Allegheny River, entered the more mountainous terrain of McKean County, Pennsylvania, and passed a sign that read "Continental Eastern Divide" that she made another attempt to divert the conversation in a different direction.

"What does that sign mean, Shephard?"

"What sign?"

"The one we just passed. The one that read 'Continental Eastern Divide'."

"That means, Katie, that on the east side of the pass, we are going through the water in the streams eventually ends up in the Gulf of Mexico. And on the west side, the flow goes into the Chesapeake Bay."

"Then Austin would be on the west side of the divide?"

"Nope. On the east side, so the pent-up waters of Freeman's Run behind the dam at Austin would come crashing down on the town, cascading down Sinnemahoning Creek into the west branch of the Susquehanna River through Pennsylvania and Maryland and eventually dump into the bay at Havre de Grace."

Katie was impressed. "How do you know the geography so well?"

"I just do," came the reply without further elaboration.

"I also know that the force of the water released from that broken damn would crush everything and everybody in its path for miles. I wonder if there has been any death toll estimate yet. Poor devils."

"Well, that's what this trip is all about, isn't it, Shephard? To find out what happened, who was responsible, and report as fast as possible."

"You've forgotten some important principles of good reporting, Katie."

"What?"

"To substantiate the facts and authenticate the sources first."

The remark stung Katie into a brief silence. She recognized it as a rebuke to her penchant to rush headlong into sensational journalism.

After enduring several long moments of insecurity, Katie attempted to go on the offensive. "Look, Shephard, I know you have more experience, but don't talk down to me as a wet-behind-the-ears rookie. I know how to gather facts, and I know how to report. I'm a damned good investigative reporter and writer."

"I know you are, Katie. I've read your stuff."

"You have?"

"Yes, I have, and I've often wondered about the spirited writer behind those stories."

"You have?"

"Yes, but I've also seen the controversy you've caused by going to print without doing due diligence."

Katie was soaking in the flattery only to be stung again by the criticism. "Well, Mr. Know-It-All," she fumed, "let's get one thing straight. I'm only here for the convenience of a ride, not for collaboration. You write your stories, and I'll write mine. And I'll make deadline while you are *substantiating* your sources."

"Okay, Katie. Back off. Whether you realize it now or not, we are going to need each other over the next several days however we compose our reports. And I don't mean simply professional support. I mean we will need to support each other emotionally as well. We might at least try to be friends for a while because we are going to face some pretty gruesome stuff together. This won't be a picnic."

Katie softened. This rival from the morning paper wasn't as evil as she once thought. In fact, she was thinking that he could be more than just a callous competitor. He might just be a pretty nice guy, a good-looking one at that with his wavy, auburn hair and chestnut eyes, who made a lot of sense.

It was twilight by the time they reached Keating Summit in Potter County. The roads had been full of ruts and mud, the small towns far between, the elevation climb steep, and the progress slow as they neared their destination.

"Here's where we turn off the main road for the last seven miles to Austin."

"This is a main road?"

"Wait until you see the next stretch. You'll think this highway is smooth as a baby's bottom by comparison." Katie was amused by his choice of comparisons.

"Let's stop at the train station here," he continued without regard to the message in her smile, "to see what they have heard from Austin and know about the road conditions."

They parked, walked across the railroad tracks, and entered the station, a flag stop on the Pennsylvania Railroad main line to Buffalo. Katie was grateful for the rest, for a bathroom, and for the warmth of the potbellied stove heating the small wood-frame building. They were not encouraged, however, by what they learned.

Telephone and telegraph lines to Austin were down, and there had been no communication. Days of torrential downpour had turned the road to Austin into a bog, not possible for horse and wagon let alone a flimsy Maxwell roadster. The tracks of the B&S Railroad line to Austin were being cleared in the hope that a train could make it through tomorrow morning.

The next Pennsy train from Harrisburg with passengers from New York, Philadelphia, Baltimore, and Washington, was due in at nine o'clock tomorrow morning. A cranky, anxious mob of reporters, the first wave from those cities, would be stampeding from that train to transfer to the few Austin-bound B&S Railway coaches. Better find a bench and a blanket and get ready to queue up early in the morning advised the station master.

Katie and Rusty called their respective newspapers, taking turns on the single phone line in the station, to report the situation. Their newsrooms in turn reported back that wire services had estimates of between seven hundred to eight hundred fatalities from the disaster. They would have to wait until morning to view the scene firsthand and get better estimates.

The station master was reluctant to use too much of his limited supply of wood for the stove and consequently the autumn chill was infiltrating the interior of the building. Rusty stumbled to his car in the pitch black of a moonless night and retrieved two blankets. A couple of hobos were asleep on a corner bench. The station master was preoccupied with paperwork on his desk in the other corner.

Katie and Rusty sat on a wooden bench, wrapped themselves in blankets, munched on hunks of bread and cheese, and readied themselves for a long, uncomfortable evening. Katie unpinned her raven hair and let it fall shining below her shoulders.

"Sorry, Shephard," she whispered in a sleepy voice. "I can't do the professional look any longer, and I'll never get it pinned back up without a mirror. This is my new look until we get back to civilization."

Katie's head soon tilted drowsily sideways and came to rest softly, delicately on Rusty's shoulder. Her hair draped riotously across the sleeve of his herringbone jacket. He looked down at the flawless skin of her neck and breathed in her scent, a mixture of ivory soap and a light lavender cologne. He found that it was not an unpleasant sensation.

* * *

EARLIER IN THE AFTERNOON, BRADY QUINN incensed by the rude behavior of Barney Anderson as the bartender had practically dragged him off his barstool and shoved him out the front door of the Goodyear Hotel, leaned against a telephone pole on lower Main Street in a drunken stupor. He heard shouts and saw people running, but he could make no sense of it.

"Run, man, run!" urged a panicked voice flying by him. "The dam's busted. Get to high ground." A minute passed, but Brady remained frozen, afraid he would fall without the support of the pole.

Another voice, this one with a decided Irish accent, sliced into his semiconsciousness. "Quinn, ye worthless drunk, move afore the comin' flood sweeps ye back to Ireland."

Where the first warning failed to stir him, the insult of the second roused enough resentment to elicit a response. "Who're you calling a worthless drunk, you son of a bitch?"

His anger, causing an accelerating his heart beat and pumping up his blood pressure, cleared his brain sufficiently to register alarm.

People were streaming from Main Street stores and scrambling up the sloping street to the hillside to the west.

Brady stumbled as he released from the stability of the pole, regained his footing, and watched a mass of terrified souls fleeing up the street. Always the contrarian, he turned in the opposite direction, moving unsteadily eastward toward the Main Street bridge. Whether it was his stubborn nature or his instinct for survival, crossing the bridge over the still-tranquil flow of Freeman's Run to the nearby hill beyond saved his life.

* * *

NOW HOURS LATER, HEAD IN HAND and tears streaming down his face, he sat near the hospital on the hillside above High Road overlooking the decimation that was once the thriving town of Austin. He could not know that Clare Benger, perched on the same hillside several hundred yards to the north, was trying to make sense of the same scene.

Unlike Clare, who never took a drink of Satan's spirits in her life, Brady was shocked into sobriety by the magnitude of the tragedy unfolded before him. For the first time on a late Saturday afternoon in many years, he had no craving for drink.

He sat shivering, knees drawn up to his chest, senses overloaded, alternately absorbing and rejecting the reality of the scene before him. A light rain intensified into a steady downpour and a heavy mist formed over the town as if the valley itself were in mourning. High-pitched sounds and billowing black smoke rose through this veil of sorrow piercing his ears and stinging his eyes. He remained suspended in a long timeless moment before he comprehended that the sounds were the cries of human suffering, and the smoke was the exhaust from fires fueled by broken gas lines.

As twilight dissolved into darkness, the reddish glows of fires created an eerie halo above the town. Other tiny specs of red seemed to float across the smog. *Movement. Movement meant life. Movement meant survivors. People were moving through the streets with oil lamps.* He could sit no longer. He rose, slip slid downhill through the mud, and crossed the swollen but now-passive creek on a few remaining planks, once part of the Main Street bridge, into town.

* * *

PEOPLE WERE WALKING AIMLESSLY, LIKE zombies, through the rubble on Main Street. A few had recovered sufficiently from shock to form bucket brigades, drawing water from ditches in a futile effort to quell the fires on both sides of the street. Brady knew that the gas mains, protruding like broken sticks from the plank streets, had to be shut off before any progress could be made in fighting the fires.

As he walked up Main Street, he saw to his left, on the south side, massive mounds of pulpwood, hundreds of thousands of stock-piled cords washed down from the mill mixed with the remains of houses and buildings, towering dike-like thirty feet high. Wooden and brick buildings alike were leveled with two exceptions

One was the Goodyear Hotel on the corner of Railroad Avenue battered by debris now piled high on its northern facing side. The other was the First National Bank building at the corner of Turner Avenue in similar condition.

The bank building housed the bank, the post office, and the telephone exchange, and was owned by the partnership of Frank E. Baldwin, distinguished attorney, banker, and state senator, and George C. Bayless, industrialist and entrepreneur. *A symbol of arrogance and greed still standing amid the rubble*, Quinn thought cynically. There was no doubt in Brady's mind who was to blame for the disaster.

Gangs of men clawed through the mounds of rubble in desperate efforts to reach people buried beneath. The few surviving horses—most had either drowned in their stalls at the livery or escaped to the hillsides—were harnessed to pull heavy chunks of pulpwood and sections of collapsed walls off the piles. The human and equine efforts combined began to uncover only bodies, not survivors.

Ironically, it seemed to Brady, there were few injuries. Residents had either survived or perished. He recognized the battered body of grocery store owner Willie Nelson as several men dragged it from the rubble.

"Poor devil," mumbled a man close by. "He was runnin' up and down the streets like a madman, knockin' on doors, tryin' to warn all who'd listen. Saved a lot a lives. Never made it home to warn his family though. We shoulda listened to old Willie. By God, he was right about the dam."

Brady counted twenty-four blanket-covered bodies on his trek up Main Street. He paused briefly to inspect the litter-filled lot on the north side of the street that had once been the location of his law office. Not only had he lost his office, but his shabby, one-room residence on the second floor as well. His shoulders slumped further under the weight of a soggy sweater and the realization that the once-proud Brady Quinn's life journey had descended to the level of a homeless, jobless, alcoholic.

In the distance he saw a group of people huddled beyond the barbed-wire fencing on the far side of Orchard Road that separated the houses on upper Main Street from a meager patch of uphill pasture land. As he drew closer, he recognized Barney Anderson still huddled with his wife and twin boys. The hillside was a mixture of mud and tears.

Cora Brooks, the brothel madam turned by tragedy into an angel of mercy, moved among stunned families and individuals, distributing blankets, compassionate hugs, and invitations to come with her to her house on the hill above the mill for food and shelter. Beyond the fence, she caught Brady's eye and motioned for him to follow as well.

Brady shook his head in silent response. He just couldn't leave this chaos without trying to help. Instead of climbing over the fence to the pasture, he turned left, walking south on Orchard Road across the hillside. He had no plan. He soon reached the crossing of the B&S Railroad and followed the tracks eastward on their winding way to town. He stopped for no particular reason as the tracks crossed Goodyear Avenue, his normally senses now on full alert as they had never been before.

He searched left and right for some sign of life. He saw none, heard none. The carcass of a horse cradled in the bough of large willow tree nearby caught his attention. As he approached the ill-fated animal, he noticed something else dangling from a higher limb on the far side of the huge tree. It was an arm. *Brady, it's an arm.*

Brady slogged to the far side of the tree to find the unconscious, barely breathing body of Pauline Lyons. He gently untangled her from the clutching branches and lowered her limp body, clad only in shreds of material, into his arms. He stripped off his sweater and slipped it over her head. It fell to knee length on her diminutive body as he slung her over this shoulder. He marched back up the tracks toward Orchard Road repeating a mantra of *please live, Pauline* with the beat of each step.

Later that evening, the warmth of Cora Brooks's fireplace hearth, the nourishment of warm chicken broth, and the caring hands of Cora's ladies, brought color back to Pauline's pallid features and hope in Quinn's heart that she would survive.

So ended the day for Brady Quinn and other survivors huddled together at Cora's house, thankful for being alive but fearful of what they would find or not find in the days ahead.

Sunday
October 1

THE PENNSYLVANIA RAILROAD PRIDED ITSELF on punctuality, and so exactly 8:59 in the morning, locomotive number 22 pulling five coach cars, two first class sleepers, and a diner car, completed its arduous climb up the three percent grade to Keating Summit and steamed into the station. The station master ran through an early morning mist to the rusted water tank towering over the tracks to fill the thirsty engine for its final lap to Buffalo.

Rusty and Katie watched from a coach car of the B&S Railway on a nearby rail siding. Disoriented passengers, juggling cameras, briefcases, and bags tumbled chaotically from the arriving cars onto the station platform, finding no one to give them directions.

"Not many going on to Buffalo today," Rusty observed. "They'll be heading our way as soon as they figure out that these four coaches are bound for Austin."

Katie was studying the crowd assembling on the platform. "Those are all reporters?"

"Mostly. I'm sure special relief trains will be coming later today with medical personnel and supplies, but these are the guys from the city newspapers itching for a scoop and a first-on-the-scene byline."

"Don't *the Times, the Inquirer, the Sun,* and *the Post* have any women reporters?" Katie asked incredulously.

"They don't send them into the hills of Pennsylvania aboard crowded, smelly, smoke-filled rail cars."

"Well, they should if they want to get the story right."

Rusty refused to engage in a gender-based debate but couldn't resist saying, "They'll be streaming this way as soon as they figure out where this train is going. Then you can experience crowded, smelly, and smoke-filled if that is your wish."

Five minutes later, Rusty's prediction proved accurate as a herd of anxious reporters waving arms, tripping over bags, and pointing in their direction started to stampede.

Katie braced for the ensuing onslaught, inwardly disappointed that her alone time and space with Rusty was about to be invaded. She clutched his arm drawing him closer as the first wave of humanity flooded into their car. Rusty was right about the smell, but he had failed to mention the assault on the ears in addition to the nostrils.

"Where I come from, reporters are a bit more genteel," she observed sarcastically.

"When guys earn their living in the raucous, unsavory, and cutthroat environment of eastern cities, they become raucous, unsavory, and cutthroat," Rusty responded. "They'll do anything, and I mean anything, to beat the competition. View them as the enemy, Katie. They'd cut your Achilles tendon to beat you to the nearest telephone or telegraph line."

Katie was about to object to Rusty's hyperbole when she was crushed against the window of the train car by the force of a burly man thrusting himself against Rusty onto their two-person bench seat. Rusty glanced at her with a see-what-I-mean look. She nodded but said nothing.

"Hi there," boomed their new seatmate without a word of apology. "Station master said to wait on the platform for the train to Austin, but when word got out that these were the cars going there, everybody got the same idea. Doesn't look like everybody's going to fit, does it?"

His question was rhetorical. Looking out the window at those trying to scramble aboard the already-packed cars, Katie knew the answer was obvious.

"Rappaport from *The Bulletin*, Philadelphia's other newspaper," the man offered by way of introduction. "Met some doctors, nurses, and telephone linemen aboard that train," he pointed his index finger in front of Katie's face in the direction of the platform thirty yards distant. Katie could almost taste the cigarette smoke that radiated from his skin. "Be nice if they made it aboard. God knows people and phone lines will need fixing down there in Austin, but I'm not about to give up my seat. Don't think any of my brethren of the fourth estate will either."

"That's a sad comment on our profession," Katie intoned pushing his hand away.

"You a reporter?" came the startled response. "Well, I'll be damned. You think you can just shake those titties to get a Pulitzer, pretty lady?"

Rusty had to restrain Katie from rising from her seat to throttle the man.

"Shut your mouth, meat head!" she flared in response. "I can out-report, outwrite, outthink, and outmaneuver your dumb ass any day of the week. And the first chance I get, I'm going to kick you in the crotch for that remark."

The man fell silent, rose, and pushed his way in hasty retreat to the back of the car. Another man of similar size took his place before Rusty could shift over. They were destined to ride this way, sardine style, for half an hour as a B&S locomotive hooked up to the cars, and then again for another half hour as the train slowly descended five miles through the misty, still-verdant, preautumn foothills of the Allegheny mountains to Austin in the valley below.

Rusty smiled inwardly at the spunk of this raven-haired emerald-eyed beauty in the window seat next to him, content for the moment to be in such close physical contact with her.

Katie, cramped as she was, felt comfort in the warmth and reassurance of his presence. She was unsure if the tingling sensation she felt was due to lack of circulation or something else.

The cry of the conductor abruptly jolted them from mindless musings to stark reality as the train rumbled into the B&S car shops on the outskirts of town. "End of the line. Austin station is washed away."

* * *

AS RUSTY AND KATIE DROPPED off the coach car onto the muddy ground of the rail yard, they observed the first signs of destruction through the low-hanging mixture of fog and smoke. Overturned freight cars and locomotives appeared ghostlike before them, scattered across the yard like toys tantrum thrown across a playroom.

"My god, Shephard, what kind of force could do that?" Katie asked as she slogged aimlessly through the mud.

Rusty was similarly amazed. "A killing force, that's for sure, Katie. A force of nature made possible by the folly of man." He grabbed her arm to steady both their balance and their nerve. They were surrounded by reporters and cameramen from the train transfixed by the sight and unsure of where to proceed.

"Town's that way, or what's left of it," croaked the conductor standing on the entry steps of one of the coaches while pointing north in the direction of Main Street. "Follow the tracks, and if you see anyone looking for the train, tell them we are loading here at the car shops to return to Keating Summit."

Rusty and Katie joined a double-file line marching along the tracks toward town. They followed the gentle curve of the tracks for about fifty yards until the rail bed straightened. At that point, a ten-foot-wide depression, litter-filled with chunks of wood, bricks, and plaster, appeared, running beside and parallel to the tracks.

"That would be Railroad Avenue," said a man ahead of them nodding to the depression while referring to a hand-held map depicting the streets of Austin. "It should cross Main Street up ahead, then Thorn, Scotville, and Elliott Streets. Turner Avenue would be west to our left, and Ruckgaber Avenue east to our right on the far side of that stream called Freeman's Run."

Ahead of them, they could see smoke rising from smoldering mounds of debris backlit by active fires refusing to be quelled by buckets of water passed hand to hand from the stream.

"All the water in the world won't stop those fires until someone shuts off the ruptured gas lines." Rusty observed shaking his head.

A huge dike-like pile of pulpwood intermixed with the remains of buildings and houses stretched for blocks on the south side of

Main Street obstructing their view. Ahead the tracks passed through an opening in the mounded debris clawed clear by crews searching for bodies.

Rusty and Katie hiked through this passageway into a macabre scene of death and destruction. Men, bone-weary from a night of unrelenting firefighting and searching for survivors, carried bodies on makeshift stretchers toward them down Main Street.

Katie felt her stomach lurch as she passed these forlorn figures with their burden of the shrouded remains of men, women, and children. She suppressed the urge to throw up and tried to focus her attention further up the street.

"Shephard, there's a policeman on the next block," she hollered over her shoulder as she picked up pace in that direction.

Rusty caught up to her just as she approached the blue-uniformed officer, a semblance of authority trying vainly to preside over the chaos around him. Katie breathed in deeply to compose herself. "Excuse me, sir," she exhaled in a breathy attempt to get his attention.

He turned toward her, assessing them guardedly. "What is it, miss?"

"My name's Keenan from the *Buffalo Evening Times*, sir, and this is Shephard from the *Express*." She nodded toward Rusty. "Are you in charge here?"

"Nobody but God is in charge here, Keenan. We're just trying to clean up the lives He took and patch up the lives He saved."

"May I quote you on that? May *we* quote you on that, officer?" Katie corrected herself as both she and Rusty started scribbling on note pads.

"Suppose so," he softened in response sensing an opportunity for some recognition. "Name's Baker. Spelled B-A-K-E-R. Daniel. Chief of Police of Austin's three-man force. Three includes me."

"Do you have estimates on the number of dead and injured?" Katie continued. Rusty remained silent, deferring to her as a professional courtesy. It was her interview.

"Hard to say, Keenan. We're still counting bodies. That there last stretcher you passed was number twenty-four. Probably a couple hundred more reported missing. Poor devils. Could be buried under this debris, washed downstream toward Costello, or sleeping off a bender in some attic on the hillside for all I know."

"Thank you for your candor, Chief." She paused, alerted by his vacant stare that the word "candor" was not in his vocabulary. "Where are they taking the bodies?"

"Across the stream, over those boards where the Main Street bridge used to be, then up the hill to the schoolhouse on High Road. Pretty sad, huh? Schoolhouse being used as a morgue. Right next to the hospital. No business there though. Not many injuries. You either died or survived. Nothing much in between. Nurses are helping in the morgue instead of treating patients in the hospital."

Katie and Rusty were writing furiously. These were dynamite quotes and the first estimates of casualties from a credible source for their stories. Rusty's report would be grounded in the facts, in what was verifiable, and he hoped Katie would report in the same manner. He was dubious.

"Thank you, Chief," Rusty finally broke his silence, impatient to get to the morgue where numerous additional story lines awaited. "Katie, let's go to the morgue, count bodies, and get more interviews. We need to know more about the cause of this disaster."

"You won't find that answer at the morgue, mister," Chief Baker intoned as they turned to leave. "Feller you want to ask about that is named Bayless. It was his dam that broke."

Rusty made a mental note of the disparaging tone in Baker's voice. He wrote a name and a word on his note pad: "Bayless" and "culpability" followed by a question mark.

Near them, flashbulbs popped from cameras capturing the devastation for tomorrow's front pages, as Rusty and Katie crossed the creek, then Ruckgaber Avenue, and started the climb up the hill to High Road and the morgue. Rusty cursed himself that, in his haste to be first on the scene, he had neglected to bring a camera. A rookie mistake. At least no other reporters were moving in their direction. It appeared that they were the first to learn of the existence of the morgue, he rationalized. Being first, but without a camera, was a small consolation.

All thoughts of cameras and first-on-the-scene scoops vanished from their minds as they entered the schoolhouse/morgue.

* * *

HE SAW HER BEFORE SHE saw him. Father Patrick O'Brien looked up from his prayer book when she entered the schoolhouse. He stopped reciting the liturgy of the last rites of the church as he stood over Willie Nelson's body, one of many stretched out in rows on the wooden floor. His mind froze in disbelief, and words would not form. For that instant, he forgot where he was and what he was doing. As he gazed at Katie, all the images of death and sounds of sorrow in the room evaporated in his mind so that he was alone with her. The prayer book slipped from his hands, landing with a thud on the lifeless chest of Willie Nelson.

Six years of loneliness and longing for her, carefully compartmentalized and buried somewhere deep within him, subordinate to his celibate life, burst forth from emotional imprisonment. Her mud-splattered clothes, disheveled hair, and faint lines of fatigue in the creamy-white skin beneath those sparkling green eyes did not detract from her beauty.

As she surveyed the room, their eyes met. A moment of hesitation. A moment of uncertainty. Finally, a moment of recognition. Her lips quivered and her eyes, never leaving his, filled with tears that overflowed and splashed softly down her cheeks.

It was Clare Benger, back in her schoolhouse not to teach but to comfort, who broke the trance for him; it was Rusty Shephard for her.

"Is something wrong, Father?" asked Clare standing beside him.

"Is something wrong, Katie?" asked Rusty standing beside her across the room.

The magic of that moment shattered, Father O'Brien and Katie released eye contact and reverted to their respective roles as priest and reporter.

"No, nothing wrong," responded Patrick O'Brien looking up at Clare who held the distraught teenage daughter of Willie and Mary Nelson in a comforting embrace.

"No, nothing wrong," responded Katie Keenan mopping her damp cheeks with a lacy handkerchief drawn from her pocket. "Just overwhelmed by the scene."

Rusty had begun to read Katie pretty well, and he suspected there was something more.

* * *

DOCTOR EDWARD MANSUEY, SERVING IN the temporary morgue as interim coroner, did not recognize the newcomers in the room, nor did he sense the intense personal dramatic dynamic touched off by their arrival. He knew that the tall, ruggedly handsome, redheaded man, and his stunning brunette companion were not locals, and he suspected with disdain that they were reporters. He resented the intrusion and swiftly moved toward them to tell them so.

"Excuse me. I'm Doctor Mansuey, and I'm in charge here. This area is restricted unless you are here to identify one of the deceased," was Mansuey's abrupt greeting and intended dismissal.

Rusty was preparing for confrontation. Katie, knowing that reporters would not be welcome, took a different tactic. She approached the doctor with a disarming smile and responded softly, "We know you are busy, Doctor Mansuey, and we don't mean to intrude. I'm Sister Mary Kathleen, a close friend of Father O'Brien." Then nodding toward Rusty, "Brother Russ and I are Maryknoll missionaries here to assist in comforting the bereaved."

Before Mansuey could respond, Katie rushed toward the startled priest, grasped both his hands in hers, announcing "I'm Sister Mary Kathleen, Father," and pulling him closer, whispered, "Please don't blow our cover, Patrick. I'll explain later."

Rusty hesitated, then followed her cue to escape further inquiry from Mansuey. "I'm Brother Russ, Father," he murmured.

Father O'Brien stooped to pick up his fallen prayer book, needing a moment to regain a modicum of composure. He stood, resisted the impulse to embrace Katie, and responded loud enough for Mansuey to hear, "Thank you for coming, Sister. Nice to meet you, Brother Russ."

What type of tragic comedy is this, Katie? Rusty Shephard wondered.

What's going on here, Katie? Patrick O'Brien wondered.

"May we have a word with you in private when you have a chance, Father?" Katie asked as if in response to the silent inquiries. Both of her admirers nodded in agreement, and shortly thereafter, the three reconvened outside the schoolhouse.

* * *

SHIVERING IN A COLD, MISTY breeze, Rusty became impatient as he watched the long embrace. "Guess you two know each other."

"Patrick and I go way back, Rusty," said Katie, her voice halting and muffled as she buried her head in the good father's shoulder. Slowly, reluctantly, she broke from his embrace, placed her hands gently on his chest, and patted a tearstained wet spot on his black cassock. "The truthful part of my little white lie to Mansuey is that Patrick and I are very good friends."

"I can see that, Katie," Rusty managed uncomfortably, "but did you have to ordain me into religious life?"

"Mansuey was about to kick us out, Rusty, if you hadn't noticed. It was all I could think of at the time."

Rusty's discomfort continued as Katie and Father O'Brien exchanged brief summaries of the past six years of their lives.

"Look," he finally interrupted, "I get that you two have a history together, but this is really not the time to reminisce. Katie and I have a job to do here, Father, and so do you, I might add. Ours is to gather facts through observation and interviews, write our reports, and send them to our respective newspapers as quickly as possible. Yours is to minister to those in need."

"Don't lecture, Patrick," came the defiant, protective response from Katie.

"Katie, I meant no disrespect," said Rusty more softly. He saw her Irish ire flare and knew it was time to back off. "I'm just anxious to get to work."

"I understand that, and I think I can be of help to you in that effort," said Father O'Brien. Not knowing how to address Rusty, he added, "Is your name Russ?"

"I prefer Rusty, Father. Rusty Shephard, and I am city editor for the *Buffalo Express*."

"Nice to meet you, Rusty. I was wondering if Katie was going to introduce us."

Katie flushed at the remark, embarrassed by her lapse of social grace and the realization that she had totally ignored Rusty during the long, emotion-filled reunion with Patrick.

"As I was saying, Rusty, I think I can help," Father O'Brien continued. "First of all, I'll introduce you to family members of the deceased victims who can tell you their stories of loss. I'll introduce you to Clare Benger, our elementary school teacher in Austin, who can tell you about her story of survival. And I will smooth things over between you and Doctor Mansuey. You must be patient with him. His dear wife is one of the bodies in the morgue and his infant son has not been found."

Rusty hung his head, joining Katie in the embarrassment of the moment. "I'm sorry, Father. I would appreciate your help."

"Another thing I can do for you, insist on doing for you, is to provide you two with a meal and a place to sleep for the night at the rectory of St. Augustine, my home. It survived the flood quite miraculously, and I have some supplies remaining in the pantry. And I have one more thing that will be of use to you, a typewriter. You can compose your news stories this evening."

"That would be wonderful, Patrick," Katie responded. She wondered, even in the midst of crisis, what it would be like to sleep under the same roof with him again.

* * *

FATHER O'BRIEN'S ANCIENT ROYAL TYPEWRITER, used mainly to peck out sermons on Saturday evenings, began hammering out copy nonstop well into this Sunday night and early Monday morning. In the parlor of St. Augustine's, Katie and Rusty shared time on the typewriter, as well as their notes and observations, to compose their reports.

Katie wrote sidebar stories on Clare Benger's narrow escape and Doctor Mansuey's tragic loss of his wife Mary and his ten-month-old son Elias. Saturday was bath day, the doctor had explained to Katie, tears streaming down his cheeks. Mary's body, still in the bathtub, had been extracted from the rubble on Main Street.

"In the second-floor bathroom, with the baby splashing in the tub, she never heard the sirens," Mansuey had choked as Katie scribbled on her notepad. "She never heard the shouts on the street below. She was just swept away and crushed by the force. I can't imagine her agony as our baby boy was ripped from her grasp. I hope they find him soon. Mary would want him to be buried with her."

Rusty wrote the story of thirteen-year-old Madge Nelson who was mourning the death of her father, Willie, and desperate to learn the fate of her mother, Mary. Standing over the shrouded body of her father and trembling in the arms of Clare Benger, Madge told of her harrowing experience of clinging to her bed as it was ripped through the crumbling walls of her house, riding the crest of a torrent, and crashing down on the roof of the First National Bank building.

"Mother was at home, downstairs in the kitchen, I think," she told Rusty. "Oh god, I have no idea where she is now." Rusty learned from her that her sister was away at college in Williamsport. "I need my sister," Madge pleaded. "Can you get word to my sister, mister? Please get word to my sister. She needs to know about father. We need to find Mother."

Rusty, a veteran reporter quite familiar with scenes of death and destruction, had difficulty maintaining composure in responding to her request. "I'll do my best, Madge," he whispered. "I'll do my best."

Clare Benger folded Madge into her arms and turned away. The interview was over.

Rusty learned a great deal more about Madge's father from Father O'Brien. Willie Nelson, it seemed, returned to town in a state of agitation following his meeting with Bob Pearson at the Bayless Mill. He brought his borrowed horse back to Silas Wolcott at the livery and closed his store on Main Street, tacking a note of warning on the front door. He then proceeded street to street, door to door, to pass his message verbally to all who would listen. Some did. Most, as usual, did not.

"For several hours before the dam broke, he spread words of warning everywhere in town," Father O'Brien related to Rusty. "Those who believed him left town or moved to higher ground. The irony is he never made it home to warn his family."

The story of Nelson's heroism made dramatic copy that Rusty pounded out on the old Royal. As he typed, he wondered out loud what Nelson had learned at the mill that stoked such immediate alarm. He made a mental note to follow up on that.

It was well past midnight when Rusty and Katie began to compose their lead stories summarizing the magnitude of the disaster.

"Katie, let's pool our notes and write a single report for both newspapers with joint bylines. It will be more comprehensive, and we can get it wired out sooner."

"How do you propose to do that, Shephard? I'm told phone and telegraph lines here won't be repaired, even temporarily, for days."

"I'll take the first train back to Keating Summit. I'm sure trains are running frequently now bringing in volunteers, food, clothing, supplies, and caskets for the bodies piling up in the morgue. I'll wire your reports to the *Evening Times*, my reports to the *Express*, and our joint report to both papers while you continue to gather facts here in Austin. We'll be further ahead if we can work as a team on this."

Katie was dubious, and her hesitation said so. Would Roy Durnstine, her editor at the *Evening Times* who hated everything about the competing newspaper, including Rusty, print a story with his byline included? Would Durnstine agree to copublish a report with the *Express*? Could she trust Rusty to wire her reports without revision—or even wire them at all? It would be a tremendous scoop for the *Express* if he failed to send the reports to the *Evening Times*.

Finally, she relented, trusting Rusty to keep his word, and trusting him to persuade Durnstine to publishing the coauthored report. Besides, Rusty's plan made sense despite her concerns.

Rusty started to type, inserting her comments and observations into the report. Their styles, his meticulously detailed and spartan, hers more flourishing and effusive, melded into a product they both agreed surpassed what they could have written individually.

Perhaps this teamwork could work, Katie thought, as Rusty departed out the door on foot to the B&S Railway rail yard in the pitch black of a moonless night.

* * *

KATIE EXTINGUISHED THE OIL LAMPS illuminating the parlor and entered the living area, carrying a candle and tiptoeing over bodies of refugees of the disaster sleeping on the floor.

She climbed gingerly up the stairs to the second floor and proceeded quietly down the hallway. As she approached the first door on her left, she paused and succumbed to the impulse to peek in through a slight opening. She could make out the form of Father O'Brien in his nightshirt, lying on his back in bed.

Katie froze. As she watched his chest rise and fall in the silent rhythm of slumber, she stood mesmerized at the doorway. Something was awakening in her that was impossible to suppress. It was as if the long-dormant embers of love she had known with him started to rekindle. She felt the warmth in her core begin to spread up and down her body. She wanted desperately to slip into the room to embrace him. She was excited. She was frightened.

Katie, what's wrong with you? He's a priest, married to the church. If you approach him, and he rejects you, you will be unbearably humiliated. If he welcomes you, you will be committing a mortal sin, and so will he. Move on, Delilah. Move on quickly.

She half stumbled down the hallway in retreat and lifted the latch on the second of three doors. Father O'Brien had reserved the two guest bedrooms for Katie and Rusty. Inside she blew out the candle, sat on the bed, and breathed deeply in an effort to dampen the embers. After a time, as the passion ebbed, and she regained control, she removed her blouse, slip, skirt, and stockings and lay on the bed in her brassiere and panties.

Here I am lying in bed half naked with Patrick only ten feet away. She concentrated on her breathing, chest rising and falling, she imagined, in unison with his. The fire began blazing again. Her full, perfectly formed breasts seemed to swell as they moved up and down. She felt a wetness between her legs. She groaned, turned on her side, inserted a hand inside her panties and found the wet spot.

It was too much. *God forgive me.* She rose, retraced her steps back down the hall in the dark, and entered his room, latching the door behind her. He had rolled onto his side facing the wall with his back toward her. He did not stir. She shed her undergarments, slid into bed, placed her arm around the waistband of his nightshirt, and pulled herself into him, knees bending into his, her pubis pressing against his buttocks, and her breasts against his shoulder blades.

She felt his body tighten, then relax as if in welcoming. *Had he been expecting me?*

"Forgive me, Patrick," she whispered. "You don't have to move. I only want to be next to you for one more night."

In response, his hand reached around his back, and he cupped the softness of her thigh. They lay that way, half asleep, in a euphoric dream state, immersed in thoughts of what might have been, through the night.

In predawn twilight, she picked her undergarments from the floor and padded back to her room. Not a word was exchanged then or later. She slipped back into bed without regret.

Perhaps it was only a venial sin.

Monday
October 2

RUSTY WATCHED THE LIGHTS OF the caboose of the B&S train bound for Keating Summit recede into inky blackness. He swore. The train, making continuous round trips transporting emergency supplies and relief workers in and desperate survivors out, had just departed from Austin

It would be two hours of wasted time sitting on tar-stained rail ties in the B&S rail yard waiting for the next train. He swore again. If he didn't make it to a telephone or telegraph line by sunrise, he would miss his publication deadline at the *Express*, Buffalo's morning newspaper. That would mean missing a complete news cycle, not being able to publish the breaking news from Austin until Tuesday morning. He spat on the ground in disgust.

It would also be the cause for an ethical dilemma. If he missed his own deadline and wired the reports to the *Evening Times* as he promised Katie, he would hand the competition the marvelous benefit of a full day's edge in publication. A cardinal sin in the ranks of the fourth estate. The next train needed to be on time. He needed to be on it. And lines of communication needed to be immediately available at Keating Summit.

His mind racing wildly slowed momentarily as he thought of Katie. What, in fact, was she to him? A professional partner? A competitor? What defined their relationship, and where could it be headed? He couldn't deny that her beauty and personality stirred some undefined feelings within him. He would have to put a check on that. He admired her talent and spirit, but he remained wary of her motives.

What kind of history did she have with O'Brien? Rusty remembered the looks and long hugs they had exchanged. Something more than a pastor-parishioner relationship for certain. Something more than friendship. Rusty could not discern why that bothered him.

He had not resolved any of these matters by the time the B&S locomotive steamed back into the railyard at Austin. Two dozen passengers stood with him on a makeshift platform waiting to board. Rusty recognized all of them, including Rappaport from *The Bulletin*, as reporters who would be scrambling to commandeer either the single phone or single telegraph line when the train pulled into the Keating Summit train station. He began working on an alternate plan.

* * *

THE RISING SUN, PEEKING OVER the crests of the rolling hills surrounding Keating Summit, cast long, early morning shadows on the train platform as the train rolled into the station. Before the train came to a full stop, Rusty hopped off the coach car and ran across the platform toward the entrance. He wasn't the only one with that idea, but he was ahead of the pack. Unfortunately, the entrance door was blocked by mounds of relief supplies ready to be loaded aboard the train for the return run to Austin.

He began stepping over and around boxes of food, clothing, and medical supplies in a desperate attempt to be first through the door to the wall telephone in the lobby or the telegraph office in the back corner of the building. His progress was stopped abruptly by a tug on his belt. Before he could turn to see what had snagged his belt, Rusty was jerked backward off his feet and deposited on the wooden planks of the station platform.

On his back, enraged and embarrassed, he looked up at a figure towering over him.

"No need to be in such a rush, sir," an authoritative voice growled from above. "We're going to be polite and orderly here. Now please get up and let me see some identification."

Rusty rose to face a giant of a man in a Pennsylvania State Police uniform who had unceremoniously hauled him off his feet. "Sorry, officer," he sputtered, anger waning, embarrassment ebbing. "I need to get to the telegraph office."

"So do a lot of people, sir. Now let me see some identification."

Rusty felt sick as approaching reporters momentarily slowed their pace, gave wide berth to the officer, and somewhat delicately stepped around and through stacks of boxes and lines of embarking passengers to the front door of the station. Through the windows, Rusty could see the stampede resume to the telegraph office and the wall phone in the lobby.

Rusty handed the officer his newspaper credentials without comment, noting the nametag "Reilly" on his massive chest. *Irishmen continue to mess up my life.*

Corporal Reilly seemed to pause for an eternity as he inspected Rusty's credentials while long lines to the telegraph and phone formed inside the station.

"Well, Mr. Shephard," Reilly said finally, "Governor Tener and the State Police Department of this state respect the role of the press, especially in times of disaster. We have a role to play also and that is to keep the relief effort safe and orderly. Your conduct was inappropriate and obstructive. Do you understand, Mr. Shephard?"

"Yes, sir."

"Then here are your credentials. You must present them again before boarding a train to Austin. Access is restricted to emergency personnel and," Reilly paused for effect, "unfortunately, rude reporters."

Rusty tipped his hat, turned his back to the train station, and walked toward his Maxwell.

* * *

PLAN B WAS TO DRIVE to Olean, the closest town of any size, to use the wire services of *Olean Evening Times* despite his reluctance to share the reports with yet another newspaper. By the time Rusty and his Maxwell roadster rolled into Olean midmorning, a plan C was forming in his mind.

Rusty braked in front of the offices of the Olean newspaper. The clock in the County Court House tower across the street chimed eight times before he made his decision. Eighty miles and three more hours north on route sixteen would put him in Buffalo before noon, before the publication deadline of the *Buffalo Evening Times*.

There were other benefits to plan C—his personal hands-on editing and page layout of the reports for the *Express*, a hearty meal, a hot bath, a few hours rest, and most importantly, the acquisition of a camera before his return to Austin.

He felt a passing wave of guilt when he thought of Katie's stay in the cold, lonely rectory of St. Augustine's. He rationalized away the feeling, however, with the thought that he would share the lead story with her paper in time for Monday afternoon publication. Certainly, she would recognize and appreciate his sacrifice in doing that. He was somewhat proud of himself in resolving that moral dilemma in her favor.

To the consternation of other motor and hoofed traffic on Main Street, he U-turned his vehicle and headed back to the highway.

* * *

KATIE SAT TENSELY UPRIGHT, AS stiff as the straight-backed chair in which she sat inside the office of the president and owner of Bayless Pulp and Paper Mill. Father Patrick O'Brien sat beside her no less tense. In an act of grim irony, nature had left the mill's office building totally intact while the paper mill sat ravaged a mere twenty yards below. Remnants of the broken dam itself dominated the landscape a half mile distant.

George C. Bayless, in an understandably foul mood, sat behind a desk in front of them. To his right sat Fred Hamlin in a similar mood as Bayless in a similar chair as Katie.

Father O'Brien handled the introductions and refrained from further comment.

"From what paper?" snorted Bayless.

"The *Buffalo Evening Times*, sir."

"Never heard of it. Let me see some proof."

Katie slid her press credentials across the desk toward Bayless. He glanced at the card and pushed it back at her.

"If it wasn't for Father O'Brien's request, you wouldn't be here, miss." Bayless nodded and half smiled at the priest. Katie knew that Bayless was a member of St. Augustine Parish and prevailed upon Patrick to use some pastoral persuasion to gain access for an interview.

"As a rule, I don't talk to the press," Bayless continued, the half smile gone.

"I am aware of that, sir. I appreciate your honoring Patrick's, that is Father O'Brien's, request. And I appreciate your seeing me. I just have a few questions."

Bayless nodded in response. Hamlin's glaring stare at the intruders never wavered.

Katie removed a notepad and pencil from her jacket pocket. "I was wondering, sir, if there had been any prior warning that the dam might be unsafe?"

"None."

"Was it subject to regular inspections by an engineering specialist?"

"Of course, it was. The son-of-a-bitch engineer who designed the dam was here just three days ago. He's the one you should be talking to. It was his goddamn design that was faulty."

"I'd like to do that. What is his name? Is he still around?"

"His name is Hatton. Chalkley Hatton, and I have no idea where he is."

Hamlin squirmed uncomfortably and rose from his chair. Although he had not uttered a word since Katie and Father O'Brien had entered the room, he abruptly pronounced, "We have no more to say on the subject. If you have more questions, you'll have to contact our attorney, Frank Baldwin."

Bayless gestured his concurrence. "That's right. Frank will be issuing a statement and answering any questions on our behalf."

"And how can he be contacted?"

"His office is in the First National Bank Building," Hamlin answered abruptly, and then turned scarlet with embarrassment and rage at the absurdity of his response. "He'll contact you," he sputtered and unceremoniously ushered the unwelcome guests out the door.

* * *

"WELL, I MUST SAY, KATIE, you come straight at a person," Father O'Brien observed as they descended the office steps onto the rutted roadway and stepped toward his horse and carriage. "You might do well to try some tact and diplomacy before you go on the attack," the priest continued in a soft, disapproving tone usually reserved for the confessional. "The interview might have lasted a bit longer."

"That's not my style, Patrick," she countered defensively. "And don't lecture me." She saw the hurt in his eyes as the rebuke registered, and she immediately regretted the outburst. "I'm sorry, Patrick. God, you are as sensitive as I am impetuous. What a pair we make."

"Don't bring God into this, Katie. And unfortunately, we never became a pair."

Katie's shoulders sagged as she turned away to avert his eyes. His words triggered a jolt of reality she had been denying. *The hurt he harbors makes him so fragile, so vulnerable to my words and actions. I love him, but I acted selfishly last night. I must be more careful.*

Katie needed to divert his thoughts from their relationship. "Patrick, we're just steps away from the paper mill. Lives were lost there also, and their story needs to be told. Let's have a look inside."

"I think we'd be pressing our luck, Katie. I don't think Hamlin would take kindly to our snooping around the mill. He's got a nasty temper."

"Let's call it investigative reporting, not snooping, Patrick. Now move the carriage around the bend and meet me inside." She ran down a path toward a sprawling complex of buildings and scattered stacks of pulpwood as O'Brien watched apprehensively. He sighed and obediently moved the carriage further down the road. In the past few years as their lives diverged, at least one thing remained constant: there was no use arguing with Katie.

Katie approached the nearest building, a long, narrow brick edifice, two stories high and lined with massive windows along its entire length. A second building, the mirror image of this one, ran parallel, separated by fifty feet. The two were connected at the far end by a substantial passageway containing three towering smokestacks.

She entered through a splintered doorway and stood awestruck, mesmerized by both the size of the building and the machinery it contained. As she anxiously waited for O'Brien to arrive, she took a few timid steps to explore her surroundings, careful not to stray far from the entrance. All the windows, both bottom and top rows, had been blown out by the hammering force of a thirty-foot high surge of water. Broken glass and debris littered the floor, but except for a few puddles, Katie found it surprisingly dry.

She felt diminished both in size and spirit by the enormity of the machinery that towered over her and stretched endlessly toward the far wall of the room. Katie didn't know the first thing about paper production, but she could imagine the power, heat, and noise generated by those massive gears, belts, pulleys, and rollers.

"That's your basic Fourdrinier machine that forms, squeezes, and dries the pulp slurry," boomed a voice behind her.

Katie resisted the adrenalin-fueled instinct to flee, breathed deeply, and turned around to face the person with the booming voice.

"Didn't mean to startle you, miss. My name's Bob Pearson. I am, or rather I was, head of maintenance here at the pulp and paper mill. This is not an ideal time for a tour. What brings you here?"

"Ah, Mister Pearson, I'm Katherine Keenan, a reporter for the *Buffalo Evening Times*." She paused to regain composure and invent some story of legitimacy for her presence. "Mister Bayless gave me permission to inspect the factory."

Pearson masked his skepticism. "Don't worry, Miss Keenan. I'm not on the best of terms with Mister Bayless myself and certainly not of a mind to report you. We lost six men working on this machine at the time of the flood. The lucky ones were on the second level in the far end of the building.

"I'm sorry."

"It could have been avoided, you know, if Bayless and Hamlin had listened to Hatton."

"Hatton? Chalkley Hatton, the engineer?"

"That's the one. From an engineering firm in Wilmington, Delaware. He designed the dam, but he had to make countless modifications that Bayless demanded to save costs."

"You sure about that, Mister Pearson?"

"You can call me Bob, Miss Keenan… I'm damn sure about it. I was in some of those meetings. Things got pretty heated between them, but Hatton usually ended up backing down."

"And you can call me Katie, Bob. What kind of modifications?" Her reporting instincts were on high alert.

"Hatton was concerned about the depth of the concrete foundation. He wanted the footers to extend deeper into the bedrock. He argued for a cutoff wall extending beneath the foundation to keep water from leaking under the dam. He recommended an accessible release mechanism. These things were rejected, and the specs for cement, pipes, steel rods were degraded, all in an effort to save money without regard for safety."

Katie started scribbling on her notepad when O'Brien walked in.

"Hello, Bob," the priest said casually.

"You know each other?" Katie asked.

"Of course, we do, Katie," said Pearson. "This is a small community. I was just telling Katie, Father, of the constant conflict between Bayless and the engineer."

"I was unaware of that, Bob, but I did understand he was recently on site to inspect the dam."

"It was more than an inspection, Father. Hatton was in panic mode to release pressure on the dam. He almost killed himself trying to blow out the cap on the clean out pipe. Bayless and Hamlin were so enraged they actually had me tie him up."

O'Brien was shocked. "You're kidding!"

Katie knew she was on the cusp of a bombshell story, but she remained silent, trying to absorb and sort out what she was hearing.

"Wish I was. I'm not too proud of what went on before the dam broke."

"This happened on Saturday?"

"Yes."

"Where is Hatton now?"

"He hasn't been seen, Father, but I have a pretty good idea what happened to him."

* * *

BACK IN THE OFFICE BUILDING, Fred Hamlin paced back and forth like a caged tiger in front of George Bayless still seated at this desk.

"Goddamn it, Fred, sit down. You're wearing holes in that expensive oriental rug, and you're making me nervous."

"You should be nervous, George, considering our situation. You realize the potential liability for negligence here? Tens of thousands of dollars of property destroyed, not to mention lives lost. Lawyers are going to line up like vultures to sue your ass, the company, and anyone involved in the construction of the dam. We're going to be run out of town broke and broken."

"No such thing is going to happen, Fred. Now sit down and listen to me!"

Hamlin sat only to start bouncing his leg in nervous agitation. He couldn't understand how Bayless could remain so seemingly calm.

"First of all, Fred, when Baldwin shows up, he is going to prepare documents that will release us from all liability."

"Who in God's name is going to sign anything like that?"

"All the mill workers and their families who expect to work for me again. All the merchants and their families who depend upon the economy that this mill supports. All those in Austin who believe that reopening the mill will save the town from shriveling up and dying."

"You're going to reopen the mill?"

"Hell no. We're going to collect the insurance money and start over elsewhere. We'll just hold out that possibility until they waive their rights. Then it won't make a bit of difference if we stay or go."

"Wait a minute, George. There's a problem with that. There will still be some, like Willie Nelson, who won't be intimidated."

"Nelson's dead and good riddance. Thank God there aren't many like him. Besides, any lawsuit for negligence will be hard to prove. As long as we admit nothing and seem contrite, we'll be fine." Bayless tweaked his handlebar mustache as he reflected upon something else. "You sure Hatton can't testify against us?"

"I'm damn sure of that, George. But there is someone else who can do us a great deal of damage. Bob Pearson."

Bayless' hand dropped from his mustache and deep furrow lines appeared on his forehead. "You've got a point there, Fred. Think you can take care of that too?"

Hamlin's lips curled up, half smile, half sneer, in answer. "And I can also take care of that Keenan bitch also if she gets too nosey. Now I'm going to find that lazy lawyer of ours and kick him in the ass to get started."

* * *

IT WAS LIKE A LOVERS' spat, except, of course, they were merely lovers long ago and not yet lovers again, but it was a spat, nonetheless. He, feeling guilty for neglecting his flock in a time of need, and she, feeling anxious to begin investigating a case of negligence and possibly even foul play, were at odds.

"I have responsibilities to attend to, Katie," Patrick O'Brien said in an uncharacteristically brusque tone as they bounced along in their horse-drawn carriage toward town. "I need to get back to the rectory. I need to get back to the schoolhouse. I need to visit suffering families. I don't have time to haul you around town. I'm not a reporter. I'm a priest."

"Thanks for the reminder, Father," came the sarcastic reply. "All I am asking is that you take me to Senator Frank Baldwin's home.

You can drop me off and be on your holy way. I'll walk back to town, thank you."

O'Brien did a slow burn but decided to avoid further confrontation. Instead of continuing on Elliott Street toward town, he right reined the horse onto Orchard Road. Katie could be stubborn and inconsiderate at times, but she always got her way.

A half mile down the winding Orchard Road, O'Brien pulled on the right rein directing the horse up a long, narrow lane leading to the residence of Frank and Gladys Baldwin. He stopped directly in front of the pillared mansion overlooking Austin.

"You can leave now, Patrick."

Predictably, he didn't. He helped her down from the carriage, still waiting for some small mention of appreciation for his help this morning, escorted her up the steps of the front porch and gently knocked on the door.

Moments passed, and Katie, true to form, began rapping repeatedly on the door until it cracked open omitting an irritated voice. "Who is it? What do you want?"

Mrs. Baldwin's voice softened considerably when she saw Father O'Brien standing behind this impolite lady banging on her door. "Oh, good morning, Father." The door opened further in a semiwelcoming gesture. "How can I help you?"

Katie took over. "Mrs. Baldwin, I'm Katherine Keenan, a friend of Father O'Brien's. We have some questions for Mister Baldwin, and as the matter is urgent, Father suggested that we come directly to your home."

Gladys Baldwin intentionally looked past Katie. "You have questions for Frank, Father?"

O'Brien, obviously embarrassed, stepped forward. "Actually, Gladys, it is Miss Keenan who has the questions."

"I'm a reporter for a newspaper in Buffalo."

Gladys immediately changed her mind about inviting them into the house. "Senator Baldwin is not here, Miss Keenan, and I'm not sure he would be inclined to answer your questions if he were."

"Do you know where he can be reached?" Katie persisted.

"I'm not sure. I would tell you if I knew, miss." Then turning her attention to O'Brien, she continued, "Father, I'm very worried about Frank. I haven't seen him since Sunday morning. He has been searching the streets, the morgue, the hospital for any sign of his sister Grace and their parents. He is sick with worry about them, and now I am sick with worry about him."

"I'm sorry, Gladys. I'm sure Grace got John and Josephine and herself to safety," he said with a decided lack of certainty in his voice. "I was at the schoolhouse almost all day yesterday." He winced with the realization he couldn't bear to call it a morgue. "I didn't see Frank, but more importantly, I didn't see the three of them either." *What an awkward way to say they haven't found their bodies yet*, he thought.

O'Brien was about to say goodbye and assure Gladys that he would tell Frank of her concern if he saw him when Katie interjected, "Could you tell me about Mr. Baldwin's involvement with the building of the dam?"

For a moment, Gladys Baldwin held the young reporter captive in her gaze. Then she slammed the door in Katie's face.

* * *

FRED HAMLIN BRAKED HIS VEHICLE to a stop on Orchard Road, shifted to neutral, pulled on the emergency brake, and got out to peer up the lane toward the Baldwin residence. Something was happening there that disturbed him. He took a dozen steps up the lane to confirm his suspicions. *That's O'Brien's carriage in front of the house. The damn reporter just won't let go.*

He considered his options. The first was to drive up the lane and throttle the bitch. Even in his rage, he realized this might not be the right time or place for that. It could wait. He was a patient man.

The second option was to drive up the lane and warn Baldwin to keep his mouth shut. But Baldwin was no dummy. He wouldn't incriminate himself. That should not be necessary.

The option that seemed best to him now was to back down the road, wait around the bend, and see how this played out. When the carriage departed, he would get Baldwin's take on how to best handle her for the moment. At the thought of Baldwin, his anger flared again. The son of a bitch had disappeared just when they needed him most! Hamlin was prepared to address that the next time he saw him.

The problem with that strategy, as he would subsequently discover from Gladys Baldwin, was that the senator's whereabouts remained a mystery. Gladys gave Hamlin the same message and the same cool reception she had given Katie. She didn't much like Fred Hamlin.

* * *

ON THEIR RIDE BACK TO town, O'Brien considered reminding Katie again about the art of diplomacy but then dismissed the thought in favor of a silent truce. He occupied himself with concern about his long absence and a plan for the remainder of the day. Katie herself was occupied with other concerns, primarily the whereabouts of Rusty Shephard. He should be back in Austin by now. Where could she find him? Did he make the deadline for her reports?

She needed to talk to him about the events of the morning. She needed his advice. She had to admit she missed him. Then some doubt crept into her thoughts. Did he file her reports at all? Perhaps he only sent stories to the *Express*. That would make sense from a competitor's point of view. But he was more than a competitor, wasn't he? Wasn't he?

The thought was way too painful to dwell upon, so she dismissed it and began to absorb the scene as the carriage rolled down Thorn Street toward the center of town.

Workers still searched mounds of debris in the hope of finding survivors, but their efforts were fraught with fatigue and fruitlessness. Crude wooden coffins lined the streets waiting for deposits of recently recovered bodies as cleanup work continued unabated.

Gas lines had been shut off and fires extinguished. Cartons of food and clothing, off-loaded from train cars, lay haphazardly beside the tracks along Railroad Avenue waiting to be distributed. Two huge tents, one serving as a commissary for clothing, the other as a kitchen and mess for refugees and workers, had been set up in the middle of Main Street, the once bustling center of commercial activity.

Several smaller tents with Red Cross emblems were left unattended as the call for medical attention was either minor or non-existent. Nurses busied themselves instead in the commissary and kitchen dispensing clothes and food to those in need.

Katie felt a certain unnerving calmness to the scene. Along Main Street, there was a state police presence on the corners of Railroad, Turner, and Kershner avenues but little need to preserve order. Lines were short, and people, zombielike, were too shattered to be rude, let alone disorderly.

"Please drop me off here, Patrick," Katie requested, dusting off her wrinkled suit and dropping to the street before he could fully rein in the horse. Only she was conscious of her disheveled appearance. Patrick thought she was the one ray of beauty amid the ugliness of suffering and desolation.

This time, he did not argue. He had a lot to do, and she could take care of herself. As he continued across the makeshift bridge on his way to the morgue, he allowed himself to think that perhaps she would sneak from her room to visit him again tonight.

* * *

KATIE INTERVIEWED ANY PERSON WHO would talk to her as the morning morphed into afternoon and the autumn sun moved across the hilltops warming the interior of the tents. She searched for any sign of Rusty while scribbling note after note about stories of anguish and loss as well as stories of heroism and reunion. She paused to grab a sandwich at the commissary hoping to find him there.

Later on a trip to the outhouse thoughtfully placed at some distance from the town center, she questioned some reporters. No one had seen him.

The outhouse reminded Katie that it would be some time before the infrastructure providing water and sewer services could be repaired, but she remained hopeful that natural gas, electricity, and most importantly, telephone and telegraph service could be restored soon.

It was late afternoon when she ran into chief of police Daniel Baker, spelled B-A-K-E-R as he had reminded her. She learned from him that the death toll was now at thirty-eight with fifty persons still unaccounted for. He also informed her that the Odd Fellows Hall at the corner of Thorn Street and Orchard Road had been set up as a homeless shelter. More importantly for her interests, Baker said it had high priority for establishing temporary phone and electric service.

Bone weary and wondering about Rusty, she hiked toward Odd Fellows Hall, disparagingly referred to by Chief Baker as "the old boys' club."

* * *

KATIE STAKED OUT HER TERRITORY amid mattresses and blankets, jealously guarding the space around the wall-hung phone in the back corner of the club. As word spread of the possibility of phone service to that building, an increasing number of boisterous reporters began to crowd the space around her. She informed them repeatedly and emphatically to back off. She was number one in line for the phone. She watched through the window as telephone and power company linesmen worked feverishly outside the building.

Sometime after dark, the overhead electric lights flickered to life and the side-mounted gas lights were turned off. She reviewed her notes hoping that phone service would soon follow and carefully crafted the stories in her head so that she would not waste a second dictating them to the newsroom at the *Evening Times*. She would have much preferred to transmit fully typed and edited copy by telegraph, but this would have to do.

Minutes dragged into hours as smelly bodies curling up around her feet began to snore and restless reporters queuing up behind her began to curse and shove. She picked up the phone's receiver every few minutes hoping for the voice of an operator. The line remained dead.

Around midnight, when she felt for certain that her weary legs would soon buckle, she finally heard the welcome sound of "number please."

With her newsroom on the line, she meticulously dictated the lead story of death and destruction in the mill town of Austin, then followed with six sidebar stories of human suffering and bravery. She was tempted but purposely avoided any mention of her interviews with Bayless, Hamlin, or Pearson. Those were stories yet to be investigated and reported.

She realized that Rusty was not only present in her thoughts, but that his influence was also guiding her journalistic judgment.

Before relinquishing the phone, with disgruntled reporters behind her shouting obscenities, she mustered the courage to ask the question most important to her. "Did Rusty Shephard, city editor for the *Express,* phone in her reports from yesterday?"

"He did," came the response. She exhaled in relief. Why would she have doubted him? "But," the copy editor of the *Evening Times,* continued, "not in time for yesterday's deadline. The *Express* got the scoop."

She banged down the receiver.

She sat exhausted on a side bench searching for a space to lie down. Too tired to dwell on Rusty's betrayal. Too tired to consider Patrick's concern if she failed to return. Too tired to venture outside. Her eyes closed, and her head nodded forward.

"Come on over here, young lady," came a kindly voice from the mass of humanity on the floor. She blinked away a sleep-deprived cloud and saw an elderly gentleman rising to his feet. "Take my place here. I've had enough sleep."

As she approached the gentleman, she reassessed her initial impression. The lines on his face, the bulbous nose, and the bags below his eyes weren't so much the result of age as they were the result of alcohol.

"My name is Brady Quinn, and my profession is the law," he offered by way of introduction. "I understand that you have been asking some leading questions about ethics and responsibility." He held up his hand noting her immediate defensive posture. "Not to worry, miss. It's a small town. Word gets around. And besides, I know a great deal about the greedy motives of George Bayless, Frank Baldwin, and their minions that destroyed this town. We have a lot to talk about."

All at once, Katie was wide awake. She needed someone to talk to; she needed an ally. If it couldn't be Rusty, Brady Quinn would have to do.

* * *

RUSTY SHEPHARD WAS SMUGLY CONGRATULATING himself on the logic of his plan as he motored north on Route 16 from Olean to Buffalo. Plenty of gas. Plenty of time to keep his promise to Katie. And even though giving their collaborative report to the *Buffalo Evening Times* for publication a full fifteen hours before his newspaper, the *Buffalo Express*, ran against his every competitive instinct, he would do it.

To compound the agony of this journalistic transgression, he would have to suffer further embarrassment when Roy Durnstine released the story to the wire services. The result would be that his newspaper would be scooped by not only the *Evening Times* but also by every other afternoon newspaper in the state, not to mention the nation. Rusty was not consoled by the fact that he might share a byline with Katie. That also would be Durnstine's decision.

Still, he intended to keep his promise. Then a flat tire literally threw a wrench into plan C. It happened only twenty miles from his destination, but the distance didn't matter, only the time required to fix the flat. It was a long and arduous procedure.

He thought briefly of hitchhiking the rest of the way, but that would mean abandoning his car on the side of this desolate section of road surrounded by cornfields. His sports car was his baby. That wouldn't happen no matter what.

The Maxwell Motor Company did supply spare tires for some of its larger touring cars but not for Rusty's Runabout. Under the bench seat, he found a jack, a lug wrench, rubber patches, glue, an air pump, and instructions. He began by reading the instructions and was immediately confused.

Two hours later, he was back on the road, quite unsure if his patching job would hold for another twenty miles. It did, but solving that problem created another. It was a few minutes past one o'clock when he finally arrived breathless in the newsroom of the *Evening Times*. Roy Durnstine, at the editor's desk across the room, was glaring at him as he entered.

"What are you doing here, Shephard?" he shouted as Rusty approached.

Rusty stopped in front of his desk momentarily to catch his breath. "I have something for you, Roy," he panted. Have you closed the front page?"

"Damn right. Half hour ago. It's been cast and sent to the pressroom. In fact," he paused to listen to the rumbling of the press two floors below, "we're printing papers and rolling them onto the street as we speak. We run like clockwork here at the *Evening Times*, Shephard." The inference was, of course, that the *Express* did not.

Rusty dismissed the insult. "Look, Roy, I did my best to get these to you before noon. He handed the lead story along with Katie's sidebar stories across the desk. You might want to stop the press and rework page one."

Before the words were out of his mouth, he knew that would be impossible. It would take more than an hour to typeset, compose, lockup, recast the front page, and make ready the press, throwing distributors hours behind schedule, and causing enormous expense and confusion in the recall of papers already distributed.

Durnstine didn't respond until he had scanned the copy handed to him. "You son of a bitch," he steamed, slamming down the typewritten sheets on his desk. "You know damn well that's impossible. You needed to have this to me two hours ago to make deadline."

"Sorry, Roy."

Durnstine was now out of his chair waging a finger in Rusty's face. "Sorry, Roy! Sorry, Roy! You're not the least bit sorry, Shephard. You damn well knew what you were doing when you waltzed this copy into me at one o'clock. Sorry, my ass!"

"Roy, I tried. I really tried."

"Bullshit! You could have phoned it in to me."

Under attack, Rusty was quickly morphing from repentant to defiant. "Actually, I couldn't, Roy. Now if you don't want these reports, which are Pulitzer caliber by the way, that reporter of yours is damn good, I'll just take them back, and you can read them in the *Express* tomorrow morning."

"Not a chance," replied Durnstine clutching the papers to his chest.

"All right then, here's the deal. The lead story gets a dual byline. You have Katie's stories exclusively, and you delay putting anything on the wire until we go to press tomorrow."

"That's no deal, Shephard. Keenan's stories belong to us anyway. It will kill me to run your name on any story we print, but I'll give you that out of professional courtesy. As for holding it off on filing for the wire services, no friggin' way!"

Rusty expected as much, but figured it was worth a try. "I'll wait here until the lead story is typeset, and then I want the copy back."

"You planned it this way, didn't you, Shephard? I'll make sure I let Keenan know what a two-faced bastard you are."

Rusty didn't respond. *She has probably come to that conclusion on her own.*

* * *

THE NEWS STAFF AT THE *EXPRESS* was beginning to file into the newsroom, assembling for their late afternoon shift when Rusty arrived. His reception here wasn't much warmer than he had received at the *Evening Times.*

"You did what?" his editor in chief exclaimed. "You gave Durnstine your bylined report?"

"It has two bylines, Chief. Their reporter was a contributor. Besides, we'll beat them to press tomorrow along with my sidebars."

It still didn't sit well with the chief. "Go edit your copy, put it on the hook, and layout the news pages for tomorrow. Then get your ass back to Austin. And take a goddamn camera with you this time."

A group of wide-eyed reporters parted like the Red Sea as he huffed his way through them on the way to his desk.

Rusty understood quite clearly that he was expected to make a quick turnaround. So much for a good night's sleep.

It was early evening when he finished his tasks in the newsroom. He called the Buffalo Central Terminal and learned that a train was leaving for Keating Summit at midnight. The clerk wasn't sure about connections to Austin. "Everything is crazy there."

Tell me about it. The train was still his best option. He wasn't about to trust the Maxwell's tires for a return trip. He'd deal with that later.

He grabbed a camera and gave a tip of the hat to the chief on the way out. He got a scowl in return.

Rusty's first stop was Al's Café for a hot meatloaf sandwich and mashed potatoes smothered in Al's rich brown gravy. He couldn't remember the last time he had eaten or had a friendly conversation.

He took Al's advice to call his mother in Rochester with apology for not showing up last weekend. He took one scolding for that and another for telling her he would most probably not be able to visit next weekend either.

He promised her he would make it as soon as he could, told her he loved her, and said goodbye.

His next stop was his apartment over the poolroom where he could tell by the clatter of billiard balls below that the evening's competition was well underway. He soaked in the luxury of warm, soapy tub water for as long as he dared, then dressed, loaded a bag with fresh clothes and the camera, and began the ten-block trek to the train station.

He hoped he could catch some sleep on the train.

Tuesday
October 3

WELL INTO THE EARLY HOURS of Tuesday morning, Katie sat cross-legged on the floor in front of Brady Quinn, absorbed by the story of the history and development of the Bayless Pulp and Paper Company. Seated on a rickety chair in the center of Odd Fellows Hall, Katie listened attentively to Brady's long-winded oration that he animated by frequent facial expressions and hand gestures. Katie thought he would be marvelously persuasive in a courtroom of law.

Brady's pontifical style was replete with digression, opinion, and a good measure of Irish humor, but for the most part, he painted a thorough and accurate account. Brady Quinn, sober or drunk, was a great storyteller. Today he was seriously sober.

As Brady described it, entrepreneur and paper manufacturer George C. Bayless from Binghamton, New York, was interested in expanding operations into North Central Pennsylvania where an abundance of good pulpwood remained in the forests from decades of timber operations. While the lumber industry had denuded the Potter County forests of their majestic hardwood trees, it left behind expanses of stacked or standing pulpwood—the raw material for paper manufacturing.

Bayless saw the opportunities, and the town fathers of Austin, led by lawyer and bank president (later a state senator) Frank E. Baldwin, provided the incentives. The town offered Bayless a large tract of land for his plant, an earthen dam to capture the water of Freeman Run necessary for operation, stone quarries for building materials, homes for employees, and a railway siding to deliver raw materials and ship finished products.

In August of 1900, Bayless accepted the offer and construction of the mill began.

"Who wouldn't take a free ice-cream sundae like that with whipped cream and a cherry on top to boot?" spat Brady, not hiding his disdain for such an outlandishly lavish offer. "It cost us a turd load to line the pockets of greedy industrialists."

"I was just hanging out my shingle on Main Street to open my law practice," he continued, "when they slapped on the heavy property taxes to subsidize the mill. I was against it. Willie Nelson was against it. We lost that battle, and every battle since. Bayless and Baldwin packed the town council with their people and ran the town for their own benefit. It was the industrial giant versus the little people. Intimidation ruled."

"But the mill created jobs," Katie interjected.

"Yes, it created jobs," answered Brady. "It also created injuries and deaths from the powerful saws, chippers, and presses. It also created pollution from the dumping of bleach, sodium sulfite, and caustic soda into our once pristine, trout-filled stream. There was no concern for safety or conservation. The single driving force was profit."

"But the greatest sins," Brady continued, throwing his arms in the air for emphasis, "were committed in the construction of the concrete dam in 1909."

"What was the need for a new dam in the first place?" Katie asked. "Wasn't the earthen dam sufficient?"

Somewhat calmer now, Brady explained, "Paper production consumes huge amounts of water for the pulp cooking vats and for the generation of electric and steam power to operate the machinery. In long dry spells, particularly in late summers, the lake behind the earthen dam shrunk to levels that could not sustain full production. Bayless was forced to cut output during these periods. Shrinking output meant shrinking profits. He hated that. He needed a larger dam."

Katie was anxious to tie in what she had heard from Bob Pearson. "I understand there were some engineering shortcuts in materials and methods in building the dam."

"I'm no engineer, Katie, but that wouldn't surprise me at all. Bayless was all about cutting costs whether it involved production or construction. What I do know is that in his rush to construct the dam, the concrete was not given sufficient time to harden. The entire project was completed in six months. All of the concrete was poured during October and November in some pretty frigid weather, the last of it only a month before the lake behind the dam began to fill. No way did it have time to cure."

Brady paused to bless himself. "I wish you could interview Willie Nelson, God rest his soul. He saw two cracks appear in December of that year. Both ran from the breast to the base, fifty vertical feet and about ninety feet apart. Nobody listened to him, but he knew the dam was not structurally sound. Every morning, until the very day it failed, he'd walk or ride to the base to inspect it and repeat his warnings."

"Did you believe him, Brady?"

"Damn right I did. I think maybe Barney Anderson, bartender at the Goodyear Hotel, did too. He talked a lot about Willie being crazy, but I think Barney was concerned."

Katie was quick to pick up on that remark as evidence of where Brady spent much of his time. She fished for more information about his professional life by asking, "Do you have a lot of clients in your practice? What type of legal work did you do here?"

Brady was no fool. He knew where this was going. "Look, Katie, I used to do a lot of litigation when I worked in Erie. I made some poor decisions there that led to huge financial losses and eventually to a divorce. With my professional and personal life in shambles, I decided to relocate my practice to a smaller town and start over at a slower pace. Mostly what I do now is prepare deeds and Wills. And yes, I spent a lot of time at the Goodyear Hotel bar."

Katie knew now what drove him to Austin and to alcohol. The Quinn Law Firm was well known in legal circles when she was growing up in Erie. She remembered the scandal involving the firm in 1900 when she was in high school. The details were a bit much for a fifteen-year-old to grasp, but she remembered reading about accusations of fraud and malfeasance, lawsuits, investigations, and threats of disbarment. She couldn't remember the outcome, but she was sure it wasn't in Brady's favor.

She didn't need to know the details now. What she did know was that this Brady, whatever his past faults, was intelligent, articulate, and witty. She suspected that the Austin disaster had shocked him out of his world of alcoholic self-pity into the world of sober resolve. Most importantly, she trusted him. She thought a jury would as well. He would be a credible witness in any legal action against Bayless.

Relieved to change the subject, she charged, Katie-like, into that arena.

"Would you consider testifying against Bayless in a court of law, Brady?"

"Same answer as before. Damn right I would."

"Because I think that between your testimony and Bob Pearson's, we could build a case."

Brady raised his eyebrows in mock surprise. "Are you a reporter or a lawyer?"

"I'm a bit of both, I guess. An investigative reporter."

"That doesn't quite qualify you for the bar, Katie, but I think you're onto something. I didn't know you had talked to Pearson, but he certainly knows the inner workings of the cabal known as the Bayless boardroom. He could provide damaging testimony if he's willing."

"I think he is, Brady, and I think his testimony would support more than just charges of involuntary manslaughter. I believe it could support a case for murder in the first degree."

* * *

RUSTY STAGGERED INTO ODD FELLOWS HALL around four in the morning, half asleep from exhaustion, crook necked from contortion in a crowded coach car seat, and cranky from another confrontation with Corporal Reilly of the Pennsylvania State Police at Keating Summit. Hopeful for a few hours rest to recover from the nonstop stress of the past twenty-four hours, he took the advice of the train's conductor and dragged himself from the platform to this hall for refugees.

He scanned the floor of the hall for a spot to crash among the slumbering bodies. He grabbed two blankets from a pile near the entrance, found a small space in a corner, dropped and curled up in a two-blanket cocoon. He was asleep in seconds.

Into the third hour of his restless, dream-filled sleep, a voice filtered through his subconscious. "That's the jerk I was telling you about."

Rusty's groggy state of mind connected the voice with an image of an angry Corporal Reilly continuing his berating barrage waged hours ago at the Keating Summit railway station. *Just be quiet and let me alone.*

The voice persisted, invading his dream. "And to think I thought he was a nice guy doing me a favor."

Rusty knew that voice, and it wasn't that of Corporal Reilly. Reilly's image dissolved in his mind's eye replaced by a gorgeous, fair-skinned brunette with emerald-green eyes and an eyepopping figure. *Katie.*

Slowly emerging from his dream state, Rusty refused to move or open his eyes. Obviously, he had some explaining to do, but he couldn't muster up the courage to face her. He continued to play possum.

"Maybe he has an explanation, Katie," another voice said. A gravely, baritone male voice. "Perhaps you should give him a chance."

"Nothing to explain, Brady. He held up filing my stories so his newspaper could scoop mine. Simple as that. Period. 'Collaboration,' he said. 'We'll work as a team,' he said. Bullcrap. At the end of the day, it was all about him. Wake up, jerk!" She put a physical exclamation point to her venting with a none-to-gentle kick to Rusty's behind.

He rolled onto his back and sat up grimacing, hurt not by the kick, but by her words. "Katie, I tried my best. I got your reports to Roy Durnstine as soon as I could." Then looking up at her in cow-eyed contrition, continued, "I wouldn't do anything to hurt you."

Her outrage subsided for an instant. She wanted to believe him. She wanted Rusty to be the person she had first imagined.

"Look," Brady interceded as the long, awkward pause persisted, "this is not a good way to start the day for civilized people. Let's amble over to the commissary tent and have a cup of coffee. Then we can talk. I think we're all on the same side here." He reached out a welcoming hand to Rusty and dragged him to his feet. "I'm Brady Quinn. Sometimes people put an 'esquire' behind my name, but for a long while, I didn't deserve that distinction."

A while later, as the coffee warmed their hands and insides on a cool cloudy leaf-colored autumn day, Rusty began his explanation. Katie's heart was not yet warmed, but she listened patiently as he told of the incident at Keating Summit, the drive to Buffalo to make her publication's deadline, the flat tire, and the cold receptions given him at both the *Evening Times* and the *Express*.

"I went to the *Evening Times* first, Katie. The press was rolling. Durnstine would not remake page one, but he did put our bylined report on the wires immediately. The report went nationwide before either of our papers went to print. Durnstine wasn't happy, and my chief wasn't happy, but the report got on the wire, and you got the credit you deserved. I hurried back here to explain what happened and to resume our reporting. I still think we make a good team."

Rusty could see that she remained skeptical. He would have to restore trust through action not words.

"Rusty, let me tell you about Brady and what I learned from him," Katie said, shifting topics without comment about ongoing teamwork. Still, the implication that they could continue to work together remained and then gathered impetus as she excitedly laid the foundation for a journalistic and legal case for negligence. The dangling of a possible case for homicide was, in Brady's words, "the whipped cream with cherry on top" for the three of them.

Rusty was warming to Brady's engaging and compassionate personality even as they had walked from the Odd Fellows Hall to the commissary. Now the thought of adding Brady's legal expertise and local knowledge to the team was doubly appealing.

They talked together for an hour as they sampled sugar cookies and refilled their coffee cups. Katie detailed the meeting with George Bayless and Fred Hamlin, the discussion with Bob Pearson, and the visit to the Baldwin residence. Brady expanded upon the insensitive, bottom-line-driven decisions that permeated all strategic planning of the Bayless organization. Rusty absorbed all of this in his slow, methodical manner.

"How would you proceed, counselor?" Rusty asked Brady.

Brady was pleased that Rusty sought his opinion. "We need more than hearsay. We need some solid evidence," he replied.

"Agreed," Rusty and Katie said in unison.

"I think our first stop should be the morgue. Let's see if any bodies have shown up with bullet holes," said Rusty.

"Agreed," Rusty and Katie repeated.

* * *

FRANK BALDWIN WAS EXHAUSTED AND heartsick when he entered the little schoolhouse on the hill early Tuesday morning. It was the same school that both he and his sister Grace had attended from grades one to eight. Frank followed the path of boys from the few families of privilege in Austin. He was sent to a private school in Olean to complete his high school education. Grace followed the path of girls from Austin from all families, privileged or not. She learned the skills of cooking and housekeeping from her mother and married early in life.

Frank went on to college and law school, took over his father's law practice in Austin, and prospered as lawyer, bank president, state senator, as in-house counsel for the Bayless Pulp and Paper Company. To the disgrace of the Baldwin family, Grace married beneath her social class, a laborer for the Goodyear Lumber Company and later for the Bayless Pulp & Paper Company. Although Michael Collins was never accepted by the Baldwin family, he was a good man and loving husband to Grace until the day he was caught in the fast-spinning, heavy rollers at the Bayless Mill and crushed to death.

On that tragic day, Grace began her slow descent from a person-able, charming middle-aged socialite engaged in community life to a withdrawn, bitter spinster, old beyond her years without purpose in life. Frank suggested she move back to their family home to take care of their aging parents. The move succeeded in giving Grace some purpose in life, and to her credit, she became a wonderful caregiver, if not a bit compulsive and neurotic in Doctor Mansuey's opinion, to her fragile parents in their midseventies.

Steps inside what was once his grade school, Frank Baldwin stood transfixed in a state of shock at its transformation from school to morgue. The ink-stained, initial-carved, bubblegum-stashed desks and chairs no longer filled the space. Removed from the building, they lay in scattered disarray in the muddy schoolyard, discarded remnants of happier days in the lives of the children of Austin.

Instead, on the bare wooden floor lay cloth-draped mounds of human remains that had been his business associates, neighbors, and friends. He had checked here frequently throughout Sunday and Monday as part of his frantic search for his parents and Grace. Each time he entered, he was engulfed in a renewed sense of dread that he might find them on the floor.

Baldwin searched the room for Doctor Mansuey, the acting cor-oner. He felt compassion for the doctor, too absorbed in the business of moving bodies in for identification and out for burial to have time for personal grief for the loss of his own wife and infant son. By default, Mansuey had assumed not only the duties of coroner but undertaker as well.

Austin's two funeral homes were gone along with their propri-etors. Mansuey had no embalming material resulting in an imme-diate need to load bodies into crude wooden caskets for families to remove and arrange for funerals and burials without delay. Since no churches remained in town, most services were conducted in the streets followed by a solemn parade of mourners accompanying the casket to the hillside cemetery west of town.

While the supply caskets brought in by train remained adequate for the moment, Mansuey's problem was that more bodies were being brought in than carried out. He had recorded sixty-two flood-caused fatalities as of this morning, many still unidentified and awaiting burial. The stench of decay was beginning to permeate the building.

Baldwin sighted the distraught doctor engaged in deliberation with Father O'Brien. Baldwin approached with apprehension. The priest and doctor looked his way then dropped their eyes toward the floor. At their feet lay three shrouded bodies. Baldwin knew intuitively that he had found his family. His cry of anguish blended with the sounds of mourning from others in the room to create a chorus of grief rising to the heavens. Father O'Brien blessed himself asking for strength as he prepared to tell Baldwin the eyewitness account of his sister's heroism.

* * *

HEARING THE SOUNDS OF SIRENS and screams of alarm in the streets, Grace Collins ran upstairs to wake her parents from their Saturday afternoon naps. She knew the meaning of the sounds of panic. The dam had broken. She knew that she had to evacuate John and Josephine Baldwin and herself as quickly as possible. What she couldn't know was the exact amount of time remaining before the turbulent wall of death, now unleashed and on its way down the valley, would exact its crushing blow to their Turner Street home. It would be slightly less than ten minutes.

Two minutes passed as she ran from bedroom to bedroom to ready her parents to leave. She placed shoes on their feet and jackets around their shoulders.

Two more minutes passed as she tried to herd them as quickly yet carefully as possible down the stairs. Leading a crippled man with a cane and a nearly blind woman from floor to floor was a delicate, time-consuming task under the best of circumstances.

Two more minutes passed before they were off the porch and onto the street. Grace headed them south to Thorn Street, then west toward the safety of higher ground. Her instincts were correct. They were moving in the right direction, but they were moving too slowly. A thunderous roar, closing in on them from the north, grew in intensity with each passing minute.

In two more minutes, they had made it to Kershner Avenue. She was practically dragging her stumbling father and pushing her sightless mother up the street. Frenzied neighbors ran past them. Ahead loomed the barbed wire fence of the safety of the patch of pastureland on higher ground. Onlookers lining that road waived frantically, beckoning them to move faster.

Frank Baldwin later reflected upon the tragic irony of the story he was hearing. Grace could easily have reached the road by herself in the two remaining minutes, but she refused to abandon her parents. A faithful daughter to the end, according to those who watched the final moments. Grace stopped her struggling attempts to escape, turned her back to the oncoming onslaught in defiance, and embraced her parents. Then all three of them were swept away.

As Father O'Brien finished the account of their final moments, he offered his condolences to the pale, shaken sole survivor of the Baldwin clan. Baldwin fell to his knees beside the last of his family members and embraced them in turn—mother, father, and sister— duplicating her last loving act on earth.

He pressed his lips against the cold, unhearing ear of his deceased sibling and whispered, "I'll make them pay for this, Grace. I swear I will."

* * *

KATIE WAS A VICTIM OF emotional overload. The professional pressure she felt to pursue the investigations of criminal negligence and probable homicide percolated at the surface of her being and kept her focused. But underneath, an emotional undercurrent that she could not define, let alone resolve, was eroding her conviction and self-confidence.

When she entered the morgue and saw Patrick, the undercurrent erupted into an overwhelming deluge. The part of her that was not altogether consumed by the investigation began flooding with latent feelings for Patrick and emerging feelings for Rusty. She didn't think these feelings should be in conflict, but somehow or other they were.

The trigger to her emotional breakdown was the smell—the smell of death. She gagged, turned, and bolted for the door brushing Rusty and Brady aside. Outside, she bent over one of the school desks scattered in the yard. There she could not contain it. Hands on the desk, she braced herself and retched again and again.

Rusty's nurturing nature begged him to follow, but his intuitive sense of place stopped him. He did not have the intimate relationship with Katie necessary to comfort her, wrap an arm around her waist, and hold her forehead while she threw up. Not yet at least. The one person in the room who did have that kind of connection rushed passed him.

The wave of nausea was replaced by a larger wave of embarrassment. She melted into the comfort of Patrick's arms.

"I have to get out of here, Patrick," she said breathlessly, pressing her face into his chest. "I have to leave this place. I need time and space to sort things out. Besides," she continued, brightening a bit, "I'm a mess. I'm sure I smell. I need a bath. I need clean clothes. I need to brush my hair." The muffled sobs returned. "Please take me to the train station. Please."

* * *

PATRICK O'BRIEN RARELY DROVE AN automobile, and never one as luxurious as the Ford Touring Car loaned to him by Frank Baldwin. Baldwin had not hesitated a moment when his pastor, the good Father O'Brien, had made the request. It was unlike the priest to be so bold, but Baldwin was pleased to grant the request, especially knowing the young lady with him was not feeling well.

As O'Brien gently assisted her into the front passenger seat, Katie turned to Rusty who was standing uncomfortably next to Brady beside the vehicle. Katie could see that the two of them were both perplexed and concerned.

"I'm sorry, Rusty. I need to get home. Listen to Brady. He has good instincts and will lead you in the right direction."

"What happened to the team of Keenan, Quinn, and Shephard?" Rusty intoned, failing to mask his disappointment.

"You two will do fine without me. Perhaps Durnstine will assign me back here after I file more reports about the devastation here in Austin."

"He'd be crazy not to. You're the best reporter he has." Color ran to Katie's cheeks at the compliment from Rusty. "And one more thing. We have unfinished business."

She thought about that remark as Patrick drove to the rectory to pick up her traveling bag and then proceeded to the railside platform now serving as Austin's makeshift train station. They remained silent throughout the trip, both too deep in thought for conversation.

Several overturned barrels served as seats on the platform. Patrick took a cushion from Baldwin's deluxe automobile, placed it on one of the barrels and motioned her to sit.

"That's so gallant, Patrick, but aren't you worried about soiling the senator's fancy pillow?"

O'Brien shrugged, his way of suggesting this was no time to worry about offending the senator. Katie obliged and took the seat.

"I so wish I could have pulled myself together long enough to interview him," Katie continued. "I made a mess of it, didn't I?"

"You have no need to apologize, Katie," he replied, sitting on a barrel next to her. "You are not a mess, and you did not make a mess. You're a victim of stress and fatigue, that's all. I'm sure Brady has introduced Rusty to Baldwin by now, and the three are in deep conversation. Let them carry the load for a while."

Once again, a bit of an Irish anger flared at one of his innocent remarks.

"I'm as strong as they are and don't think I'm not," she blurted, struggling to control tears welling up from a mix of emotions.

He did not rise to comfort her as she expected. Instead, he stayed seated opposite her, observing her intently and allowing the crying to diminish to a whimper, then to silence.

Finally, to break the silence, he said, "Where are we going, Katie?"

"What do you mean, Patrick? I'm going back to Buffalo, and you are going to minister to these poor grieving souls who have lost everything." She gestured with a sweep of the arm at the stacked rubble on Main Street that had been the center of a vibrant community three days ago.

"No, I mean what's going to happen to us, Katie?"

She knew where this was leading and was unprepared to deal with it now. "Nothing's going to happen to us, Patrick. We are going to remain friends, and I'm going to continue being a reporter, and you're going to continue being a priest."

"I don't know if I can."

She was shocked by his frankness. *Not now, Patrick, please.* "Of course, you can."

His forlorn glance back at her was his wordless response.

She knew she could not end this conversation without some resolution. In fairness, she needed to be as honest with him as he was with her. And she needed to be honest with herself. Without fully knowing what she could, or would, say, she began.

"Patrick, you must remain a priest. It is your calling. You are such a compassionate, loving person. This is who you are. This is what you do. Your people need you, especially now."

"I have needs too, Katie. I need you."

She couldn't stop now. "Patrick, what we had once was beautiful. We were deeply in love, and the memory of that is something I will always cherish. When I saw you again, I was consumed with those old feelings, partly from loneliness, partly from passion. I know now that I was wrong. I was being selfish. I don't want to tarnish the memories with something cheap and degrading. I don't want to steal you from the church."

"It wouldn't be stealing, Katie. I would come willingly."

"No, Patrick. It will never work. Not now."

"Not now? Not now? Is there someone else?"

It was Katie's turn to allow a wordless silence to speak for her.

Patrick O'Brien absorbed the meaning of the moment, then rose, stepped off the platform, and returned to the car. She sat alone, seated in unintended parody of a queen on a cushioned throne, tears trickling quietly down her cheeks, waiting for the next train.

He didn't even say goodbye.

* * *

FATHER O'BRIEN WAS RIGHT ABOUT one thing. Only moments after he and Katie departed the schoolyard, Brady had introduced Rusty to Baldwin. It didn't take long for the deep conversation O'Brien had predicted to begin.

The history between Baldwin and Quinn was marked with distrust and distain. Baldwin viewed Brady as a loudmouthed drunk. Brady, in turn viewed Baldwin as an arrogant, conceited, pretentious opportunist. The extraordinary aspect of their relationship was the undercurrent of mutual respect between the two.

Baldwin knew of Brady's former status as a managing partner in an elite law firm in Erie. He also knew firsthand of Brady's quick mind and sharp tongue when he was sober. Brady's persuasive and on-target criticisms of the Bayless operation affected public opinion and rankled Baldwin endlessly.

Despite Baldwin's misguided ambition and formal bonds with George Bayless, Brady detected at least a minimal sense of decency in Baldwin and a more observable recent distancing from his association with the industrial mogul.

These mutual assessments didn't exactly set the stage for amicable discussion let alone cooperation, but Rusty Shephard's laidback style of diplomacy moved the conversation in that direction.

"Look gentlemen," Rusty began as they stepped from the suffocating atmosphere of the morgue into the fresh air and hazy sunshine of a late-morning autumn day, "we are from different backgrounds, but I think we share some common goals in our desire to uncover the truth and pursue justice. If we join forces, our combination of perspectives and talents can be a great asset."

"Truth and justice. Don't forget 'the American way', Rusty," Brady deadpanned with his tongue stuck firmly in his cheek. "Look, we aren't supermen, any of us, but I do agree with you that we are stronger together. Justice here means accountability. And people responsible need to be held accountable for this loss of life and property. Frank, with your insider knowledge, and Rusty, with your investigative instincts, I think we can develop a strong case for criminal negligence that will hold up in court."

Baldwin responded without hesitation. "If you are asking if I would be willing to testify in court against Bayless and Hamlin, the answer is an emphatic 'yes'. Beyond that, I would suggest that I prepare a petition to the court asking for arrest warrants to be issued against them immediately."

After a brief pause, he directed a complimentary afterthought to Brady, "I would be pleased, Brady, for you to review the draft of the petition and join me as cocounsel in presenting it to the County Court in Coudersport. Let's meet at my home at four o'clock this afternoon."

Brady, surprised and genuinely flattered by the suggestion, nodded.

"I can't help with the legal matters," Rusty interjected, "but I can spend some time investigating the crime scene. I'd like to take a closer look at the dam."

"I'll take you there, Rusty," Brady volunteered.

"How do you propose to do that?" Rusty asked.

"By borrowing the car of my esteemed new colleague," Brady winked at Baldwin, further cementing his reputation for bold behavior.

Baldwin nodded back at him. Brady's forthrightness, a character flaw that sometimes got him in trouble, could also be disarming.

"Good," said Brady punctuating the end of the conversation and the beginning of an unlikely alliance. "And on our way, Rusty, I want you to meet a friend of mine."

* * *

"WELL, WELL, A NEWSPAPER MAN you say, Brady?" queried Austin's most distinguished and only brothel owner upon introduction to Rusty Shephard. "From the great city of Buffalo. I've done some business there in my early days." She winked at Brady. "My name's Cora Brooks." Cora extended her hand to Rusty. "Any friend of Brady's is a friend of mine, but if you're looking for ladies, mine all left after the flood. Not much call for business under these pitiful circumstances. I can offer you gentlemen a beverage, however."

"Too early in the day for me," Rusty responded. Brady just shook his head.

"I know it's not too early for you, Brady. What's the matter?"

"Guess, I've just lost my taste for it, Cora. 'Pitiful circumstances' can do that to a person."

"Affects me just the opposite, Brady, but to each his own. Now what can I do for you gentlemen?"

Rusty fished his notepad from his pocket. "Brady tells me you actually saw the dam break, Cora. Can you tell me what you saw?"

"Let's step out on the porch, fellas, and I'll describe it to you."

Rusty and Brady followed her through the front door where many a satisfied customer had departed with a smile and into the dull late-afternoon light of a cloud-covered autumn day. A cold breeze greeted them as Cora marched them to the corner of the porch overlooking the mill and the dam.

"It's a clear view of the dam from here as you can see. I was standing in this exact spot sipping my morning coffee on Saturday when it happened.

"I think it was in the afternoon, Cora," Brady interjected.

She scowled at Brady. "Anything before five o'clock is morning to me, honey. My day starts late and ends late. Anyway, my ladies were lounging in the parlor waiting for their daily inspection and a little speech about proper etiquette in the bedroom. I have my standards here, you know."

Rusty finally got the picture. He wished Brady had briefed him.

"Anyway, I was deep in thought with my back to the dam when I hear a loud crack."

"The dam breaking?" Rusty asked.

"Just let me tell the story, darling. No, it was a gunshot. I'm sure of it. So I turned in that direction, toward the dam, and I saw an object falling down the face of the breastworks."

Once censored for interrupting, Rusty still could not contain himself. "An object, Cora? Could that object have been a person."

"I never thought about that. Why do you ask?"

"An associate of mine talked to Bob Pearson. He thought he saw someone standing on the spillway platform just before the dam gave way."

Cora pondered the possibility, seemingly reluctant to draw that conclusion. "I guess it could have been, but if it was, the poor devil got crushed in midfall when the dam burst. But why would anyone be on top of the dam?" She paused, then made a connection. "I'll bet it was the same idiot I saw there swinging from a rope earlier in the morning."

Both Rusty and Brady were on full alert. This was new information. "Tell us more about that, Cora," said Rusty.

"I saw it from my bedroom window. I wasn't quite awake, but I'm sure it wasn't a dream. It looked like he had a rope tied around his waist and someone on the platform catwalk was lowering him down the face of the dam. There were some other people on the platform too.

Brady, always afraid of heights, shivered as he closed his eyes to get the picture. "That's crazy. Insane."

"Right about that," Cora continued. "He seemed to be swinging back and forth out over the breastworks, and then he released something he held in his hands. I couldn't see what it was, but it fell like a rock into the pond at the base. Just after it hit the surface, the water erupted like a geyser. The guy at the top began hauling him in like a dead fish at the end of a fishing pole. Then they all scampered across the breast of the dam and disappeared. It was the damnedest thing I ever saw. None of my ladies believed me."

"Well, we do, Cora." It was Brady. "My guess is that they were inspecting the dam and were trying to relieve some of the pressure. That might have been a dynamite package you saw dropped, but I can't imagine why. We need to talk to Bob Pearson about who was there and what they were doing."

"Katie and I were asking about him at the Odd Fellows Hall and at the food commissary tent this morning," Rusty added. "He seems to have disappeared. We found out he lives by himself. His home got destroyed, but nobody knows where to find him."

"Did you come here to talk about Bob Pearson or the dam busting?" asked Cora, a little perturbed that they kept interrupting her story. Both Rusty and Brady nodded and leaned in to encourage her to continue.

"Well, just after the gunshot and the person or whatever it was falling, there was this tremendous rumbling, like an earthquake. I could see cracks on either side of the spillway widening. They opened up like giant jaws as the dam gave way, and water burst forth with a roar that was deafening. Pauline could barely her me when I called."

"Pauline?"

"Pauline Lyons at the switchboard at central. God bless her. She saved a lot of people by spreading the word.

"God bless you, Cora," said Brady. "You alerted her first, or she couldn't have done that."

"And since we're giving medals here," Cora responded, "God bless you, Brady, for rescuing her and bringing her here. It took a while to nurse her back to health, poor child."

"I left her in good hands, Cora," said Brady. "You sheltered a lot of people here until they could relocate. Including me."

Rusty was getting impatient. "Anything else you can add, Cora?"

"Only to invite you gentlemen back to stay the night if you have nowhere to go. It's pretty lonely here with everyone gone, and I'm a pretty social person as you know."

"We might take you up on that," said Rusty. "It would sure beat the cold floor at the Odd Fellows Hall. In the meantime, Brady and I have some investigating to do." He motioned to Brady. "Let's walk down to the base of the dam for a closer inspection."

* * *

THE TREK TOWARD THE DAM, traversing down the hillside from Cora's house, was a bit precarious, especially for Brady whose regular exercise in recent years had been limited to getting on and off the barstool at the Goodyear Hotel to visit the bathroom. The terrain was uneven, and the slope moderately steep, particularly as they neared the bottom. With no trail to follow, Rusty guided Brady through the ankle-high vegetation and around bushy outcrops, looking for footholds free of rocks.

Brady stumbled into Rusty frequently, once knocking them both off their feet.

"Look, Brady," Rusty exclaimed as he brushed himself off, "I know you're no mountain goat, but do you think you could try to watch your step a little better?"

"I should have worn my jungle boots, great white hunter. You didn't tell me we were going on safari."

The final descent, laced with more grumbling and a few more falls, landed them near the base of the dam on the recently reclaimed gravel banks of the stream called Freeman's Run.

"Three days ago, we'd be standing in the middle of a pond churning from the overflow of the dam," Brady observed. "Actually, we'd be underwater."

Great slabs of concrete, sections of the broken dam, thrown apart at oblique angles by the explosive force of unleashed energy, towered above them in both directions. In the midst of this concrete graveyard, a tranquil stream now emerged, lapping at their feet, unfettered and free once again to meander happily down the valley toward town.

Rusty noted numerous reinforcing steel rods poking out like quills from the slabs of concrete. He would learn in subsequent court testimony that if the rods had been larger and more numerous, they might have held the dam together. Without an engineer's eye, he simply viewed them as grotesque gargoyle-like protrusions, symbols of mayhem and destruction, and perhaps, he thought, even evil.

"I wish we had an engineer here to explain all of this," said Rusty.

"Don't worry, Rusty. We'll recruit plenty of expert testimony for the trial. The mother-lode of which would be from the design consultant himself. He might incriminate himself, but I'll bet we'd find that he was strong-armed by Bayless to cut a lot of corners."

"Who was the chief architect?"

"An engineering firm from Wilmington, Delaware. The main guy's name is Hatton, and people saw him in town Saturday morning."

"You mean he was here when the dam broke."

"Looks that way, Rusty. It would be nice to interview him, wouldn't it?"

"Damn straight. Excuse the pun. Let's follow the stream and see what we can find."

"Why not? My shoes are ruined now anyway."

They trod downstream, sometimes stepping into the slow-moving water when brush-filled terrain impeded their path along creekbank.

They were less than one hundred yards downstream, Rusty later estimated, when he saw it. A whitish, leaflike protrusion on the far bank caught his eye. "That doesn't look natural, Brady. I'm going to have a look."

Rusty carefully picked his way, rock to rock, across the slippery bottom of the stream. Fortunately, the water was clear, only knee-deep, and the current minimal. He reached the other side without incident.

Brady watched as Rusty secured a foothold on the bank, looped one arm around a hanging tree branch, and reached for the white object submerged in mud. He yanked. A hand, then an arm, then a shoulder, and a then head appeared out of the mud with a sucking sound.

"I think we may have found Mr. Hatton, Brady, but I don't think he's in a mood to be interviewed. He's got a bullet hole through his head."

* * *

BRADY WASN'T HAPPY TO BE part of a two-man crew tasked with dragging a two-hundred-pound body up the hill back to Cora's house. It was dusk by the time they arrived, and Brady practically collapsed on the threshold. Frank Baldwin wasn't happy either when he later learned that his new touring car had been used as a hearse to transport a mud-infused, decaying corpse to the morgue.

It was dark by the time they arrived at the morgue, and another unidentified body was presented to Dr. Edward Mansuey. The body count was now sixty-two, most now identified, even travelers staying in town on Saturday, but twenty residents were still missing.

The only person in Austin who seemed happy this night was Cora Brooks as she welcomed Rusty and Brady back to her infamous house on the hill. Infamous or not, the house provided them a hot meal, a warm, a steaming bath, and a change of clothes while theirs were washed and hung to dry near the hearth of a blazing fireplace. They learned that Cora had quite a collection of men's clothes, left behind as calling cards by hastily departing guests over the years.

Most welcome were the downy-soft beds and the privacy of separate bedrooms. As he drifted off to sleep, Rusty wondered how many visitors had slept in this bed. None that stayed overnight, he presumed. And none that slept alone.

Wednesday
October 4

BOB PEARSON, HEAD OF MAINTENANCE at the Bayless Pulp and Paper Mill, was comfortable with machinery but not so much with people. From the first day Fred Hamlin hired him, Pearson remained aloof from the other workers. He was content in keeping the machinery—the saws, the chippers, the presses, the boilers, the two Fourdrinier machines—and thus the factory itself in running order.

Pearson's mechanical skills far outweighed his social skills. He talked to the machines as he lubricated, adjusted, and repaired their gears, rollers, and pulleys, but he avoided lunchtime conversation and camaraderie with the work crew. He preferred opening his lunch pail in the solitude of a corner near a Fourdrinier machine. The men joked that the Fourdrinier was his only friend. Perhaps Pearson had friends in a past unknown and unknowable life, but today he well earned his reputation as a loner.

And so it was that when Pearson was anxious or troubled, he withdrew rather than seek comfort in human companionship. In the days following the dam's collapse, he had withdrawn to the comfort of his machines in the damp darkness of the ravaged remains of the mill. Then on Monday, he was alarmed to find the intruder—a reporter at that—in his sanctuary.

He had let down his guard when he learned she was a friend of Father O'Brien. He regretted now being so open with her about his opinions and suspicions. He'd have to be more careful. It was certainly clear that Hamlin didn't trust her.

He had watched Hamlin load a rifle in his car and follow her and the priest as they departed the mill grounds in a carriage that day. He suspected that Hamlin had seen them coming from the factory. Pearson feared that Hamlin might return to inspect the premises. He knew his machines could no longer protect him.

Around midnight, his flight instinct kicked into high gear, and in the pitch blackness of a moonless night, he fled to the safest spot that came to mind.

* * *

FATHER PATRICK O'BRIEN TOOK HIM in of course. Pearson knew he would. The priest, silhouetted by the light of the candle in his hand, had led him down the dark corridor of the second floor of the parish house. Despite the brain-numbing fear that enveloped him, Pearson remembered counting the doors as four figures, two men and their candlelit shadows, marched in lockstep down the hallway. The first door, he had presumed, was the priest's bedroom.

Father O'Brien had paused as they approached the second door, looking into that bedroom with what Pearson thought was expectation followed by a discernable disappointment as he pulled the door shut with unnecessary force. They proceeded to the third and last bedroom on the hall where Pearson spent the remainder of the night.

Cloistered for the next day and night in the confines of the parish house and constantly reminded by the priest that his protected asylum was assured, Pearson nevertheless seldom ventured from the security of his bedroom with the exception of hurried visits to the outhouse. Father O'Brien brought meager meals to him from the house's dwindling pantry when Pearson deflected all pleas to dine in his company downstairs.

So it was on Wednesday morning that Pearson lurched to a far corner of his bedroom at the sound of knocking on his door.

"Who's there?" he demanded in high-pitched nervousness.

"It's me, Bob, your friend and pastor, for goodness sake. Will you please open the door?"

"I'm sorry, Father," Pearson responded meekly as he unlocked the door. "I thought Bayless or Hamlin might have found out I'm here."

"That's nonsense, Bob. I've told no one. Besides, you can't hide in here forever."

"I'm afraid for my life, Father."

"Excuse me being blunt with you, Bob, because priests are allowed to do that, but I think you're being paranoid. Bayless and Hamlin haven't been seen in days. They're probably holed up at the mill offices along with their esteemed attorney trying to concoct a defense against the many lawsuits about to come their way. Believe me, you're the least of their worries."

"You may think that, Father, but I have become a greater threat to them than all the lawsuits combined."

Father O'Brien stood frozen on the threshold of the bedroom trying to make sense of Pearson's remark. A moment passed as he considered whether to pursue it further. Instead, he simply shook his head and continued. "You must come out now, Bob. They need you at the morgue. I mean at the schoolhouse."

"Who is they?"

"Doctor Mansuey, the coroner, and Dan Baker, the chief of police, among others," the priest responded, a hint of irritation creeping into his voice. "Now come on! They need you now to identify a body."

* * *

SOMEWHAT COMFORTED BY THE THOUGHT that the law would be present in the person of Chief Baker and further fortified to be escorted by the clergy, Bob Pearson half ran the short distance to the schoolhouse, glancing left and right for any sign of trouble.

"Good God, Bob, slow up," the priest panted trying to catch up as they neared the entrance. "The deceased isn't going anywhere."

"Maybe not, Father, but I would just as soon be inside," Pearson shouted over his shoulder. Finding the door locked, Pearson waited impatiently for someone to answer his knock.

The door opened, and the two stepped into a chilly, dimly lit room that was intentionally kept unheated to better preserve the bodies.

"'Bout time you got here, Pearson," boomed the baritone voice of Chief Baker ushering them in and slamming the door behind them.

Pearson hastily scanned the room, then exhaled in relief when he saw only two other figures in the room. Both he recognized; neither he feared. Rusty Shephard and Dr. Mansuey were engaged in conversation in a far corner. Mansuey was seated on a stool; Rusty was standing beside him. The newspaper reporter was nosey but nonthreatening. The doctor, eyes bloodshot from fatigue and grief, was simply doing his duty as coroner.

With a nod of his head in greeting, Mansuey rose and proceeded to the center of the room where a solitary, blanket-draped body lay. Business had slowed here at the morgue. Pearson presumed that four days after the disaster most bodies had been recovered, identified, and buried.

As if reading his thoughts, Mansuey spoke up, pointing to the corpse. "Looks like there won't be many more coming in. This one is number seventy. We may never find those still missing. Some moved on before we could account for them." His voiced cracked and he bowed his head. "Others, like my little boy, were simply washed away without a proper burial."

Father O'Brien blessed himself and moved wordlessly toward the center of the room. Pearson followed. They remained standing on one side of the body. Rusty and Brady joined Mansuey on the other side. The doctor bent and pulled the blanket back far enough to expose a bloated blackened face. A sickening stench rose from underneath the blanket.

Brady gasped. Baker stifled an impulse to retch. The other three remained stoic. Looking directly at Pearson, Rusty spoke first, "Can you tell us, Mister Pearson? Is that the engineer who designed the dam?"

Pearson took a long look at the distorted features of the deceased, paused with seeming uncertainty, then turned toward Rusty and responded, "Decidedly not, Mister Shephard. That man with a bullet hole in his temple is not Chalkley Hatton. He's a mill worker by the name of Charlie Rennicks."

Mansuey remembered placing toe tags on Charlie's family three days ago—wife, Mayme, seven-year-old Arnold, and three-year-old Evelyn. *At least he was spared the grief of burying them*, he thought.

* * *

PENNSYLVANIA GOVERNOR JOHN K. TENER, a tall Irishman and former professional baseball player, was only ten months into his first gubernatorial term when he received the news of the Austin catastrophe. John Tener's keen mind and engaging personality had served him well in the political arena. A two-term congressman and newly elected governor of a key northeastern industrial state, he was a rising star in the democratic party.

Tener, self-assured and assertive by nature, was seldom indecisive. Today was an exception. He wasn't at all certain that this trip to Austin was a good idea.

Despite the outward facade of calm, he was churning inside. He dreaded the approaching on-site contact with death and destruction, fearing he would succumb to a show of emotion totally unfit for a strong and confident leader. He wished he were back in the security of the governor's office in Harrisburg, signing declarations of sorrow and support.

Opposite him in the plush upholstered seats of the governor's private railcar sat the man responsible for uprooting him from his familiar, safe surroundings. T. Chalkley Hatton, senior partner of the engineering firm of Hatton, Bixby, and Rollins, classmate of John Tener in their undergraduate days at Harvard, and known as Whitey to his close friends.

"I'm still processing all of this, Whitey," the governor said, scratching his clean-shaven chiseled chin of a movie star. "Your call on Saturday warning of the outrageous conduct and total disregard for safety procedures at the Bayless Pulp & Paper Mill was an eerie harbinger of the collapse of the dam two hours later. Did you really think the breach was imminent?"

"I didn't know it would be at that very moment, John, but I did know that if the pressure wasn't released, it could not hold. I called you to issue an evacuation order. Unfortunately, it was too late."

"Are you sure this is a good idea to confront George Bayless? He was a big contributor to my campaign, you know."

"Damnit, John. Put politics aside for once. This is about justice and fair restitution for families who suffered loss of loved ones, property, and livelihood. Bayless needs to be held accountable, and you should use the power of your office to see that it happens."

"I'm not used to being lectured to, Whitey."

"Well, get used to it until you do what is right."

Sitting mute throughout this dialogue, the third person in the parlor car, seated beside the Tener, spoke up, "You don't need to worry, Mister Hatton. I'm here to support the governor and assure that justice is served."

Hatton turned his attention to the state police commissioner, a bulldog of a man both in build and facial features. "Thank you, Captain Dixon. We appreciate your personal intercession. I understand that you already have a significant presence of officers in Austin."

"That is correct, sir, both in Austin and at Keating Summit to prevent looting and to limit access to authorized personnel only. We have been successful at both."

"Thank you, Captain. It's now my hope, and I'm sure the governor's wish that you conduct a thorough investigation into criminal culpability."

Tener pushed back in his velveteen cushioned seat, clearly uncomfortable with the topics of confrontation and criminality.

"I do indeed, sir. Justice will be served," Commissioner Dixon repeated.

The governor's railcar shook as if in emphatic response to the statement, but as the three passengers looked out the windows, it was apparent that the movement was no more than an uncoupling and reconnecting of their parlor car to an engine of the Buffalo and Susquehanna Railroad.

They fell into silence for the duration of the final leg of their trip from Keating Summit to Austin, each contemplating what "justice" meant, what roles they might play, and what consequences they might face.

* * *

HAD FRANK BALDWIN AND BRADY QUINN known that Chalkley Hatton was on his way to Austin, they might have rescheduled their appearance before Judge Willard Wainwright, president judge of Potter County, at noon at the county courthouse on Main Street in Coudersport. Hatton's testimony would have strengthened their case immensely.

On the thirty-mile drive to the county seat, Baldwin and Quinn reviewed the points of their petition for an arrest warrant jointly drafted the night before. The petition argued that George C. Bayless, major stockholder and chief executive officer of the Bayless Pulp & Paper Company, and Fred Hamlin, superintendent in charge of operations, should be held criminally liable for the deaths of sixty-two mill workers and residents of the town of Austin resulting from negligent practices in the supervision of construction of the dam owned by the company. The death toll was still rising, but the attorneys agreed that even one death from such negligence should have criminal consequences.

The petition presented written testimony from Baldwin as company legal counsel, hearsay evidence from maintenance personnel including Bob Pearson, and some documentation in the form of correspondence between Bayless and Hatton during the construction process. Baldwin and Quinn agreed that the petition was strong enough to merit the issuance of arrest warrants by the judge.

The Honorable Willard Wainwright, impatient and irascible on his best of days, disagreed and proceeded to dress down the appellants as part of his summary orders concluding the hearing. Despite Baldwin's massive physical size, he seemed diminished both in size and spirit as he stood before the judicial bench looking up at Wainwright. Quinn, likewise, standing beside Baldwin, seemed to shrink before the judge's reprimands.

"I am not indulgent of hastily prepared and sparsely supported briefs presented to me, counselors. Hearsay evidence is not permissible in this court. I am not convinced that you have proved a prima facia case for unlawful killing, nor am I of a mind, with the evidence presented, which by the way is primarily based upon your testimony, Mister Baldwin, to issue warrants for arrests of the two named individuals."

Judge Wainwright leaned forward on his elbows. His bushy gray eyebrows rose upward furrowing his already deeply rutted brow and his lips pursed accentuating the frown lines around his mouth. Baldwin and Quinn took involuntary steps backward.

"Now here's the way it is, boys," he intoned in his best breathy, conspiratorial, off-the-record voice. "Your case is not without merit, and I am not a heartless bastard inclined to disregard the potential for both criminal and civil remedies for those poor suffering souls in Austin. But you should realize, especially you, Senator"—he nodded at Baldwin—"that the evidence presented does not approach the threshold of proving probable cause in determination of criminal negligence. I will, therefore, not grant your petition for warrants for arrest."

Following a short pause for dramatic effect, the judge continued, "Here is what I will do, however. I will issue a warrant for search of the offices of Bayless Pulp & Paper Company in an effort to secure adequate evidence to present to a grand jury. I will order the district attorney of Potter County to impanel such a jury to further investigate the matter. The jury will be instructed to review all relevant documents, hear all relevant testimony, and consider the possibility of criminal conduct before issuing or denying issuance of indictments for further prosecution."

Another pause coupled with a finger-pointing gesture. "Now this is what you need to do. Build a stronger case. Dig for more evidence of negligence. Get the dam's design engineer on the stand. Support his conclusions with more expert testimony. Question the integrity of the accused. And before you leave, stop at the clerk's office to pick up the search warrant that I will execute immediately. Now get out of here."

Baldwin and Quinn, afraid to utter another word, did an about face and proceeded to the prosecutor's table to collect their papers in preparation for a hasty retreat.

They were halted in their tracks by the booming voice from the bench. "By the way, Mister Baldwin, be aware that if you agree to testify in this investigation, you are likely to incriminate yourself, and that may lead to an indictment for criminal culpability. Likewise, you may be disbarred for violating attorney-client privilege in offering your testimony."

Baldwin shrugged in acknowledgment.

"And finally," the judge concluded as he rose to retire to his chambers, "there is one more matter that may be of interest to both of you. I have signed papers deputizing Doctor Edward Mansuey as acting Deputy Coroner in Austin and authorizing him to schedule a coroner's inquest for Friday regarding the unusual circumstances in the death of a certain," he paused to peruse a paper in his hand, "Charles Rennicks. I am directing District Attorney Jacob Wiley to attend as well to determine if this is a matter for prosecution."

* * *

FROM HIS EXPERIENCE WITH THE legal system, George Bayless had learned to use the plodding nature of the grinding wheels of justice to his advantage. He had sidestepped many a potential lawsuit for negligence by delay, persuasion, payouts, and where necessary, strong-arm tactics throughout his tenure at his first venture into the paper manufacturing business in Binghamton, New York.

"Sometimes if you just wait it out, Fred," he often said to his superintendent of operations, "it will just go away. But sometimes you have to employ some persuasion to make it go away." Such was his reasoning in posting numerous handwritten notices in Austin on October first and second, even as the search for bodies was ongoing.

ANY MAN, the posters said, WHO DESIRES CONTINUED OR NEW EMPLOYMENT AT THE RECONSTRUCTED BAYLESS PULP & PAPER MILL SHOULD APPLY AT THE COMPANY'S OFFICES IMMEDIATELY. SIGN-UP BONUSES WILL BE OFFERED.

What the posters did not say, what Bayless, even without the advice of Frank Baldwin, knew not to say directly, was that anyone filing suit against the company would never be hired. If the unstated part of the message needed reinforcement, Bayless made sure that the word-of-mouth message he spread along with the posters made it clear.

Thus intimidated and in desperate need of income, nearly four hundred men lined up at the mill's offices on Monday and Tuesday to seek the promised employment. Bayless had no intention of reopening the mill. What he wanted was the protection from lawsuits that the so-called employment contract provided.

The printed documents, which Bayless had used effectively at the Binghamton operation, were simple hold-harmless agreements, fully executed by an unwitting signature and payment of five dollars characterized as an employment bonus.

Bayless had backup plans ready for those who refused to sign and for others who remained as potential adversaries. Meager payments for family burial expenses in return for signatures was a favored tactic. And of course, he would not hesitate to press forward with blacklisting, blackmail, threats, physical force, and whatever additional measures of "persuasion" he deemed necessary.

Believing that Chalkley Hatton was permanently out of the picture, Bayless was reasonably certain that once these little fires were extinguished, he could move forward free of potential liability. He hadn't even considered the possibility of a grand jury being impaneled for further investigation. Even so, he had one more club in his bag he was prepared to use to limit liability. A declaration of bankruptcy.

He was feeling this sense of smug confidence late Wednesday afternoon as he sat in the secure haven of his office explaining the strategic steps to Fred Hamlin when Edith's squeaky voice interrupted to announce a visitor in the outer office.

"Another applicant?" Bayless inquired.

"No, sir, we finished with the last of them this morning," Edith reminded him. "This gentleman has some type of legal document for Mr. Hamlin."

Alarmed, Hamlin stood up with a what-the-crap expression on his face. He looked to Bayless for any kind of reprieve. None was forthcoming.

"Show him in," Bayless said, insensitive to the Hamlin's obvious alarm.

A tall lanky teenage boy with greasy hair and bad complexion dressed in an ill-fitting gray courier's uniform, stepped tentatively into the office. "M-m-mister H-h-hamlin?" he stuttered looking directly at Bayless seated behind his massive mahogany desk. "He's Hamlin," snarled Bayless, pointing to the man standing beside his desk. It felt like a Judas kiss to Hamlin.

"M-m-mister H-h-hamlin," the boy continued, now looking in the right direction. "I have a s-s-summons for you from the d-d-district a-a-attorney's office that I was d-d-directed to h-h-hand to you p-p-personally." He extended his hand toward Hamlin, holding an official-looking envelope with two fingers as if it were some stinky substance he couldn't wait to drop. Hamlin didn't move.

"P-p-please, s-s-sir, I need to hand this to you and get y-y-your s-s-signature on this r-r-receipt." The messenger extended his other hand holding a single piece of paper.

Hamlin still didn't move. The boy inched timidly toward him. Bayless sat motionless with a bemused expression on his face as he watched this snake dance play out.

Finally, Hamlin stepped forward, snatching both documents from the boy's outstretched hands. A corner of the receipt, torn free in the unexpectedly quick exchange, fluttered to the floor. "T-t-that's all right, s-s-sir," the boy stammered as if responding to an apology. "Y-y-you can just s-s-sign the main part." He hesitated and then added, "P-p-please."

"Just sign the damn receipt, Fred. Then we can look at the summons. Where the hell is Baldwin, anyway?" Bayless had been stewing about Baldwin's disappearance for days.

Hamlin scribbled his signature and unceremoniously dispatched the messenger. He plopped his bulky frame back down on the chair beside the desk. He opened the summons and studied it with stone-faced deliberation.

"Well?" Bayless interrupted after allowing more than ample time for Hamlin to read the one-page document. "What does it say?"

"It says I have to appear at a coroner's inquest regarding the death of Charles Rennicks. At the Odd Fellow's Hall here in Austin. At eleven o'clock on Friday."

"Jesus Christ, Fred! Charlie Rennicks! What the hell happened to him?"

"I'm not sure, George, but I think I may have shot the wrong man."

"Jesus Christ," Bayless repeated, buying time to consider the ramifications of this development. "What a mess you've created, Fred."

"I've created?" Hamlin bounced off his chair to confront Bayless at close range. "I've created? It was your order to eliminate Hatton."

Bayless rose from his chair and backed away in a physical and symbolic way to distance himself from Hamlin. "I said no such thing, Fred. I suggested that Hatton was a problem for you to deal with."

"Screw the words, George. You and I both know what you meant!"

In this instant of heightened tension, Bayless suddenly realized that alienating Hamlin now would not be to his advantage. He still needed him. It wouldn't be too difficult to incriminate the stupid bastard at a later time and then walk away.

"Okay, Fred, let's calm down and think this through. If Rennicks is indeed the man you shot, we have two problems. You said that you thought Pearson may have followed you to the dam. If that's the case, he may have witnessed something as well. This inquest could embolden him to come forward. Our first problem is that Pearson might testify at that hearing. Our second problem is that Hatton is still alive and could implicate us in any ongoing investigation. "I suggest you take care of those two problems in that order."

"Is that a suggestion or an order?"

"I worded it as a suggestion, Fred, but if you don't cover up the mess you made, you'll be facing consequences you don't want to consider."

"What about you, George? You don't think you'll face consequences?"

Bayless didn't respond immediately. He was already thinking about ways to extract himself from this mess at anybody's expense, including and especially Hamlin's. "Just one last word of advice, Fred," he said finally, and then paused again before spitting out his final directive. "Don't fuck it up this time."

* * *

KATIE DIDN'T WAKE UP UNTIL noon on Wednesday, a full twelve hours after her fifteen-minute walk from Buffalo Central Railroad Terminal to the boarding house on Susquehanna Street where she leased a room from the kindly but far-too-inquisitive, some would say nosey, Mrs. Pearlmutter. Immediately upon climbing into bed, she fell into the restorative embrace of escape into deep dreamless sleep.

It was a loud knock on her door by the same Mrs. Pearlmutter, whose curiosity could not be contained a minute longer, that woke her.

"Are you all right, dearie?" Mrs. P. inquired in her smoking-induced, raspy voice outside the door. "I heard you enter last night, but you were up the stairs so fast I couldn't catch up with you. Hello, hello, dearie."

Katie grudgingly swung her feet from bed to bare floor, winced at the cold shock that shot up her legs, and started to the door. She stopped several feet short and reconsidered her instinctive response to open it. She just couldn't deal with the predictable barrage of questions from her landlady, nor did she wish to be seen in her current disheveled condition.

"I'm fine, Mrs. P.," she shouted back through the door. "I just need some time to put myself together. I'll stop to see you on my way out."

"Are you sure, dearie? It's so unlike you to sleep so late. Were you out drinking last night?"

Katie stifled the impulse to tell the nosey landlady that not only had she gotten sloppy drunk, but also engaged in a sexual orgy for most of the evening. Instead she responded honestly and hoped that would end the inquisition. "I returned by train late last night totally exhausted from a difficult assignment, Mrs. P. I need to get ready now to go to the office."

Mrs. Pearlmutter sensed dismissal and reluctantly retreated downstairs to her living area. Katie waited until the footsteps fell silent, stripped off her clothes, wrapped a large Turkish towel around her, tucked the top tightly against her, and trotted down the hall to the tenant-shared bathroom.

She turned the tap on the bathtub, mumbled a prayer of thanks for the urban convenience of indoor plumbing and hot water, watched steam rising as the tub filled, dropped the towel, and slowly immersed her body into the luxurious warmth. She allowed her head to slip under the water. Her luxurious raven hair floated to the surface and swirled riotously with the motion of her body.

She scrubbed her skin with bar soap until it turned a tingling pink, then she stood and drained the tub. She watched the sudsy water swirl her sweat and soil down the drain and wished the pain and ugliness she had endured for the past four days would wash away as easily. She filled the tub again.

This time she attacked her hair with a rich shampoo, lather, and submerged again. She lingered there, eyes shut tight in underwater suspension while a kaleidoscope of images flashed through her head. Images of death. Images of destruction. And an image of the pain on Patrick's face when she left him. Katie bolted out of the bathtub full of resolve to do whatever she could to ease his pain. She needed to talk to him again, to better explain her feelings, to minister to the minister in a gentle, loving way.

Before she could begin to think of returning to Austin, however, she had some professional obligations that needed attention. Rusty had given her the gelatin dry plates from his camera to develop, print, and share with both newspapers. She had to translate her notes into stark stories full of descriptive detail of tragedy as well as tender stories full of compassion for the suffering souls trying to rebuild their lives. In short, she had to report to an irritable and impatient Roy Durnstine who would be less than empathetic to the accumulated stress of her emotional involvement.

She towel-dried, wrapped her shimmering, still-damp hair in a bun, dressed in one of her customary business suits with a crisp white blouse and heels low enough to make a dash down the stairs into Mrs. Perlmutter's kitchen. As she munched on a muffin spread with apple butter and sipped strong, steaming coffee, she allowed Mrs. P. to unwrap her hair, redry it with a vigorous massage, brush it to a glossy sheen, and allow it to fall softly over her shoulders.

"There, that's better," wheezed the landlady puffing on her tenth cigarette of the day. "You can look professional and feminine all at the same time, dearie."

Katie nodded her thanks, took a deep breath, and headed out the door for the four-block walk to the offices of the *Buffalo Evening Times* and an anticipated unpleasant encounter with the editor in chief.

* * *

ROY DURNSTINE'S GREETING WAS PRETTY much what Katie expected.

"Where the hell have you been, Keenan? We haven't heard from you since Monday night. Readers are begging for more eyewitness reports from Austin, and I get nothing from you yesterday or this morning. Look at today's front page."

Durnstine hopped from behind his desk and waved the latest edition of the *Buffalo Evening Times* in front of Katie's face, slapping the front page with his free hand for emphasis. "Nothing. Nada. No byline stories from Austin. No photos. The only piece I could use was a generic blurb about body counts from the wire services. That's not reporting. That's not what sells papers. What do you think we're paying you for, Keenan?"

"Are you done, Chief?" Katie's lower lip was quivering.

"No, I'm not done. Do you realize how badly the *Express* scooped us this morning? That son of a bitch Shephard had reports with banner headlines."

Katie thought later that it must have been Durnstine's berating barrage that triggered her breakdown, but she acknowledged in self-reflection that his calling Rusty a "son of a bitch" might have contributed. The quivering spread from lips to shoulders and she burst into tears.

Durnstine stood dumbfounded. He had no reference in his hard-ass journalistic experience of how to react. Scolding reporters and countering their lame excuses was second nature. Thinking of Katie as self-confident, thick-skinned, and headstrong to the point of impudence was normal. But not this.

She stood before him, stripped of her outwardly composed veneer, shaking and sobbing. He did what he had always wanted to do in his fantasies, but never thought possible. He folded her into his arms. He felt the softness of her breasts press into him and the dampness of her tears soak into his shirt. The shaking subsided, but he didn't want to let go.

It was she who finally pushed back. "I'm sorry, Chief. That was so unprofessional." She breathed deeply to release some embarrassment and compose herself before continuing. "I should have reported in this morning. I meant to. My body just shut down until noon. That's on me, but I'll make up for it, Roy."

Her fresh, soap-scrubbed scent lingered with Durnstine, and the last of his defenses crumbled with her use of his first name. "That's all right, Keenan," he managed to mumble. "What do you have?"

"First of all, I have these for processing, printing, and screening." She pulled a half dozen dry photo plates, protected by their light-shielded cases, from her brief case. "They are photographs of the broken dam itself, of the destruction in the streets, and of bodies in the morgue." She paused, then added sarcastically, "That son of a bitch took them."

"I suppose that we have to share them with the *Express*?" was all that Durnstine could manage in response.

"No. Three of them will be exclusive to us. Your choice. The remaining three prints will go to the *Express*. That's all that Rusty asked, and that's more than fair, Chief."

Durnstine noted that she had returned to professional mode and that he was "chief" again.

"And what's more," Katie continued, "I have material for at least that many stories. Let's say three for tomorrow and three for Friday. I should be back by Saturday."

"You're going back?"

"Of course, I'm going back. There's a lot more to report, Chief, and I'm the one you want on the scene."

"Like what, Keenan. This story is losing legs already."

"Like investigating criminal negligence in the construction of the dam, Chief. Like investigating the suspicious disappearance of person of interest, Chief."

"When can you leave, Keenan?"

"I'll wrap up these stories tonight and catch the first train for Austin in the morning."

"Is business the only reason for going back, Keenan?"

She didn't answer.

* * *

IT WAS BOB PEARSON WHO discovered the other body—the body no one was looking for, the body no one wanted to find.

Pearson was like a bulldog unleashed once Father O'Brien had lured him from his seclusion in the parish house earlier in the day. After identifying the body of Charlie Rennicks in the morgue, he had shed his cloak of reclusiveness and replaced it with an air of renewed confidence and purpose.

First, he accompanied chief of police Dan Baker in a fast-paced walk from the morgue to Odd Fellows Hall, bending Baker's ear all the way in a cathartic outpouring of his distrust and suspicion of Fred Hamlin.

It was at the Odd Fellows Hall in late afternoon that he received his summons to appear on Friday morning of the inquest into

Rennicks' death. He learned from the messenger that not only would district attorney Wiley be present at the inquest but also that Wiley planned to impanel a grand jury to investigate the circumstances of the collapse of the dam.

Pearson was further encouraged and emboldened by the news that Chalkley Hatton was back in town. The thumbs that George Bayless and Fred Hamlin had forever pressed on the scales of lady justice were being pried away bit by bit, witness by witness. If only he could find evidence that would lead to the conviction of Hamlin for the murder of Charlie Rennicks, he would be content to allow the district attorney to prosecute the case for criminal liability against Bayless.

Consumed in such thought and planning, Pearson walked slowly down Main Street, crossed the bridge to the east side of town, and passed the remains of St. Augustine Church on Ruckgaber Avenue. He entered the front door of the adjacent church rectory as the sun sank behind the rolling hills on the western side of the valley and dusk descended upon what remained of the little mill town of Austin.

He trudged up the stairs to his room, weary but inwardly energized by the day's events. As he passed the pastor's bedroom, a brisk breeze swept from the half-open door. Thinking it would be well to close the bedroom window to ward off the oncoming chill of night, he gently tapped on the door in case Father O'Brien was in the room.

Pearson's knock inched the door open farther allowing him to see that the priest was indeed in his room. Patrick O'Brien's feet dangled eighteen inches from the floor. Below him was an overturned chair and to either side, as if dropped in despair from his lifeless hands, were a crucifix and a picture of a lovely lady with long dark hair. In the dim light, Pearson could barely detect the strip of bedsheet knotted around the priest's neck and extending to the rafter above.

Thursday
October 5

GEORGE BAYLESS FELT HIS COVER-your-ass plan was going well despite the absence of his long-time attorney Frank Baldwin. He had the legally binding hold-harmless agreements from most of mill workers—those who survived, anyway—and others with the false hope of future employment. Fred Hamlin and several of his henchmen would provide the persuasive muscle to convince those who had yet to commit.

Where payouts might be necessary to quiet the critics, he needed a smooth-talking negotiator, not a brute like Hamlin. He had always relied on Baldwin for that role, and now the bastard could not be found. After five days of being trapped in his office, Bayless wanted to return to his hometown of Binghamton to rest, to recruit additional legal resource, and to lay low for a while, actually, for a long while. He'd leave Hamlin here to take the heat.

Austin had been a profitable venture. It was time to collect insurance money, file for bankruptcy, find another opportunity, and move on.

After he had dispatched Hamlin on assignment yesterday, he unceremoniously and permanently dismissed Edith, much to her chagrin. Then he cleaned out and burned the bulk of the contents of his files, particularly the incriminating correspondence with Chalkley Hatton during the construction of the dam that clearly documented his refusal to accept the engineer's recommendations while continuously choosing cost cutting over safety.

He was about to depart the office on Thursday morning when he heard a knock at the door and the ominous summons. "Mister Bayless, this is Captain Dixon of the Pennsylvania State Police. Please open up."

Bayless, bereft of his usual buffers in the persons of Edith, Hamlin, or Baldwin, faced the door alone and without a plan. The usually unruffled titan of industry broke into a sweat.

In an effort to show the confidence he did not feel, he straightened to his full height of five feet eleven inches, puffed out his robust chest and belly in peacock fashion straining the buttons on his vest and marched to the door.

"Yes. What can I do for you, Captain?" he asked in a shaky voice that betrayed the image he sought to convey.

Chief Daniel Baker stepped from behind Captain Dixon. "Actually, it's what you can do for both of us, Mister Bayless. We have a warrant here signed by Judge Wainwright, which gives us permission to search these premises. Please step aside."

Baker loathed Bayless, and the feeling was mutual. Given this opportunity to serve up some humble pie, Baker did so with flourish and unmasked satisfaction.

"By all means, Dan," Bayless seethed, stepping aside with an ushering motion. "Be my guest, gentlemen. Always glad to accommodate the law."

Bayless was not a religious man, but he said a silent prayer to the gods of unfettered capitalism that he had the foresight to destroy the evidence.

* * *

BOB PEARSON THRASHED HIS WAY through the brush along the overgrown trail from the mill to the dam on the western side of the valley. It was the same trail Pearson had seen Hamlin take last Saturday afternoon. Hamlin, rifle in hand and rage in his heart, had been on a mission that day. Pearson, controlled and calculated, was on a mission of his own right now.

A quarter mile from the mill, the trail forked with the right fork descending another quarter mile to the base of the dam and the left fork ascending to the top. Pearson chose the left fork, certain that he was following in the footsteps of Hamlin.

The trail switchbacked up what was disdainfully dubbed by the righteous folk of Austin as 'prostitute hill,' Cora Brooks' place being on its highest point. As the path switched back and forth up the hill, Pearson could catch intermittent glances of her house through patches of trees above him. He could not know that Rusty and Brady's route of helter-skelter descent through briars and brambles two days before had cut across his path of travel today.

Neither could he know that he had a fellow traveler on this trail today who had followed him at a safe distance since he left the mill.

As he neared the western bank of the spillway, the trail leveled out. It was along this straight and level portion that Pearson paid close attention to his surroundings. He saw an outcropping ahead to the left and slightly above the trail. He detoured to inspect it.

As he moved closer, he discovered a flat rock perched high above the valley with a clear and direct view of the spillway. A perfect sniper's post. He searched the flattened vegetation around the rock and found what he was looking for nestled in the grass. Shell casings. Casings he was sure would match up with Fred Hamlin's rifle.

Had Pearson looked behind him on this exposed section of trail, he would have seen a figure approaching. Had he not been so intent in his search, he might have distinguished the rustling of the wind-blown grasses from the rhythmic fall of hiking boots behind him.

Pearson's first awareness of another presence was the feel of something cold around his neck. As wire cut through throat tissue, tendons, and carotid arteries, he looked up to see the sneering features of Fred Hamlin. It was the last vision registered by his oxygen-deprived brain.

* * *

FOR HOURS AFTER THE STATE police captain and the chief of police departed, George Bayless sat immobile at his desk, confidence draining from him with each breath. The officers had removed nothing because they had found nothing incriminating in his files. That was not his concern. He was stunned by the mere fact that a search warrant had been issued and further by the stern warning of Captain Dixon not to leave town while an investigation continued.

Bayless was not controlling the situation. Instead he was being controlled, and he had no frame of reference on how to react to that. Bayless had always operated from a position of power and control. Removed from that, anxiety began to fill the void.

He was plucked from this sea of self-doubt by a loud knock on the door of his office. Self-doubt turned to anger at the prospect that the law had returned. Anger then morphed to confusion as he was certain all the outer entrance doors were locked. When he heard the voice outside his door, his anger returned, yet now mixed with a measure of relief. He knew that voice belonged to a once-trusted advisor who possessed keys to the building.

"George. It's Frank Baldwin. May I come in?"

Standing in tense anticipation behind his desk, Bayless slumped back down into his chair. "Frank, you son of a bitch. Where the hell have you been?"

Baldwin took the gruff response as an invitation to enter. He did. "I've been searching for my parents and sister, George. They were finally found huddled together in a pile of rubble."

Bayless was unmoved. Sympathy was not inherent to his personality. "I've needed you, goddamn it. I was just served with a search warrant, and god only knows what else is brewing in that simmering legal caldron stirred by guess who? The commissioner of the Pennsylvania State Police, that's who!"

"I heard he was in town, George. Now calm down and let's discuss the situation."

"Calm down, my ass! How do you expect me to calm down when the law is breathing down my neck and Hamlin's flying off the handle?"

At the mention of Hamlin, Baldwin's massive frame straightened attentively. "What do you mean by that, George?"

"Don't worry about that, Frank. Just sit down and tell me where we're vulnerable and how to protect our soft underbellies."

Baldwin tried to redirect the conversation back to the reference to Hamlin. There was something new here that might be of importance to the authorities. "Did Hamlin do something that's bothering you?"

"I said forget about Hamlin! Just tell me how we cover ourselves. And that includes you, Frank. If I go down, I'm taking you with me."

Baldwin ignored the threat. He'd already chosen his path and was willing to accept the consequences. "Well, in civil action, you are exposed to lawsuits for damages, injuries, pain, suffering, and possibly wrongful death."

"I think we have most of that covered, Frank. I've been down this road before, and I was prepared even without your sorry ass. We have hold-harmless agreements from the vast majority of employees and applicants. Hamlin and I have prepared a list of the holdouts and the likely troublemakers in town. Hamlin knows the ones who'll cave when he applies the thumb screws. We have another list for you and a pile of cash to persuade them to back off. Then there is always the filing for corporate bankruptcy."

"The corporate shield may not be sufficient, George, if the claimants can prove reckless disregard for safety standards on your part. That could wipe you our financially. Beyond that, you have an even more serious problem."

"Christ, what's that?"

"Prosecution by the district attorney for criminal liability."

"That's ridiculous. On what charges?"

"Could be manslaughter or even accessory to second degree murder, George, depending on the strength of evidence and testimony."

"There's no evidence, Frank. I destroyed all of the construction drawings showing the modifications we stipulated as well as all of the correspondence between Chalkley Hatton and me on those topics. There is no other evidence. And there certainly are no witnesses to testify."

"You are basing that conclusion on some false assumptions, George. Hatton has copies of all the material you destroyed."

"He's not around to produce those files."

"But he is, George, and he will produce the incriminating evidence. And in regards to testimony, both he and I will state under oath that you blatantly disregarded the engineer's recommendations, recklessly modified construction plans, intentionally mandated use of inadequate and substandard materials, and ordered the dam filled prematurely before the concrete had time to cure. Altogether your cost cutting, greed-motivated control of construction activities shows a pattern of willful and knowing endangerment to life and property."

Bayless's eyes glowed with the intensity of embers embedded in a blaze of anger and hatred. "Get the fuck out of here, Frank."

* * *

RUSTY SPENT MOST OF THE morning and early afternoon at the Keating Summit train station and the telegraph office, alternately phoning and wiring material to the newsroom of the *Buffalo Express*. He was pleased to learn that Katie had delivered photos for this morning's edition. The stories he sent for tomorrow's edition focused on hope—the hope for the future, the hope for recovery, rebuilding, and healing for the devastated community.

He intentionally withheld any reference to the ongoing investigation into the cause of the dam's failure, the potential liability of the owner, and the suspicious death of an employee. He hoped that Katie had heeded his advice. "Katie, don't print speculation, only the facts."

Katie. His thoughts kept returning to her in waves of gratitude, admiration, and if he were to be truthful with himself, affection. He wondered if she would return to Austin. He wondered if their relationship would develop beyond a guarded, professional alliance. They had shared their reports. They had depended upon one another. They had been a good team.

He shook his head as if to discard these thoughts as wishful thinking. It was over. She wouldn't return. The pressure and emotion of her time in Austin had depleted her. This newspaper business, the reporting of human suffering, carnage, and tragedy should remain man's domain. She was a nice girl and a good reporter but better equipped to write feature stories for the society page than to be involved in an action-oriented investigation of a developing story.

Deep within, he didn't believe any of that, but these rationalizations helped insulate him from the pain of disappointment and the admission of a growing emotional attachment.

He shared her hesitation to return to the gruesome scene called Austin. Perhaps it was because of that, or perhaps it was because of an improbable, undefined hope, but whether from fear or anticipation, he remained fixed on the platform as the 2:30 B&S train bound for Austin steamed out of the station. He would catch the next one in two hours he told himself. There would still be plenty of time tonight for Brady to bring him up to speed on today's developments in the investigation and on pending legal matters.

A half hour after the B&S train departed, the Pennsylvania Railroad train from Buffalo, straining from its long climb to Keating Summit, emitted a final gasp as it rolled into the station on a separate track. Still standing on the platform, absorbed in thought and conflicting emotion, he barely noticed its arrival.

* * *

FROM INSIDE A COACH CAR on that train, Katie was jolted from sleep as the engineer braked to a final stop. She rubbed her forehead that had been resting on the glass window nearest the platform. In self-conscious embarrassment, she turned toward her seatmate, a shy, diminutive doctor from Buffalo on a mercy mission to Austin. She was relieved to see him standing in the aisle preparing to exit the train.

Had he cared to engage in conversation during the trip, she would have told him of the futility of his mission. Five days after the disaster, no surviving victims remained untreated. Doctors were not needed for the other victims—now numbering seventy-eight—only the coroner, casket makers, and funeral directors.

In a delaying tactic to allow the red pressure mark on her forehead to diminish, she turned back to the window casually, watching people on the platform. Arriving passengers stepped from the train and started walking toward the terminal while departing passengers queued up to board. A sudden, sharp tension shot through her body, straightening her from a slouched to a full upright position as she fixed her attention on the back of a man in clerical attire. Surely, Patrick wouldn't be here to greet her. Would he? Please no. She wasn't prepared.

The man pivoted sideways revealing a profile that was decidedly not Patrick's. For the second time in as many minutes a sense of relief washed over her. This one, however, was mixed with an overriding sense of guilt. Why should she be anxious about seeing her friend, her former lover? She had long since recognized the need to talk with him, to better define their relationship in a gentle, considerate manner. But at this moment of insight, she realized that needing to do it, as opposed to wanting to do it, were decidedly different feelings. She felt ashamed.

The shout of "all aboard" startled her from reflection into action. She grabbed her bag and hustled from the train running rudely into a man standing on the platform. She was about to apologize when the man put his finger on her lips and wrapped his arms around her. It was Rusty. She allowed her tension to release, her knees to buckle, and her body and being to be drawn into his embrace. A totally different set of emotions washed over her this time.

* * *

BRADY, WAITING IMPATIENTLY AT CORA'S house for Rusty's return, was delighted to learn by Western Union messenger that both Rusty and Katie would be arriving on the five-thirty train. He began to brief them on recent developments the moment he loaded them and Katie's bag onto the horse-drawn carriage. Katie leaned toward him in rapt attention as he slapped the reins to begin their journey to Cora's house. Seated on the far side of Katie. Rusty tried to pay attention but was repeatedly distracted by the soft caress of Katie's lustrous windblown hair on his cheek and the signature crisp scent of Ivory soap mixed with a hint of lavender cologne wafting from her. While he had been aware of the feminine beauty she usually chose to camouflage beneath the tailored suits and pinned-up hairdos, he now inhaled the new Katie in a stylish skirt and blouse with flowing hair.

Brady told them of the early afternoon strategy session he had attended at the Baldwin residence along with Frank Baldwin, Chalkley Hatton, Governor John Tener, and District Attorney Jacob Wiley. He ticked off his summary of the main points of their discussion, finger gesturing with one hand while holding the reins loosely with the other:

- Baldwin was willing to testify against Bayless and Hamlin despite the risk of self-incrimination.
- Hatton was willing not only to testify under the same circumstances but also to present written documentation of Bayless's flagrant disregard of his recommendations and warnings as to the structural integrity of the dam.
- Specifically, Hatton would cite Bayless's refusal, together with Hamlin's complicity, to construct a cutoff wall on the upstream side of the dam to reduce infiltration, his rejection of an accessible, reliable gate mechanism to relieve pressure, his insistence on cutting construction costs by substituting inferior materials, his orders to add to the height of the dam while disregarding the engineering requirement of adding the breadth to the base, and his rush to fill the dam before the concrete was sufficiently cured.
- Based upon this testimony and the supportive evidence, Wiley had sent a wire to Judge Wainwright requesting arrest warrants for Bayless and Hatton for criminal negligence.
- Wiley would instruct Captain Dixon to place them under arrest following the coroner's inquest tomorrow morning.

* * *

BY THE TIME THE CARRIAGE pulled up in front of the former brothel of Cora Brooks, Rusty was convinced that the case for both criminal and civil liability was solid.

Now seated at Cora's dining room table, warmed by fireplace embers and a hearty meal of beef stew and corn bread, he reviewed correspondence between Bayless and Hatton that Brady had spread before him. He scanned through the letters, noting the incriminating excerpts:

Hatton to Bayless, March 9, 1909:

> In building a concrete gravity dam of this height, it is quite necessary to secure as firm a stratum of rock as possible for the purpose of preventing leakage and to support the excessive weight. From the evidence of test drilling, this type of solid bedrock cannot be obtained within six feet of the surface of the valley. It will most likely be between twelve and fifteen feet.

Bayless to Hatton, March 15, 1909:

> Your estimate of the depth necessary for the foundation is duly noted, but I feel that you are being unnecessarily excessive in suggesting any depth over six feet. Our experience with construction of an earthen dam showed the transition of the shale line to solid rock was at about six feet. I think that depth should be sufficient. Please remember that we want to put in as cheap a dam as we can to supply roughly four million gallons of water daily to boost our non-stop production by about sixty percent.

Brady Quinn's annotation to the above correspondence:

> Engineer's recommended depth for foundation of dam—twelve to fifteen feet. Actual construction depth authorized by owner—six feet.

Bayless to Hatton, March 22, 1909:

> I had a meeting with our directors, and they seemed unwilling to expend more than about $85,000, so we will have to cut every possible corner. Can we eliminate the cost of a gate mechanism? Please do everything that you can to reduce the cost of this construction.

Hatton to Bayless, March 30, 1909:

> Yes, I can cut out the gate house with sluice gate entirely and put a thirty-six-foot cast iron pipe through the dam at its base with a valve for the purposes of periodic cleanout and regulation of pressure in case of emergency. This will cut off $1,800 from the estimate. This method, controlled by a manually operated wheel on the breastworks, is not optimal, but if you insist on this modification, I must caution you that the valve mechanism must be tested regularly and maintained in good working order. It is my purpose to keep the cost of this dam down to the lowest point, but I must insist, so long as I am consulted by you, upon being safe both now and hereafter, not only for your safety but for my own reputation as an engineer.

Brady Quinn's annotation to the above correspondence:

> Engineer's recommendation for a gate house mechanism not included in final construction. Manually operated relief value not regularly tested or maintained per engineer's recommendation.

Hatton to Bayless, May 21, 1909:

> I found upon investigation while at Austin that we had struck a very good stratum of rock at a depth of about eight feet below the natural surface of the ground, and so I directed that this be used for the permanent foundation of the dam, but that the stratum was not sufficiently thick to allow us to use it for the cutoff wall, and that this cutoff wall to prevent water infiltration beneath the dam would have to be put down deeper. The indications are that it may have to go three or four feet below the stratum we are building the concrete on.

Bayless to Hatton, May 24, 1909:

> I am sorry that the rock you found was not sufficiently thick as to make a cutoff wall unnecessary. This is an expensive part of the job, and I am anxious to hold the price down to the minimum cost wherever we can.

Brady Quinn's annotation to the above correspondence:

> Engineer recommends a cutoff wall. Cutoff wall not incorporated in final construction.

Hatton to Bayless, July 12, 1909:

> As your consulting engineer, I feel a responsibility in having this work professionally carried out, and while I am anxious to have the dam constructed in the shortest possible space of time and with the least cost, yet I must insist upon it being built in a safe way. Of course, you are having this dam built and paying for it, and if I am constructing it in any way that is objectionable to you, and you write me a letter directing me to build it in a contrary way, I would, of course, follow your instructions, but the responsibility is taken from my shoulders and put on yours.

Brady Quinn's annotation to the above correspondence:

> Owner employed cost cutting in methods and materials without notification to or consent of engineer.

Hatton to Bayless, November 1, 1909:

> Last night I received a telegram from the contractor stating you desired to raise the spillway for the dam by two feet. I have made a computation of the structure, and I find that it would be dangerous to the stability of the structure to increase the height of the water above what we have provided. If you expect to add to the height of the dam, so as to raise the height of the water without correspondingly broadening its base, of course the dam will be unsafe. I, therefore, cannot make any changes to the dam unless you instruct me to do so over your written signature, thus relieving me on all responsibility.

Bayless to Hatton, November 6, 1909:

> From your letter I judge that the dam is hardly safe at the point we expect to carry the water. If this is the situation, it is your fault it was built this way. We expected there was a good factor of safety in this dam and that the raising of the water a foot or two would not make any particular difference.

Brady Quinn's annotation to the above correspondence:

> Owner instructed the contractor to add two feet to the spillway of the dam without written notification to the engineer, blatantly ignoring the warning of jeopardizing the integrity of the dam.

Hatton to Bayless, November 22, 1909:

> I have been advised by the contractor that the construction work on the dam is completed and that he will send me the request for final draw for review and approval. The dam may be complete from a construction standpoint, but I caution you that the foundation will not be property set for many months, and it will not be safe to fill in the construction ditch allowing water from Freeman Run to pool behind the dam until that time. I would advise waiting for warm spring weather before beginning to fill the dam.

Brady Quinn's annotation to the above correspondence:

> Contrary to the advice of the engineer, the owner began filling the dam on November 26.

As Rusty read through the correspondence, he felt a presence leaning over his shoulder that radiated far more warmth than a meal or a fireplace. Once again, Katie's delicate touch on his shoulder and her hair brushing his cheek distracted and excited him.

"What do you think, Katie?"

"I think we have the bastards right where we want them, Shephard," she whispered playfully in his ear. Rusty felt her breath on his neck as she shifted to place her lips close to the other ear and continued with the same breathy, conspiratorial inflection, "And when Bob Pearson testifies at the inquest tomorrow, and Hamlin is locked up as the prime suspect in a first-degree murder case, perhaps we can celebrate."

Katie's teasing tone and gestures didn't escape Brady's notice. "Knock it off you two and sit upright. I have some very distressing news that I've kept from you.

Flushed with embarrassment and startled by the grave tone in Brady's voice, they did as they were told, turning their attention to Brady who was seating himself at the head of the table. His face was furrowed with concern and compassion as his eyes locked and lingered on Katie. The long pause made it obvious that he was struggling to find the right words.

"There is no way to sugarcoat this. Katie, I am so sorry. Bob Pearson found Father O'Brien's body last night hanging from a rafter in his bedroom."

* * *

BRADY LIT THE LAST OF the six kerosene wall lamps in Cora's parlor and dining room before returning to the table. He began collecting the papers still spread in front of Rusty who had not moved for the past hour. The sounds of uncontrolled sobbing from a bedroom upstairs had subsided somewhat, but Rusty sat immobile in a state of empathy for Katie's suffering.

Brady attempted to distract Rusty with another topic. "I saw two huge gasoline-driven generators being unloaded from a railcar last night. I understand that the General Electric Company donated the equipment and crew to establish an emergency lighting plant in town. They must have it set up because I can see a glow in town from Cora's porch."

Rusty did not respond. The awkward silence was broken only by the muffled sounds of Katie's crying interspersed with Cora's soothing reassurance floating down the stairs.

Brady cleared his throat and continued. "The search for bodies can continue through the night now although I doubt many more will be found."

Rusty remained mute and motionless.

"With the additional man power to make connections, string the wire, and climb the poles, full utilities could be restored soon. Even old Cora may have electric and phone service here on the hill next week."

Brady finally got a response, but it wasn't from Rusty. "Who are you calling 'old', you no-good, decrepit drunk?" Cora's voice, no longer floating, now came booming down the stairs as she descended.

Brady flinched but recovered quickly. "Well, if it ain't Cinderella coming in search of her glass slippers. Your charming prince awaits to keep you from turning into a wrinkly old bag. Oh, I'm sorry. I see that has already happened."

"Shut up, Quinn. Go to the kitchen and bring me a wet a wash cloth to wipe away some tears and sooth some swollen eyes. I need to talk to Rusty."

Brady stifled a response and retreated to the kitchen. Cora sat beside Rusty.

"How is she?" Rusty asked.

"She's brokenhearted and filled with guilt, Rusty."

"Why should she be?'

"Which? Brokenhearted or filled with guilt?"

"Both, I guess."

"Men are such insensitive creatures. I shouldn't have to spell this out, Rusty, but she's brokenhearted because Patrick O'Brien, before he become Father O'Brien, was her first love, and guilt-filled because she feels she caused his death."

"That's absurd, Cora. He killed himself for crying out loud."

"Because he was prepared to leave the priesthood for her."

Rusty sat confused and out of questions.

"And because," Cora continued, "she rejected the idea, and in doing so, he felt she rejected him. She didn't mean to hurt him, but she did. She wanted to see him again to better explain herself, to let him know she would always love him as a friend."

"What's to explain? He's a priest. He's married to the Church."

"He was willing to divorce the Church for her. In essence, he was proposing to her."

"She told him no, right? He should have accepted it and moved on."

"Easy for you to say. You're not in love with her. He was."

Cora wasn't expecting any response to that, but when it came, it was her turn to be confused and out of questions. "I don't know. I may be. Was she still in love with him?"

Cora paused to sort out her thoughts before answering. She was not used to being asked about affairs of the heart. Love had no place in her business, and it had been decades since it had been a part of her personal life. "I can't answer for her, dearie. I think you two need to talk."

"Maybe. Later."

* * *

LATER WAS SOMETIME AFTER MIDNIGHT when Brady and Cora had retired to their separate bedrooms. Rusty rose from a couch in the parlor, half-awake from a restless slumber, vaguely remembered that he needed to talk to Katie, and started stumbling up the stairs. The dying embers in the fireplace fought futility to ward off the late-night chill in the house. He shivered, whether from cold, fear, or excitement he did not know, as he walked to the door where Katie's distress had now dissolved into a soft whimpering.

He hesitated, unsure of himself, unsure of what he would say, unsure he would be welcomed. He tapped lightly on the door. The whimpering stopped.

"I'm fine, Cora. Please go to bed," came the whispered voice from within.

"It's not Cora. It's Rusty." He was surprised to hear the tremor in his own voice, his confidence eroding along with his resolve.

"You shouldn't be here."

"I know. I'll go now."

"No, please don't go. Come in. Let's talk."

He turned the knob with shaking hands, pushed the door open, and stepped inside. She sat up and lit a candle by the bedside. Suddenly he was embarrassed by both his presence and his appearance. He had risen from the couch without a thought to pulling on his trousers, socks, or shoes. He stood before her barefoot in one-piece, dingy-cotton long underwear, frayed at the neck, wrists, and ankles.

Katie giggled despite the past hours of misery and mourning. He turned to leave.

"Wait. Don't go. It's okay." She patted the edge of the bed, sat up, and shifted to the center to make room for him. "Sit here."

He turned back to her again, still unsure but less self-conscious, and saw the flickering light of the candle reflect off her shining raven hair and dance across the curves on the front of her nightgown. "Then please blow out the candle."

He sat down beside her and felt the sweetness of her breath caress his cheek as she extinguished the candle. Not a word was spoken, but he heard her breathing quicken. His hand found hers, and she drew him to her. His lips gently brushed hers. Her lips parted and accepted his with a growing need.

She pulled back. "You must think the worst of me acting like this and in a whore's bed at that."

He shook his head in response and then gently ran his hands through the silkiness of her hair down to where it cascaded off her shoulders. He slid the straps of her nightgown down her arms. The nightgown fell to her waist.

He stood, unbuttoned the front of his garment, and stepped out of it. She eyed the nakedness of his tall, lean, muscled body in the faint light of a cloudless night filtering through the window. "You're beautiful," she murmured, pulling back the bed sheet in invitation to him.

He sat on the bed beside her. Their lips touched, lingered, and explored over and over, slowly, softly. His lips left hers and moved down her body, lightly touching her neck and shoulders. She moaned, folded her arms around his neck, pulled him into her, and reached up to his shoulders. They fell in an embrace of ecstasy. Their bodies danced together to a heart-pounding symphony that went beyond passion.

They rested in a peaceful afterglow without a word. The second time was longer, more controlled, and even better. The third, as dawn approached, was the best.

Friday
October 6

RUSTY DID NOT APPRECIATE THE knowing glances that Brady shot his way across the breakfast table. Cora and Katie, chatting amiably at the other end of the table, seemed oblivious to the Brady's atta-way-bro silent messaging.

To disguise his mild irritation and bring the entire table into conversation, Rusty pointed to the hands of the grandfather clock in the parlor. "Just three hours until the coroner's inquest at eleven. Who is planning to be there?"

Brady and Katie both cast are-you-kidding looks at Rusty. Cora spoke first, "Wouldn't be proper for me to be there, darlin'. I'm not the most popular person in town, and besides, I sort of shy away from things where the law is involved. Not that I don't know Chief Baker pretty well." She winked at Rusty and Brady.

Rusty, fed up with the winks and knowing glances, rushed to return to the topic. "Where's the inquest being held, Brady?"

"At Odd Fellow Hall. Doctor Mansuey, as acting coroner, will preside, confirm the identity of the deceased, present his medical opinion for cause of death. Rusty and I will describe the location and circumstances of discovery of the body. Bob Pearson's testimony concerning motive and opportunity should be quite enough for District Attorney Riley to instruct Captain Dixon to arrest Fred Hamlin on suspicion of murder in the death of Charlie Rennicks."

"That should take place right at the inquest," Brady continued, "since Hamlin's presence was required by subpoena. Riley also has a warrant to arrest him on the charge of criminal negligence in the deaths of some seventy poor, innocent souls residing in Austin on September 30. That same warrant, which also applies to the pompous Mister Bayless, will be executed immediately should he be attending the inquest or at the early convenience of Captain Dixon should he not."

"Thank you, counselor," interjected Rusty whose respect and fondness for Brady was growing daily. "Continue."

Brady nodded acknowledgment to Rusty. "With the weight of evidence against Hamlin, I doubt the judge will set bail on the first charge, meaning Hamlin will await trial in jail. Bail will probably be set for Bayless in the matter of criminal negligence, pending a grand jury investigation and determination of the exact charges to be brought to trial. In the meantime, Miss Keenan and Mister Shephard, let's prepare for a trip to Odd Fellow's Hall. And, Madam Brooks, allow me to help you clear the breakfast dishes before we depart."

Rusty observed another wink and nod between Brady and Cora that made him consider how Brady had spent the night.

* * *

AN UNEXPECTEDLY SMALL, BUT RESTLESS, crowd of observers that included Governor John Tener, Chalkley Hatton, Frank Baldwin, District Attorney Jacob Wiley, Captain Samuel Dixon, Chief Dan Baker, Clare Benger, Pauline Lyons, Lena Brinkley, Barney and Nancy Anderson, Brady, Rusty, and Katie, along with a smattering of other curious town folk, milled around the vast, open space of Odd Fellow's Hall.

Brady, struck by the stark difference of the hall since he slept here in cramped conditions last Monday night, was engaged in a conversation circle with Clare, Pauline, Lena, Barney, and Nancy. He hugged Pauline long and hard, amazed and grateful at how well she looked following the intense physical trauma she had suffered.

Doctor Edward Mansuey, the appointed presider at the inquest into the death of Charlie Rennicks, paced back and forth behind a wobbly, wooden table in the center of the room. On the table sat a Bible for the purpose of swearing-in witnesses and a folder containing his notes for the purpose of establishing the cause of death. He paced behind a chair intended for the presider and glanced at the vacant chair at the side of the table intended for witnesses. He pulled a watch from his vest pocket and frowned. It was ten minutes past the scheduled time to convene.

Notably absent were George Bayless, Bob Pearson, and Fred Hamlin. Mansuey was not overly surprised about Bayless who had not made a public appearance since the dam breached. He was both surprised and concerned, however, by the absence of Pearson and Hamlin. Pearson was the star witness, and Hamlin, absent in defiance of a court subpoena, was the prime suspect.

Hatton, Baldwin, Dixon, Baker, Brady, Rusty, and Katie, all aware of the anticipated outcome of the proceedings meticulously scripted by D. A. Wiley, shared his concern.

Governor Tener, on the other hand, appeared to be relieved. Present only as a favor to his friend Hatton, but never comfortable with the situation since his arrival in Austin on Wednesday. He had successfully avoided any confrontation with Bayless, a major campaign contributor but was not as successful in avoiding this inquest that might involve an arrest of a murder suspect. He was inwardly pleased that chances of that occurring were diminishing with each passing moment. His plan now was to board his personal train car bound for Harrisburg immediately following the inquest.

Dixon and Baker, arrest warrants in hand and handcuffs in pocket, were anything but pleased by the truancy of Bayless and Hamlin. Their very next stop would be the offices of Bayless Pulp & Paper Company.

Five more minutes passed before Doctor Mansuey resignedly called the meeting to order. Brady, Rusty, and Katie exchanged troubled looks. Their concern for the outcome of the proceedings had taken a back seat to their concern for Pearson's safety. They knew how badly Pearson wanted to testify. Whatever kept him from showing couldn't be good. Katie suggested that they should begin searching for him at the mill. Brady and Rusty nodded their agreement.

Mansuey went through the perfunctory motions presenting the medical findings and taking testimony from Brady and Rusty regarding the discovery of Rennicks' body. Brady was ruled out of order for his comments about Hamlin's heading for the dam with gun in hand on Saturday. "Hearsay," ruled the coroner.

Mansuey concluded for the record that death was attributed to a single gunshot wound to the head with the bullet entering the temple above the right eye and exiting the cranium along with a sizable amount of brain matter from a hole the size of a baseball. The bullet was not recovered for identification, but the evidence suggested that it was fired from a high-powered rifle. Time of death could not be determined due to the decomposed nature of the body.

The coroner advised the district attorney to classify the death as a homicide, but that the evidence was inconclusive as to a suspect or motive.

All assembled parties quickly departed for their predetermined destinations.

* * *

THE NIGHT'S CLOUDLESS SKY HAD morphed into a mist-covered morning and then into a dull gray blanket now hanging low over the valley as Katie, Rusty, and Brady approached the Bayless Mill. Katie motioned the other two to follow her to the entrance she had discovered on her last visit.

Several boards had been tacked across the doorway in an apparent but ineffective attempt to bar access. Rusty kicked the boards loose, and they entered. The same sense of vastness that she had experienced on Monday halted Katie momentarily.

The huge Fourdrinier machine with its massive gears, belts, pulleys, and rollers, towered before them and seemed to stretch endlessly into a void beyond their view in the dimly lit building. What little light there was filtered in through the mud-caked and soot-covered windows lining the first and second levels of this section of the two-story structure. A three-foot wide iron catwalk, presumably built for ease of maintenance of the Fourdrinier, was bolted to the far brick wall just below the roof.

Katie surveyed the scene and breathed in the damp, musty air that smelled of rotting wood, rusting machinery, and ripening mold. She stifled a gag reflex but could not rid herself of the apprehension building within her.

Rusty's reassuring voice somewhat restored her wavering resolve. "If Pearson's here, let's not spook him with a lot of noise. Let's find him or evidence that he was here recently. I suggest we quietly search the building on both sides of this, this…what is it, Katie?"

"A paper-making machine, Shephard."

"Okay, a paper-making machine. And what's beyond? You've explored this building before and in better light."

"This ceiling height continues the entire length of this machine. Located at the far end are several smaller pieces of equipment, beaters, and chippers I think Pearson called them. At that point, a wall separates this room from a two-floor section of the building. I don't know what's in that section, but Pearson did say that the boilers and steam-driven generators are housed somewhere beyond in a building connected to this one."

"You've got the photographic memory of a reporter, Katie," Brady chimed in.

"I try to pay attention to detail, Brady. It's part of my job."

Katie's uneasiness had not escaped Rusty's notice. He was put at ease to hear by her voice, knowing then she was back in the business mode that matching her appearance in the business suit she had donned for the inquest earlier this morning. "I'll take this side of the machine while you two explore the other side," Rusty instructed. "We'll meet at the other end and make a plan from there to cover the rest of this building and then make our way to the other buildings."

Katie was not overly pleased to be separated from Rusty, but willing to accept the security of Brady's company as the second-best alternative. As they made their way across the twenty-foot face of the Fourdrinier to the far side, they could no longer see Rusty who had begun his search on the other side of the machine.

Brady was intrigued by the complexity of the mammoth machine, keeping his attention focused on it as they walked down its length. Katie, on the other hand, was more interested in searching along the wall underneath the catwalk. Brady was moving at a faster pace that put some distance between them when the shot rang out from above.

Katie heard Brady scream and knew instinctively that he had been hit. The same intuition told her the bullet had been fired from the gun of a sniper on the catwalk above her. Another shot pinged off the machine near the spot where Brady lay motionless.

Katie's spontaneous reaction, darting from the relative safety of her position, placed her in the sniper's direct line of fire. She fell to her knees in front of Brady and then shoved him with adrenaline-fueled strength, rolling his unresponsive body under the crawl space beneath machine. Two more bullets clanged the iron structure inches above them, and then it was quiet, eerily quiet.

Where was Rusty? Had he fled? She wrenched her thoughts away from Rusty and back to the bleeding body lying face up beside her. On her knees, head bumping against gears above her, she searched his body for a wound and found a puncture on the right side of his chest just below the clavicle. She ripped open his blood-soaked shirt and was instantly splattered by blood squirting in heartbeat rhythm from the exposed torn flesh.

She knew that the blood was life draining from Brady's body. She shed her suit coat and threw it onto the concrete floor between the machine and the wall. Another shot rang out from a position further down the catwalk, tearing through the coat and ricocheting off the concrete. She neither flinched nor hesitated. Pulling her blouse over her head, she shredded it into strips saving one large piece to fold into a pad and press into the wound.

Maintaining as much pressure as possible on the pad to arrest the flow of blood, she wrapped strips of her blouse around his back, under his armpits, and across his chest. Once, twice, three times she wrapped each strip and tied it snuggly over the pad. Blood still oozed from the puncture, but the makeshift bandage had stopped the hemorrhaging.

Satisfied she had done all she could, Katie lowered her profile to a prone position beside Brady, creating the smallest possible target for the sniper. It was then that she heard scuffling on the catwalk.

She risked exposing her head to see what was happening. She saw two figures near the far end of the catwalk struggling for possession of a rifle. Her vision cleared sufficiently to identify the figures as men, one tall and lean, the other stocky and muscled, each with a two-handed death grip on the rifle between them.

In that instant it became clear to Katie what had happened. As the beefy gunman was firing on her and Brady from above, he had backpedaled further down the catwalk for a better shooting angle, totally oblivious to what was happening behind him. The tall man had scaled the ladder at the far end and bulldozed the short distance down the catwalk crashing into the gunman. The gunman, caught off guard, had time to raise but not fire his rifle before the collision. The tall man was Rusty. The gunman was Hamlin.

Katie watched in terror as Hamlin forced Rusty against railing, back bending him precariously over the edge. Just as it appeared that Rusty could no longer maintain his balance, he startled Hamlin by abruptly releasing resistance and dropping down to a position of leverage on Hamlin's lower body. Rusty grabbed both of Hamlin's legs and thrust upward with all his strength. Hamlin went airborne, headfirst over the railing, screaming obscenities until he landed with a thud and went silent.

The sounds of combat echoing in the enclosed space had masked the quiet entrance of Captain Dixon and Chief Baker, drawn to the mill by the sound of gunfire as they were searching for Bayless in the adjacent office building.

Now on high alert with guns drawn, their eyes and weapons swept the building as they tried to assess the situation. Dixon and Baker both pointed their guns at the lone remaining figure on the catwalk.

"Stop. Stop. Don't shoot. That's Rusty," came the cry from beneath the machinery in front of them.

Startled, they lowered their weapons and turned toward the source of the urgent plea. Nothing could have prepared them for the sight of a woman, clad in dirty suit trousers and bloodstained, lacy brassiere rising to her feet in front of them.

"Don't just stand there," Katie shouted, oblivious to her appearance. She pointed toward Brady, hidden beneath the machine. "Help this man. He's been shot."

Dixon and Baker may have thought that nothing more could shock them until they discovered the body of Fred Hamlin. As fate would have it, the superintendent of the Bayless Mill had fallen on the razor-sharp steel blades and knives protruding from the bay of the chipper machine directly beneath the catwalk. They had to extract his body in pieces.

Bob Pearson's beloved machinery had taken its revenge upon his killer.

* * *

THE AMBULANCE TAKING BRADY TO the hospital located adjacent to the school on High Road was no more than a one-horse buckboard. Brady was strapped to a mattress in the center while Rusty and Katie, seated on hay bales on either side of him, tried to anchor him during the jarring ride. It seemed to Rusty that the driver hit every rut along the way.

Brady, half conscious, groaned with every bump. His physical pain was obvious. Rusty and Katie were suffering too, but their emotional pain was not as obvious. There was little conversation between them. For the moment they were consumed with their concern for Brady. Processing what had just occurred at the mill would impact them later.

Rusty put his coat on Katie to ward off the chill of the autumn day and, most especially, to cover her state of undress. He seemed to care more about her modesty than she did. The coat failed to conceal completely the red markings streaking her skin from neck to navel.

When they arrived at the hospital, the buckboard driver hopped down from his seat and ran to the main entrance to alert medical personnel. Within moments, Doctor Horn and two nurses rushed from the hospital to the wagon. The nurses appeared to be more stunned by the state of Katie's appearance than the medical condition of the wounded patient.

At the back of the wagon, the doctor and nurses lined up on one side with Katie, Rusty, and the driver on the other. In tandem, they slid the mattress off the buckboard and carried it along with the patient, pallbearer style, into an examination room on the first level.

Horn sighed audibly, ordered the patient's legs elevated, stripped the makeshift bandages off Brady's chest, and observed the damage caused by the rifle bullet. With nurses assisting, he removed Brady's jacket and tattered shirt, lifted him on to an exam table, and rolled him gently on his side. Brady was no longer responsive. His skin was nearly as pale as the white sheet beneath him.

"Clear through exit wound," the doctor noted as he looked at Brady's back. "That's good. It's also good, Miss Keenan, that you compressed the wound and contained blood loss. You saved his life," and after a pause, "for the moment anyway."

Horn dismissed Katie, Rusty, and the driver with a wave of his hand. When they had withdrawn from the room, Horn began a closer examination. He placed a stethoscope on Brady's chest and probed around the wound. A nurse sat poised to record the doctor's findings on a chart.

"Patient presents anemic condition indicative of loss of blood and poor circulation, breathing rapid and shallow, heart rate elevated, puncture wound between third and fourth ribs upper right chest approximately one centimeter, back exit wound between fourth and fifth ribs approximately two centimeters, no evidence of bullet or bone fragments, no evidence of bone or organ damage, significant tissue damage and blood loss, hemorrhaging arrested, clotting normal, body temperature—"

Horn threw a questioning glance at the second nurse who had just removed a thermometer from the patient's mouth. "One oh two point one," she announced.

"Elevated," he continued. "Treatment, clean, stitch, pack, and wrap both entry and exit wounds. Impression, shock from trauma and blood loss, onset of infection. Prognosis, survival unlikely."

Horn completed dressing the wounds and ordered the nurses to make a room ready for patient admission. He threw unused fragments of pads and gauze into a nearby basket in obvious frustration. He had read in medical journals about recent advancements in blood transfusion medicine. Something about antigens and classification of blood types. The patient needed blood, but he had neither the equipment nor the knowledge for such a procedure.

What more could he do? Horn found the answer in the Hippocratic oath he had pledged to uphold: *do no harm*. He would monitor the patient's progress or decline. He could do no more. He relinquished responsibility to God.

* * *

HOURS LATER, KATIE AND RUSTY positioned themselves on either side of Brady's bed, alternately sitting and standing, and sometimes pacing the few steps allowed in the confined space of the hospital room. The dull light of dusk filtered through the room's single window casting shadows on the patient's distressed facial features.

Rusty watched Katie dip a cloth in the wash basin on a small table beside the bed, wring it out, and place it on Brady's forehead.

"He's still really hot," she said.

The corridor outside the room suddenly brightened sending shafts of light though the open doorway. Rusty rose and walked into the corridor.

"Electric ceiling lights," he observed. "Looks like the town's recently rigged emergency generating system is working here."

As he stepped back into the room, he refocused his attention from Brady to Katie. In the newly added light, he could clearly see the signs of fatigue and stress. She sat motionless, appearing very tiny in his now fully buttoned coat. The emerald-green irises of her eyes floated in a sea of pink. The normally smooth skin of her forehead wrinkled with concern. The usually self-assured, square-shouldered posture slouched under the weight of worry.

"Katie, you should go back to Cora's place, get cleaned up, and get some rest."

"I'm fine, Shephard."

"Really. Please. I'm sure one of the nurses would be happy to take you back."

"Shut up, Shephard. I'm not leaving Brady."

That ended the argument and most of the conversation for the remainder of the evening. Around midnight, Brady began moaning and thrashing in bed. Fearing that he might open his wounds with the violent movement, Rusty leaned over and pinned his arms to the bed. In response, Katie, somewhat roughly pushed Rusty aside.

"I'll take care of this, Shephard." She placed another wet cloth on Brady's forehead, gently framed his face with her hands caressing his cheeks and whispered soothing sounds of reassurance into his ear. It seemed to Rusty, somewhat to his undefined discomfort, that this went on endlessly.

She lifted her head momentarily to speak. "He's perspiring profusely now, but he doesn't seem as hot."

Rusty noted a change as well. While beads of sweat rolled down Brady's face and the moisture of his body began dampening his chest bandages and the sheet beneath him, his tremors seeming to slacken. Gradually, almost imperceptibly, his body calmed into a state of peaceful rest. His breathing became deeper and more regular.

Katie finally sat up. Her cheek glistened with moisture from its close contact with Brady. "I think he's going to be all right, Rusty."

The expression of optimism and the tone of tenderness her voice encouraged Rusty to try again. "Will you go back to Cora's now, Katie?"

"Let's talk to the nurse."

When the nurse confirmed that Brady's temperature had indeed returned to a normal range, and when she agreed to give Katie a ride in her motor car, Katie relented.

Hours after Katie departed, and not long before sunrise, Rusty heard the first mumbled words from Brady's mouth. "I dreamed I was kissed by an angel."

"You were, Brady, you were," Rusty said. "You weren't dreaming."

Satisfied, Brady returned to a deep healing slumber.

Saturday
October 7

ONE WEEK REMOVED FROM THE disaster that all but wiped out the borough of Austin in North Central Pennsylvania, the sun rose over the small mill town nestled in the Freeman Run valley of the Appalachian mountain range. Oblivious to the devastation and uncaring about the misery, its rays reflected off the color bursting forth in the surrounding forests.

Nearly five hundred of its three thousand residents had fled in the past week, unable to cope with the lingering aura of sorrow and unwilling to face the difficult tasks of rebuilding.

Those who remained welcomed the sunshine both for its warmth and for the promise it conveyed new day of hope. They were a hardy lot full of grit, determination, and optimism. They were not about to give up on the town or themselves. The restoration of structures and infrastructures as well as the healing of souls was beginning.

Rusty was filled with these thoughts as he looked out the window of Brady's hospital room and observed the bustle of activity on Main Street. Debris had been cleared and building begun. The dead had been buried and properly mourned. The spirit of the town had been crushed but not extinguished. It would survive with or without the Bayless Pulp & Paper Mill.

A nurse's aide entered the room carrying a breakfast tray of hotcakes, sausage, and steaming coffee. Rusty's stomach growled in response to the aroma. He had forgotten all about food, and at its sight, he suddenly became famished.

"I don't think the patient can tolerate food at the moment, miss," said Rusty, trying to suppress the hunger pangs.

"This is not for the patient, sir. This is for you. We will begin giving him fluids when he wakes. You can enjoy the breakfast now."

The food made the vigil for his friend far more tolerable, and the coffee started to stimulate his dormant brain cells. He wondered if Brady would fully recover. Or Katie for that matter. Her injuries were emotional, not physical but just as real. He wondered about the future. Would they be a part of his future?

A nurse appeared at midmorning to check Brady's vital signs and change the dressings. Brady stirred at her touch but did not wake. "The wounds look good," she reassured Rusty. "There's no evidence of infection. He's likely to sleep for a while. Why don't you go home and get some rest? He'll still be here when you return. We'll take good care of him."

Rusty gladly accepted the invitation. He guessed "home" meant Cora's. His belongings were there and so was Katie. That sounded like home.

He walked out of the hospital onto High Road, breathed in the crisp, fresh autumn air, and then remembered he had no transportation. It didn't matter. He felt released, relieved, and ready for a long walk.

He saw activity in the building next to the hospital and realized that the temporary morgue was being restored to its former purpose. Clare Benger was standing in front directing what appeared to be a group of volunteers as they sanitized the interior and carried desks back inside. *It won't be long*, Rusty thought, *until Clare will be standing in front of a class of students sitting at those desks.*

He turned onto Main Street, crossed Ruckgaber Avenue, and paused on the rebuilt bridge over the tranquil waters of a slow-flowing Freeman Run. It was the same stream whose pent-up fury had crushed the town a week ago.

He crossed Railroad Avenue and the rail tracks. He passed Wolcott's Livery that was being repaired. A workman was tacking up a sign on the unfinished front. He could see additional workmen on the roof and more inside pushing horses aside while working on the stalls. An impulse, in sync with his lighthearted mood, directed him into the livery. Crazy maybe but practical as well. Why not?

A half hour later, he sat uncomfortably astride a leased, sway-backed gray mare who was far steadier than her rider. "Gentlest horse here," Silas Wolcott had assured him, eyeing the city fellow with a glint of amusement in his eyes. Rusty imagined laughter trailing him as he made his way down Main Street. He prayed that the mare—Nellie was her name—would not embarrass him by dumping on the street.

It wasn't that Rusty was entirely inexperienced at horseback riding. He just couldn't remember the last time he rode. Sometime at summer camp as a kid, he supposed.

He leaned back too far in the saddle as Nellie trotted up the incline toward Orchard Road. At the intersection, he tugged on the right rein and was relieved when Nellie obediently responded. All he had to do now was stay on the road that led to Cora's.

Brimming with false confidence as he neared the house, he envisioned himself as a knight approaching on a white steed to rescue a damsel in distress.

That fantasy evaporated quickly when Cora greeted him with unwelcomed news. Nellie morphed from a white stallion to an old gray mare and he from a shining knight to Don Quixote.

* * *

"IF YOU ARE LOOKING FOR Katie, Rusty, she's not here."

Startled as he tried to dismount, Rusty caught his shoe in the stirrup and landed on the ground, face up with Cora towering over him.

"What do you mean 'she's not here'?" he sputtered.

Cora felt too sorry for him to laugh. "I mean she's gone. I took her to the train station an hour ago."

Rusty slipped his foot out of the shoe still stuck in the stirrup and righted himself. "Why would she do that?"

"She's confused, Rusty. She's overwhelmed with anxiety and anger and grief and guilt and other feelings she doesn't even understand."

Rusty paused to process what Cora was telling him. "Anxiety" would be about Brady. "Anger" would be about Hamlin and Bayless. The rest was a puzzle.

"What's she grieving about? What does she feel guilty about? She's a hero for god's sake. She saved Brady's life."

"Men are morons. You just don't get it, do you, Rusty? She may have saved one friend, but she lost another, and she blames herself for his death."

"O'Brien? That's crazy."

"Crazy to you. Real to her. I think the emotional tipping point for was when I told her this morning about the funeral service yesterday for Father O'Brien. She burst into tears. 'I should have been there for him,' she said. 'I've failed him again.'"

Rusty couldn't respond. Perhaps he had been insensitive to her feelings for O'Brien. Perhaps he had selfishly focused on himself. Perhaps he had assumed wrongly that she had feelings for him. He looked at Cora for help. Cora read it in his eyes that conveyed, *what do I do now?*

"Look, Rusty, the feelings she does not yet understand are for you, but they're buried right now under a pile of emotional rubble, not unlike Austin after the dam broke. And like Austin, she needs time to heal. Given time, those emotions will rise to the surface. They are emotions based upon the future, not rooted in the past. Let her go for a while. She needs time."

Rusty considered this.

"And one more thing," Cora continued, "Katie asked me to thank you for taking care of Brady. She's sorry she had to leave so abruptly, but she knows he's in good hands."

Rusty looked down to the ground and then at his rented horse. Again, Cora read his mind.

"Don't even think about chasing her to Keating Summit on that horse, cowboy. You'll probably kill yourself. And besides, you don't want Katie to have a lasting image of you trying to dismount. Now go in the house and take a nap. I'll take care of the horse, then after I fix you a nice meal, you can lead her back to the livery with my carriage and go visit Brady. Tell him Cora can't wait for his return."

Distraught as he was, Rusty had to smile at that. He submitted to Cora's logic with the same bemused resignation as Brady would to her charms. He wrestled his shoe from the stirrup, slipped it on, and trudged into the house thinking that Brady had the better deal.

Saturday
October 14

RETURNING TO AUSTIN AFTER WORKING in Buffalo for five days, Rusty was amazed at the transformation in the appearance and spirit of the town. Houses were being repaired or rebuilt. Many residents had returned to their homes; others would soon be returning. Much to parents' delight, the school would be reopening on Monday. Electricity, phone, water, and sewer services had been fully restored.

On Main Street, the sturdy brick buildings of First National Bank and Goodyear Hotel, which had survived the deluge, were being renovated and would soon be open for business. Other businesses along the street were preparing to reopen as well. Both the commercial and residential centers were coming back to life.

"People are resilient," Brady reflected sitting on a couch in Cora's parlor. "They have to be. Life is a mix of good times and bad, and if you stop living because of the bad times, you can kiss the good times goodbye as well."

Seated across from him, Rusty nodded. "You're becoming quite a philosopher, Brady."

"Not like me, is it? Too much time to think. I hate sitting around like this, arm in a sling and sore as hell. I really want to get going."

"Well, listen to the doctor and to nurse Cora. A wise person once told me, 'It takes time to heal.'"

"Did you know Cora's moving, Rusty? After I'm better, she says."

"Really?"

"Makes sense. There's nothing to keep her here. Business isn't exactly booming, and prospects are dim. She says she's too old to recruit ladies and start up again."

"Her plans?"

"She's tired of small-town life. She'll get a good price for this house. Then it's on to a city and plan from there. I'll miss her. She has become a good friend."

"You're staying, Brady? What's to keep you here?"

"Frank Baldwin for one thing. He's asked me to join him in his legal practice. He says there will be plenty of litigation from this Bayless mess for both of us to handle. Frankly, I think I'm part of his contingency plan in case he loses his license to practice. Despite his cooperation with the grand jury investigation, that's a real possibility. At minimum, he'll be censored by the Pennsylvania Bar Association."

"What about the grand jury, Brady?"

"It will convene next week with Baldwin and Hatton both testifying against Bayless."

"Bayless was arrested?"

"Didn't take long. He might have been a cunning businessman, but he was a lousy fugitive. Went back to Binghamton, and the New York State Police nabbed him there on a warrant for manslaughter, not to mention contempt of court for fleeing. He is now safely ensconced without bail in the Potter County jail in Coudersport."

"Couldn't happen to a nicer guy. I didn't see anything on the wire."

"Just happened yesterday. They informed Baldwin, and he informed me. One more thing on the legal front. Cases are closed on the murders of Charlie Rennicks and Bob Pearson. Fred Hamlin was convicted of first-degree murder in both. He saved the state from the expense of frying him in the chair. And by the way, they found poor Bob's body chopped into pieces and scattered around a field not too far from here. Guess Hamlin figured the coyotes would find the body parts before the law did."

"Thanks for bringing me up to speed, Brady. I'll be pounding out copy for Monday morning's edition of the *Express*, not that I have to worry about beating the competition. Austin's not a story any longer. Two murders in rural Pennsylvania isn't sensational enough for the press.

"That mean you're going back to Buffalo tonight?"

"Hell no. Tomorrow. Cora's promised me a home-cooked meal and a warm bed for the night, and I'm not going to turn that down."

"Not with her in it, I hope."

Rusty frowned. "No not with her in it, Brady."

"Then I can toast you with a glass of milk tonight while you two are sipping bourbon. How's Katie by the way?"

"I don't know. She took a leave of absence from the *Buffalo Evening Times*. I think she went back home to Erie to spend time with her parents. I haven't seen her."

"She has a lot on her plate, Rusty."

"I know. I've been told that before."

"She's a hell of a reporter, and the gold standard for women in the profession. I hope she doesn't give up on journalism. I hope she doesn't give up on herself."

"I know and agree with that too, Brady."

"Will you take some advice from a guy who's been around the block a few times?"

"If I refuse, you'll tell me anyway. Is it legal advice you're offering?"

"Nope. Personal."

"Go ahead."

"Don't let her go, Rusty. Fight for her. She's worth it. She's not just a good reporter. She's a good person and one who is very fond of you."

"You think so?"

"I know so. She didn't have to tell me. I've seen it in those gorgeous green eyes."

Rusty swallowed hard. "I'll take your recommendation under advisement, counselor."

Wednesday
November 15
Buffalo

SITUATED ON THE EASTERN SHORE of Lake Erie, Buffalo, was known for its lake-effect blizzards and it's long harsh winters. Even so, residents weren't prepared for this preseason snowfall that blew in off the lake in the early afternoon. By six o'clock, it had piled up half a dozen inches of snow with no sign of letup.

Rusty sat at the counter of Al's Café, purposely positioned with his back to the large street window, depressed by the early winter storm and life in general. It was an odd hour for Rusty to be at Al's place where he usually stopped for a late-morning, afterwork breakfast rather than a late-afternoon, before-work sandwich. Much as he loved the newspaper business, he had to admit that at age thirty-one, the night-shift routine was wearing on him.

The pool game below his modest, second-floor apartment down the street had started unusually early for a Wednesday. When he had finally surrendered to the clatter of billiard balls, tumbled out of bed, washed, shaved, dressed, and hustled down the stairs, he was greeted by the unpleasant sensation of stepping into an ice bath of ankle-deep snow. After retrieving a pair of ugly but practical galoshes to pull over his shoes, he set out once again for some anticipated warmth and conversation at Al's place.

Now he wished he had gone straight to the office. Upon arrival, he found that he wasn't hungry and just didn't feel like talking. He absently stirred his coffee and ignored his half-eaten egg salad sandwich. Al, behind the counter, was rambling on about an adventurous aviator by the name of Calbraith Rodgers who had just completed the first ever cross-country flight from Shepherd Bay, New York, to Pasadena, California.

"Took him fifty-six days with a couple dozen stops, some scheduled and some not, but the son of a bitch did it. Trouble was, he didn't get the prize money."

Al waved a copy of the *Evening Times* in Rusty's face, stabbing at a picture on the front page. "Look. Here's a picture of the crazy bastard."

"I know, Al. I'm in the news business. If you had purchased a copy of the *Express* this morning, you would have seen a better picture and a more complete story."

Mistaking Rusty's sarcasm as a sign of interest, Al plodded ahead. "I dunno. Seems pretty complete to me. I'll bet you didn't report about the prize money."

"Yes, Al, we did."

"Says here that William Randolph Hearst offered a prize of fifty thousand dollars. Imagine that, fifty big ones, for the first person to fly across the country in thirty days or less. Old Rodgers only missed it by a mere twenty-six days."

"I know, Al."

Switching topics without segue way, Al continued his nonstop chatter. "By the way, Rusty. Whatever happened to that brunette bombshell you had your eyes on?"

"What brunette?"

"Don't play coy, Roy. You know exactly who I mean."

"Yeah, well, I haven't seen her in quite a while." Rusty didn't feel like sharing details with Al. Having seen several of Katie's bylines in the *Evening Times* this week, he knew she had returned to Buffalo. He also assumed that she didn't care to see him again.

"Maybe that's the reason you're so glum, chum." Al thought the singsong name rhyming game was amusing. Rusty didn't.

At that moment, Rusty heard the chiming of bells hung on the front door. A cold blast of air it his back.

Al looked up and said, "Well, I think your wait is over, rover."

Rusty spun around on his stool and there was Katie, the luster of her dark hair sprinkled with specks of fresh white snow. She stood motionless for a moment framed by a curtain of white in the open doorway behind her, tiny droplets of melting snow falling from her hair to the fur collar of her winter coat.

"Hi, Shephard. Thought I'd find you here."

* * *

SHE SHED HER COAT, EXPOSING the curves of a tight wool-knit sweater. He liked the casual look. She looked quite relaxed and sure of herself. He liked that too. They moved to a booth and talked nonstop for an hour, feasting on each other's words and gestures with untouched coffee cups before them.

She had recovered nicely, thank you. The breakaway from the office had done her a world of good. She got a promotion in the newsroom. A regular beat and a column on the opinion page. How was he feeling? He looked tired.

Finally, the talk of relationship surfaced. He led. "Katie, I'm sorry if I came on too strong when we were in Austin. It was a time of stress. That's my only excuse. I liked working with you, and I enjoyed your company."

"Ditto, Shephard, and I don't want you to think I'm that kind of woman. You're right. It was the stress."

"Agreed."

"Shephard."

"Yes."

"I think we should start over again and do this properly. You know, we've never had a date."

"I never thought of it. Could we call this a date?"

"You never asked me."

"Okay. Katie, would you like to have coffee with me sometime? Like right now?"

"Shephard, I would love that."

"Okay, that's over. Now what?"

She leaned over the table and pulled closer. Their knees touched. She reached for his hands on the table. His hands turned sweaty and he felt a quivering sensation shoot down his back. "Let's go for a walk," she said.

* * *

THE SNOW CONTINUED TO FALL as they strolled down the center of the deserted street, playfully kicking mounds of light fluff left and right. The moon was bright and full and high above them. *Beautiful*, Rusty thought. *Life is beautiful.*

"A penny for your thoughts," she said.

"Nothing. Just something silly."

"I have a silly thought," she said.

"What?"

"Are you thinking about trading in your Maxell?"

"Are you crazy? Of course not!"

"I talked to Cora. She said you were thinking about getting a horse instead."

It took a moment for Rusty to register the teasing comment.

He burst into laughter and put his arm around her. They stumbled down the street, giggling uncontrollably as if they had just rolled out of the corner tavern at midnight.

"I love you," he said.

She didn't know if he were teasing. Neither did he.

Epilogue

THE FINAL COUNT OF LIVES lost in the Austin Dam disaster was seventy-eight—including Willie and Mary Nelson, Mary Mansuey, and her infant son Elias, Grace Collins, John and Josephine Baldwin, Ralph and Angelina Donafrio, and their children Emma, Virginia, Mona, and Joseph, Adam and Jennie Broadt, Mayme Rennicks, and her children Arnold and Evelyn. From infants to the elderly, the raging torrent of death played no favorites. The deaths of Bob Pearson, Charlie Rennicks, and Father Patrick O'Brien were considered collateral damage and not included in this count. George C. Bayless was indicted by the grand jury and convicted at trial by a jury of his peers on seventy-eight counts of second-degree murder, a more severe level of felony than anticipated by the warrant for his arrest. He was sentenced to life imprisonment. T. Chalkley Hatton was exonerated of all charges for his role as design engineer. Frank E. Baldwin, Esq. was censored and lost his license, but his law practice flourished with a succession of favorable verdicts in civil suits litigated by his partner Brady Quinn. Gladys Baldwin did clerical work in their offices. Frank lost his bid for reelection to the state senate. Both doctors Mansuey and Horn remained in Austin to practice medicine. Pauline Lyons and Lena Brinkley resumed their positions with the telephone exchange. Clare Benger was named teacher of the year. Dan Baker resigned as chief of police but remained on the force as a patrolman. Barney and Nancy Anderson and their twin boys moved to Rochester where Barney got a job managing a large hotel. Madge Nelson, orphaned by the disaster, moved to Williamsport to live with her sister.

In 1918, the *Buffalo Express* ceased publication, a result of insufficient man power caused by men marching off to war. Roy Durnstine retired as editor in chief of the *Buffalo Evening Times*, and Russ "Rusty" Shephard was hired to replace him. In 1920, the *Express* resumed publication, and Katherine Keenan Shephard was named as its editor in chief, the first woman to hold that position at any metropolitan newspaper in the country. The Shephard's remained professional rivals.

> *Cracked, ruined dam above out town,*
> *Symbol of hope which came tumbling down*
> *Crusher of dreams not meant to be—*
> *You stand in silent testimony.*
> *A reminder of what was before,*
> *Broken dam, you are a threat no more.*
> *You still are there, but so are we—*
> *Unbroken.*

—Dixie Ripple

About the Author

IN HIS PROFESSIONAL CAREER, JASON GRAY, JR. has served in executive positions in the newspaper, radio broadcasting, commercial printing, and lodging industries, including twenty years as president and publisher of Courier-Express Publishing Company and president of Tri-County Broadcasting Company, both serving a three-county area in Western Pennsylvania.

Gray earned a BSBA degree from Bucknell University and an MBA degree from the Wharton School of the University of Pennsylvania. Upon "retirement" from the newspaper publishing and radio broadcasting industries, Gray contributed his management skills to Catholic education as a school administrator. His lifelong passion for writing began as a reporter for the Associated Press.

Gray is a published author of short stories for young adults and a recent science-fiction novel, *A Journey Beyond.*

He has been actively engaged in leadership roles in community service and business organizations including the Pennsylvania Newspaper Publishers Association, the Foundation for Free Enterprise Education, and Penn State Public Broadcasting where he served as board chairman. He is chairman of the Gray Family Foundation.

His awards for service include the Service to Humanity Award from the Bucknell University Alumni Association, the Paul Harris Fellow Award from the DuBois Rotary Club, Distinguished Service Awards from the DuBois Area JayCees and DuBois Area Catholic Schools, and the Knight of St. Gregory Papal Award for service to the church.

Gray resides with his wife, Libby, in DuBois, Pennsylvania.

CPSIA information can be obtained
at www.ICGtesting.com
Printed in the USA
BVHW080044050719
552635BV00001B/5/P

At 2:30 on an unseasonably cool, partly cloudy afternoon in late September 1911, the cement dam located a mile above the mill town of Austin, Pennsylvania, gave way, unleashing a wall of water cascading down the narrow valley toward the town and sweeping away everything in its path with the explosive power of a nuclear bomb. Lulled by the assurance of engineering experts that the dam would forever withstand the pressure of the pent-up waters above the town, three thousand unsuspecting residents of Austin went about their slow-paced Saturday routines.

Some floundered and drowned in the raging waters that consumed the town, some were battered to death by logs and debris swept up by the torrent, and some, the lucky ones, raced to the safety of higher ground. Stories of heroism, sacrifice, cowardice, and selfishness emerged from the aftermath. The residents of Austin represented; after all, simply a crosscut sample of humanity, exposing the best and worst in times of crisis.

Washed Away is a work of fiction that unfolds in the historical context of this real-life tragedy. Committed to go beyond the sensational journalism of that era, two enterprising young reporters from Buffalo, Rusty Shephard and Katie Keenan, join forces to investigate the causes and determine accountability for the disaster. As their investigation begins to unmask the deceit and greed of those responsible, they encounter desperate acts of coverup, recrimination, suicide, and murder, placing their own lives in mortal danger. In their journey to uncover the truth and seek justice, they are absorbed in the emotional turmoil of the town and of their own relationship.

page publishing

$17.95
ISBN 978-1-68456-987-8
51795

9 781684 569878